meet me at Sunset Cove

praise for
Meet Me at Sunset Cove

"What an awesome read involving a designer and a contractor who share a history, a fake engagement, misunderstandings, and second chances. The characters were well-written and the storyline drew me in."

—ALLYSON, GOODREADS

"Wonderful, adorable, cute story set on Jonathon Island with fall in love with characters. Loved this one in this series. Read as stand alone or treat yourself and read the series."

—JONI, GOODREADS

"This is quite possibly my favourite of the series! Congratulations to Sarah May Warren for a stellar installment in a great series. Warren has written a 5-star novel highlighting family legacy and rebuilding, and then tied it together with the fake engagement trope and faith threads. This fantastic novel about giving the Bad Luck Barrett house a new lease on life is one you'll want on your reading list!"

—THE LITERATE LEPRECHAUN, GOODREADS

JONATHON ISLAND ◆ SEASON 1

meet me at Sunset Cove

SARAH MAY WARREN

sunrise
PUBLISHING

Meet Me at Sunset Cove
Jonathon Island, Book 5

Published by Sunrise Publishing
Copyright © 2025 Sunrise Media Group LLC
Print ISBN: 978-1-963372-87-8

This book is a work of fiction. Names, characters, places, and incidents are either products of the author's imagination or used fictitiously. Any similarity to actual people, organizations, and/or events is purely coincidental.

Scriptures taken from the Holy Bible, New International Version®, NIV®. Copyright © 1973, 1978, 1984, 2011 by Biblica, Inc.™ Used by permission of Zondervan. All rights reserved worldwide. www.zondervan.com The "NIV" and "New International Version" are trademarks registered in the United States Patent and Trademark Office by Biblica, Inc.™

For more information about Sarah May Warren please access the author's website at the following address: SEWarrenFiction.com.

Published in the United States of America.
Cover Design: Sunrise Media Group, LLC

To my hubby, my kiddos,
and our bad luck house.

But he said to me, "My grace is sufficient for you, for my power is made perfect in weakness." Therefore I will boast all the more gladly about my weaknesses, so that Christ's power may rest on me.

2 CORINTHIANS 12:9

Jonathon Island

Meet Me on Jonathon Island (prequel novella)
Meet Me at the Grand
Meet Me on Lilac Lane
Meet Me at the Fudge Shop
Meet Me on Blueberry Hill
Meet Me at Sunset Cove
Meet Me at the Christmas Cottage

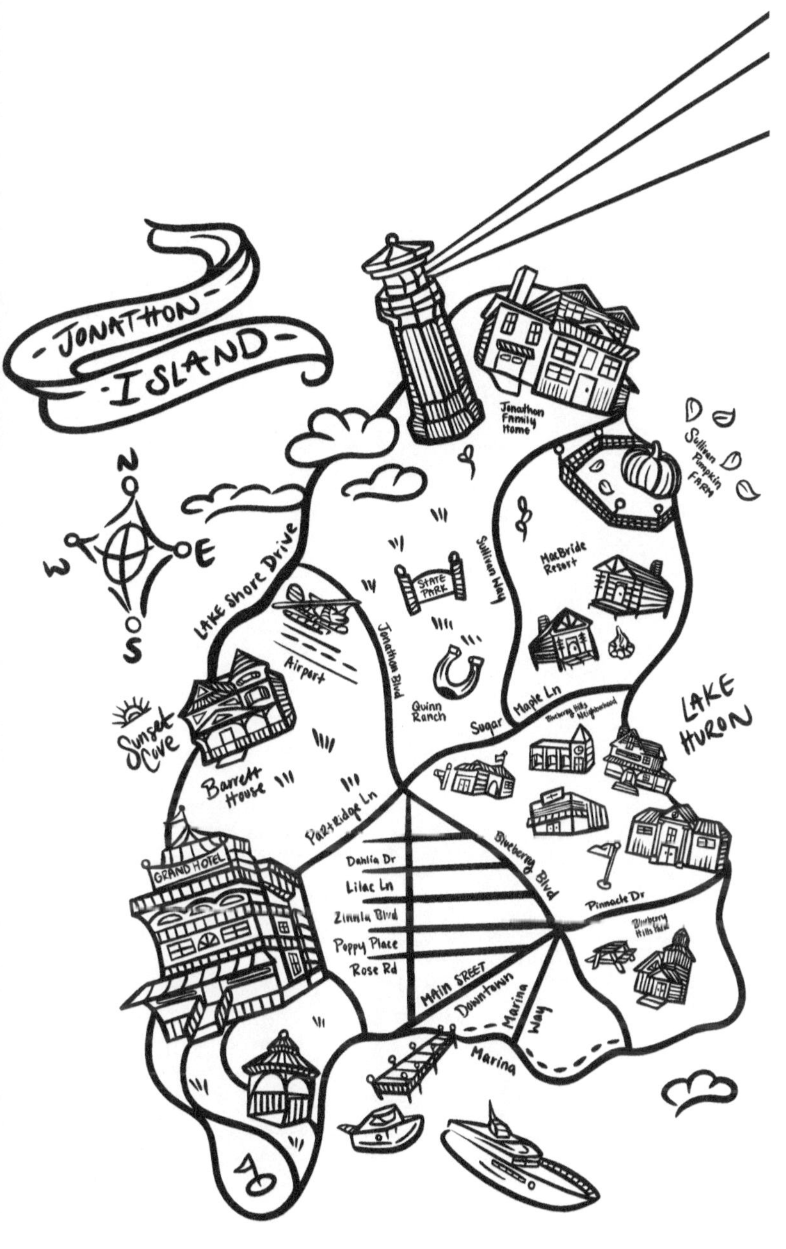

- JONATHON -
- ISLAND -
Jonathon Family Home
Sullivan Pumpkin Farm
N
W
E
S
Lake Shore Drive
STATE PARK
Sullivan Way
MacBride Resort
Airport
Jonathon Blvd
Quinn Ranch
Sunset Cove
Barrett House
Sugar Maple Ln
Blueberry Hills Neighborhood
LAKE HURON
Partridge Ln
GRAND HOTEL
Dahlia Dr
Lilac Ln
Zinnia Blvd
Poppy Place
Rose Rd
Blueberry Blvd
Pinnacle Dr
Blueberry Hills Hotel
MAIN SREET
Downtown
Marina Way
Marina

One

DAISY DECKER HAD ALWAYS BEEN A girl with a plan.

So why did she feel like she was drifting aimlessly in the middle of nowhere?

Outside the window, gusts of wind sprayed icy water against the side of the vessel, carrying the scent of pine and autumn leaves through the nearly empty ferry. Daisy let out a shiver and wrapped her sweater closer to her body, wishing she'd taken more than five minutes to research her destination before tossing a few "cute fall girlie" outfits into her suitcase and fleeing the city. Apparently, Michigan had a very different definition of fall than California.

A vibration from her smartwatch tugged her attention away from the mesmerizing swells of Lake Huron, and she glanced down to see the preview of a text.

Robin 🖤
Stop hiding from me. Answer your phone.

Daisy rolled her eyes, cracking a smile for the first time in what felt like days at her friend-slash-agent's dramatics. She was not hiding. She was just taking a strategic retreat while she tried to formulate a plan to salvage the wreckage of her career.

That's what she was good at. It was sort of her "thing": Daisy Decker—the girl with all the plans. She cringed at the memory of that slogan being slapped across half the HGTV billboards in the Midwest a few years back.

Her watch buzzed again, flashing the name Robin ♥ across the screen.

Taking a breath, Daisy fished out her phone and winced as she answered it. "Hi . . ."

"Hi?" Robin asked from the other end. "You dump your boyfriend, quit your job, and then vanish into thin air for forty-eight hours, and all you have to say is 'hi'?"

"Hi . . . How are you?"

Her friend let out a groan. "You infuriate me."

Daisy grinned, relaxing for the first time in twenty-four hours at the sound of a friendly voice. Well . . . friendly-ish. "I'm sorry, Robin. I should have talked to you before bolting." A swell of water splashed against the glass as the ferry passed beside an enormous bridge. In the distance, the outline of an island was just starting to come into view. "I just . . . I had to get out of there." Like, immediately. Because the moment she'd stood up in that conference room and laid down that ultimatum, making them choose between her and her hunky costar-slash-very-fresh-ex-boyfriend Logan, she'd known it had been a mistake.

"I know," Robin said softly, followed by a heavy pause. "He's a jerk. And they're idiots for picking him over you."

Daisy sucked in a breath, trying her best to smother the sudden ache in her chest. "Thanks, babe . . . but honestly, I think I'm over him."

"Sure. Because it's just that easy to get over someone you dated for over two years."

Daisy stared out across the choppy water, searching for the right way to explain it. "Really. I think we've been over for a while now . . . I just didn't want to admit it, you know? It felt like we were this package deal—Double and Decker—but something was never quite right. And I kept waiting for things to click, but they just . . . never did."

The truth was, it wasn't seeing Logan with his arms around another woman that had made her run. It was her pride. It was standing in that boardroom, Jerry McGuire–style, with the heavy silence of rejection pressing in on every side, that kept her awake at night. She couldn't let that be the end of her career.

She heard her friend take in a breath of her own and then, "Okay, so what's next? I can start making calls . . ." Her tone turned suddenly optimistic.

"I'm glad you asked," Daisy said as the docks came into view. "Priority number one is damage control. I'm sure social media is already spinning out stories about the way I stormed out. The longer I avoid the public, the more power Logan has. That brings me to priority number two. If I'm going to get back on the radar without the network's help, I need content. And I need it ASAP. So, the plan is as follows:

"Step one, find myself an adorable little house on an adorable little island. Step two, film myself giving the house a total 'Decker' remodel and slap it up on YouTube. Step three—"

"Absolutely annihilate Logan and *Double Decker* in ratings until the network realizes they made the wrong choice and comes crawling back?" Robin suggested.

Daisy grinned. "Bingo."

"I guess it's a start," Robin said. "So where are you going to find this adorable little house?"

Before Daisy could answer, an automated voice echoed through the ferry speakers. "On behalf of everyone at Jonathon Island, we'd like to welcome you to the island. We'll be docking in just a few minutes, so please remain seated until the vessel has been secured to the dock and luggage carts have been unloaded. Please take this opportunity to collect your things. And lastly, please be courteous to your fellow passengers as you exit the ferry. Thank you, and have a nice visit."

"What was that?" Robin asked, her frown sounding through the receiver. "Daisy, where are you?"

Daisy shifted in her seat, trying to get a glimpse of her destination. "Jonathon Island, Michigan."

The ferry slowed as they passed a pair of buoys bobbing in the water. Daisy's eyes trailed up to the shore, where the water faded from blue to teal, lapping against a white pebbly beach. Above that, a wall of pine trees hugged the shoreline with pops of orange and red.

"The place Eli Noble was spotted a few weeks back?"

"That's the one!"

"It's a little off the beaten path, isn't it?"

Daisy's gaze caught on a Victorian-style turret poking through the trees as the ferry rounded the edge of the island. "It is. But I've got a good feeling about it. Who knows, maybe this place has exactly what I need to make a comeback."

The boat passed the breakwater as their destination came into view, and Daisy's breath caught in her chest.

Tucked in the crook of the bay, Jonathon Island sprawled out along a picturesque boardwalk. Blue and yellow storefronts lined Main Street, while sailboats bobbed along the marina. Victorian-style homes climbed the hill that rose up behind the town, and at the end of Main Street stood a massive historic-looking hotel. Although the structure was obviously still under construction, it didn't take much for Daisy to imagine the completed estate.

It was breathtaking.

It was no wonder the townsfolk had been working so hard to rebuild. It was a place worth fighting for. And from what Daisy had learned from the news article covering Eli Noble's recent reappearance here, the townsfolk were doing everything they could to do just that. Including selling houses for a dollar.

What better way for her to make her HGTV comeback?

"I gotta go," Daisy said, slinging her backpack over her shoulder.

"Call me when you're ready to put this plan of yours into action," Robin said, her voice touched with worry.

"You know that I'm still your best friend first. Agent second. I just want you to succeed."

There was that word. *Succeed.*

Daisy smiled. "I know. I'll call you." She ended the call, watching through the window as a rough-looking man pulled her lone piece of luggage out from the cargo space and set it on the dock for her, and she felt a flurry of excitement as she made her way to the door.

Please, God, don't let this be a dead end.

She sucked in a hopeful breath.

The ferry worker stood at the gap, his calloused hand extended to help her down the ramp.

Here went nothing.

That hopeful feeling followed her as she stepped out of the Island House Inn onto its charming wraparound porch the following morning. From the front steps of this historic building, Daisy could see the entire harbor laid out ahead of her, the late sunrise spread across the water in hues of blue and purple. A light fog crept across the pebbly beach, dissipating at the cobblestone street and the docks where the ferry, with its faded blue stripes, sat waiting for the commuters making their way down the boardwalk, chatting each other up with neighborly smiles and rosy cheeks.

This place really was a dream.

Daisy slipped her phone from her pocket, turned so the water lay behind her, and posed for a picture. The morning light touched her cheeks, giving her practiced smile a hopeful glow.

This was going to work out. It had to.

She opened up her socials and posted with a caption that read:

Big things coming, friends! Stay tuned for more from the girl with a plan!

And it was time for the first step of that plan.

Daisy dialed the number she'd looked up after settling into her hotel room the night before.

A woman's voice answered the call. "Hello?"

"Hi, this is Daisy Decker. I left a voicemail last night, but—"

"Oh, hi! Of course," Mia said warmly from the other end of the phone. "I—" She broke away, her voice suddenly distant. "Maggie, sweetie, let's keep our food on the table"—and then back to Daisy—"Sorry about that. Yes, I was just about to call you back. I hear you're interested in moving to Jonathon Island?"

Moving to Jonathon Island? Daisy bit her lip. "I'm definitely interested in buying a house . . ." Moving to an island a thousand miles from her home and her career, not as much.

"Great! I've got a couple hours—Finn, off the chair. Feet on the floor, bud—free next week. When can you get out to the island?"

Daisy felt a little of her excitement deflate. "Actually, I'm on the island right now. Any chance you might be available today?"

"Today?" Daisy heard a rustling of papers and then,

"I've got a couple of minutes open this morning. But I've got to catch the ferry at ten-fifteen. I can give you a quick show of the houses available so you can get a look before we take the next steps. How does that sound?"

A grin split Daisy's face as she pushed away from the railing. "That sounds perfect! Thank you so much!"

"No problem. I'll drop the kids with a friend for a while and meet you at the corner of Jonathon Boulevard and Main in twenty."

"See you then!" Daisy agreed and ended the call, slipped her phone back into her pocket, and practically skipped down the remaining steps.

"Morning," a gruff voice called from the cobblestone walkway leading from the street. Augo, the man who'd been working the front desk the evening before, stood outside the white picket fence, a bundle of flowers in one arm and a paper sack in the other. The man looked to be in his late sixties, with a flat cap, thick white mustache, and flannel. A small red-haired Dachshund padded along at his heels, her tongue contentedly lolling from the side of her mouth. If Daisy remembered from the night before, the dog's name was Lucy.

"Working again this morning?" Daisy asked, hurrying down the path toward the gate, swinging it open for him. Lucy ran through first, her little tail wagging as she looked up at Daisy, expecting pets. Daisy happily obliged, giving the dog a scratch behind the ears.

"Thank you, Miss . . ." The man paused, shifting the paper bag in his arm. "Remind me?"

"It's Daisy." She smiled.

He returned the smile, his own buried under his bushy mustache. "Thank you, Daisy." He turned back toward the inn. "And to answer your question—Sarah's our regular day shift. But Caleb said she's not feeling too great, so it looks like you're stuck with me again." He grinned, pausing at the first step of the landing. "You up for some breakfast? I just stopped at Doug's Market on my way in, got some eggs, some smoked salmon. You like salmon?"

Daisy cracked a genuine smile at the man's candid invitation. "Sounds amazing, but I've got somewhere I need to be—Actually, you wouldn't mind telling me how to get to Jonathon Boulevard, would you?"

"Big plans, eh?" Augo raised an eyebrow, grinning mischievously.

Daisy shrugged. "Something like that." Everything like that, actually.

He tilted his head. "You know what they say about plans."

"No, what?"

"If you want to make God laugh, just tell Him your plans." The old man let out a hearty hoot, giving her a warm wink before finishing his ascent up the stairs, Lucy once again at his heels. "Head down Blueberry Boulevard, when you find a turn, take it and keep walking. You can't miss it!" he called back over his shoulder as the front door shut behind him.

"Can't miss it, indeed," Daisy grumbled as she spun on the heel of her Dr. Martens once again. The wind swept her ponytail across her shoulders, and Daisy adjusted the neckline of her turtleneck sweater, wishing once again that she'd brought something a little warmer than a cardigan and high-rise, ripped jeans. If this thing panned out, she'd have to stock up on a few choice clothing items, starting with a warm jacket.

Admittedly, Daisy had never been great at directions, but she shouldn't have needed a GPS to take a single-turn walk through a zero-stoplight town. She huffed again, tucking her chin into her collar.

Per Augo's directions, she'd gone "up" Blueberry (whatever that meant) and taken the first turn she could find, which had brought her down to the marina and right up to the water until she couldn't "keep walking," so she'd hopped onto the boardwalk and followed it toward town.

On her first pass up the boardwalk, Daisy had stopped to admire the stunning views. The golds and reds of the trees poking around the Victorian houses up the hill. The picturesque sight of wooden boats bobbing in the bay. The pops of blue and yellow winking from the main stretch of buildings in town.

It was all much less charming on her third pass through.

Finally, after popping into a cute little coffee shop and being given three simultaneous sets of directions by three different well-meaning townsfolk, none of which were the same, proceeded by a handful of probing—also well-meaning—questions about who she was and what she was doing, she arrived on the corner of Jonathon and Main.

A woman rose from a bench under a nearby awning,

her warm plaid jacket of gold and blues complementing the fall decor peppered throughout Main Street. Daisy stepped toward her, assuming she must be the realtor.

"I was starting to wonder if you'd changed your mind," the woman said with a smile. She held two coffees, one extended toward Daisy as she stopped at the curb. "Got you some coffee. It's a chilly day, and we'll have some walking to do, so I thought you might need something warm." This with a glance at Daisy's ripped jeans, the skin beneath already turning a rosy pink.

"Thank you," Daisy said, taking the cup in her chilled hands. "I'll admit, I did get lost. But it's not my fault—I think the front desk guy gave me bad directions."

The woman frowned. "Caleb?"

Daisy winced as she took a sip of her coffee. "Augo."

"Ah, well, that explains it," she chuckled. "Augo can't be trusted with directions."

Daisy raised her brows.

"He likes to make them intentionally vague. Says it helps people 'find the town.'"

Oh, Daisy had found it all right.

"We should get going," the woman said, nodding toward the street hidden between two false-front buildings. "I'm Mia, by the way."

"Daisy." She held out a hand and Mia shook it.

"I'm excited to show you around, Daisy," Mia said, leading the way up the cobblestone street. Daisy took a hesitant sip of the still-scalding coffee as the fall breeze nipped at her neck. "What brings you to Jonathon Island? Other than your house search, of course."

Daisy's coffee caught in her throat.

That was a big question.

She went with the simple answer. "I'm a designer. I'm on the hunt for a renovation project."

The cobblestone street soon gave way to a residential neighborhood. A row of cozy houses sat nestled between a mixture of maple and pine trees. Many of the yards here were overgrown, the picket fences wrapped with invasive vines, boxwoods stretching toward the sky in front of empty bay windows. But Daisy could see it. The potential was there in every property they passed. The potential for these houses to become homes again, with the right kind of love and care they'd obviously once had.

"That sounds like a really fun job," Mia said, stopping in front of a faded-blue craftsman-style house, the covered porch overtaken by foliage that climbed toward the second story.

It looked the way a perfectly rainy day felt.

It reminded Daisy of the first house she had ever remodeled. Warmth grew in her chest at the memory.

"Well, we have a few cute little options to take a look at. Do you have a budget in mind?" Mia asked.

Daisy shot her a tentative look. "Um . . . well, I heard about the dollar house program . . ."

"Oh." Mia blinked, her eyes widening. "I'm so sorry for the confusion. The dollar house program is over. There aren't any more storefronts left."

Daisy tilted her head, her brows drawing together. "Storefronts?"

Mia matched her confused expression. "Yeah, you

know. To open your business . . . That's the dollar house program. It was for business owners who wanted to open shops on the island. They all had to apply and get approval from the town council. But all the spots have been filled. I'm so sorry. We do still have houses for sale though." She gestured toward the craftsman hopefully.

Daisy's heart sank, the plan slipping. "I don't have a very big budget . . ."

The wind picked up, shaking the trees. Through a gap in the tree line, Daisy spotted the same Victorian-style turret she'd seen from the ferry the day before.

Mia followed her gaze. "Let me make a call. I might just have something."

The fifteenth time's the charm—or so Hunter Barrett kept telling himself as he stared at his father's red ink massacre of yet another perfectly good blueprint. The red marks on his latest blueprint were becoming almost comical at this point. Three weeks, fifteen revisions, and his father had rejected each one for increasingly microscopic issues—a quarter-inch variation in the support beam placement, a slightly too-wide window trim, and yesterday's complaint about the "aesthetically concerning" spacing between floor joists that literally no one would ever see. But version fifteen? Hunter had spent half the night adjusting measurements that were already well within code, knowing his father would scrutinize every detail like he was renovating the White House instead of a midwestern-suburb, ranch-style house.

He carefully rolled up the document and slid it into his backpack. The old man couldn't possibly reject this one.

Hunter groaned as he stepped over his brother's gym bag in the hallway of their small two-bedroom apartment. "Come on, Waylen," he grumbled as he slid the bag out of the traffic zone.

"Talking to yourself again?" Waylen asked from the kitchen table, where he sat with his dirty-socked feet kicked up on the handcrafted oak, one arm slung over the back of his chair, eating an Eggo waffle with his bare hands.

Hunter slapped his brother's feet to the floor as he crossed to the fridge. "I'd talk to *you* if I thought you'd listen," he grumbled into the dark refrigerator. "And I thought you were going to fix the light in here?"

Waylen balked. "Why me?"

Over his shoulder, Hunter cast him a look of disbelief. "How about because *you're* the one with time on your hands?"

Waylen scoffed. "What's that supposed to mean?"

"It means you could afford to take a minute to fix a lightbulb between shifts of donut eating down at the police station. Or is there a recent crime streak I haven't heard about?"

"You know, the whole cops and donuts thing is a common misconception," Waylen said, threading his hands behind his head as he leaned back again. "I'm more of a Danish guy myself."

Hunter shot him a teasing glare over his shoulder. "How about you become an electrician guy, or I'm gonna start charging you your full half of the rent."

"Yeah, yeah . . ."

Hunter cracked a smile, rolling his eyes.

Giving up on a nutritious breakfast, he snatched a bagel from the top of the fridge and popped it in the toaster.

"Speaking of appointments," Hunter said, leaning back against the counter. "You said you'd help out at the River-front project tomorrow. Dad really can't afford any delays, so don't forget."

Waylen appeared completely taken aback by the reminder. "What makes you think I'd forgotten?"

The bagels popped out of the toaster, and Hunter spun to retrieve them, butter knife in hand. "Because one of the sticky notes you use to keep appointments ended up on the bottom of my shoe last night."

Waylen shrugged. "So?"

"That, and you forgot to show up to the last two projects you agreed to help out with." He finished slathering the bagel with butter, wrapped it in a napkin, and stuffed it into the pocket of his jacket. "I mean it, I don't want the demo team giving me any dirty looks by association when you forget again."

Waylen waved him off with a sheepish grin. "Thanks, *Mom.*"

"You joke, but maybe if you had a mom around, you'd know better than to put your feet up on my handcrafted hardwood table." He pushed Waylen's feet aside again and picked up a stack of papers from the table, sliding them into his backpack. "You need anything from the mainland today?"

"I'll survive," Waylen replied, finishing his last bite of waffle.

Hunter gave a nod and checked his watch. Right on time. He'd have exactly forty minutes to catch the 10:15 ferry.

Hunter soaked in the morning light as he stepped out of Good Day Coffee with a warm cup of joe steaming into the air. Overhead, the sound of seagulls mixed with the lapping of water on the shore, and across the street, Jack, the town dog, was getting some morning affection from Dani Sullivan. She rose, giving him a wave as she stepped into the Tourism Bureau.

It was another beautiful day on the island.

Hunter made his way down Main Street, his eyes gazing over the wild blue of the water. The wind flicked at his hair as he rounded the corner at the end of the street and hurried up the hill. His boots creaked over the wooden ramp, leading up to the old post office building. The small, cream-colored house sat nestled on the corner with lilac trees, now past bloom, framing the walkway. A bell rang out as Hunter stepped inside.

"Morning, Hunter!"

"Morning, Roger," Hunter replied, waving at the white-haired man behind the counter.

"Some exciting mail today!" the older man said, leaning over the desk to watch as Hunter opened his PO box.

"I keep trying to tell you, Rog." Hunter slid the contents out of the small metal box and closed it back up. "You're not supposed to look at people's mail while you're sorting it."

Roger scoffed. "First of all, I'm too old to waste away of boredom. Second, it just jumped out at me."

Hunter frowned. "What did?"

"See for yourself." He rapped a knuckle against the counter and wandered back into the office.

Hunter sorted through the pile, not sure what he was looking for.

And then he did.

His address was written in gold cursive, with a floral stamp in the corner. A wax seal weighed it down, but that was nothing compared to the weight of the sender's address.

Hunter's heart jumped into his throat as he opened the envelope and pulled out the thick cardstock.

Lisa Sherman
And
Carlisle Hansen
Joyfully Invite You
To Celebrate Their Wedding
Saturday, December 7th,
Twenty Twenty-Four
Four o'clock in the Afternoon
The Teachout Building
Chicago, Illinois

Hunter dragged a hand through his hair and flipped the card over, half expecting some sort of handwritten note with something like *I know I abandoned you and your brothers, but I'm sooooo much happier. Please bring gifts.*

He was going to throw up.

His phone rang, pulling his attention away from the invitation long enough to catch his oldest brother's name flashing across the screen.

"She's out of her mind if she thinks I'm going to her wedding," Hunter growled into the phone.

"Wow, and good morning to you too," Miles said on the other end.

"It was." Hunter stuffed the mail into his backpack, unable to summon the energy to look at the rest. With his luck, the rest were probably all consecutive jury summonses or IRS audit notices. "Until I checked the mail."

Hunter pushed back through the door, sucking in a breath of cold air as he started back down the hill.

Miles paused. "I think you're being a little hard on her, Hunt. She's still our mom."

Hunter couldn't help the eye roll. Miles had always been too forgiving for his own good. Together, his brothers could cause a real mess. Evan and Jude found the strays. Miles and Waylen kept them. And Hunter cleaned up the pieces when it was all said and done. Mom was no exception.

He rounded the corner, the docks coming into view. Across the boardwalk, commuters and a nearly non-existent handful of tourists were gathering for the 10:15 ferry. He crossed the street to join them.

Hunter stopped at the docks, out of earshot of the

crowd gathering below. "Listen, Miles, you can go if you want, but you can count me out."

His brother's silence spoke volumes. "Okay."

Hunter pushed out a breath, trying to force the tension out of the conversation. "How are things out there? Gone on any fancy hippie retreats lately?"

"Oh, ha ha. I go on one nature retreat and suddenly I'm a hippie."

"Your words, not mine!" Hunter chuckled, relaxing just slightly.

"For your information, the adventure tours are going well. I led a kayak group out this morning for the sunrise."

"Brave kayakers. It's freezing on Lake Michigan."

Miles barked a laugh of agreement. "You should come out here sometime."

Hunter made a face despite knowing his brother couldn't see it. "Eh, I think I'm still a little jaded toward the Windy City."

"Still hung up on that stupid contest?" his brother teased. "You know, it's not the city's fault."

"Even so, I'd prefer not to relive my greatest embarrassment every time I come to visit you. You'll have to come to us. Dad's been perfecting his smoked ribs for just such an occasion."

"How is Dad?"

Hunter turned, leaning his elbows on the edge of the boardwalk railing, switching the coffee to the hand that had grown cold. "You know Dad. He works too hard. I wish he'd take a break."

"Sounds like someone else I know," Miles poked.

Below, Mia Franklin caught his eye from the dock and gave him a wave, gesturing for him to come down and talk to her. "Hey, Miles, I wish I could catch up more, but it looks like Mia needs to talk to me."

"No problem, let's talk later."

"Sure thing." He hung up and strode down the dock as Mia made her way to meet him, two kids in tow. It was still hard to see an old friend, now a widow, managing on her own. Then again, she wasn't on her own anymore. She and Cody Hart were getting pretty serious, from the sound of it.

"Hey, Mia, what's up?"

"Sorry to cut your call short. Was it important?"

"Nothing to worry about." Hunter shrugged. "What's going on?"

She released her son's hand to brush a strand of dark hair behind her ear, and he dropped into a crouch, stalking the seagull a few feet behind them. "I was hoping you might ask your dad to give me a call. I couldn't get through to him just now, but I have someone who's interested in the house."

Hunter frowned. "Interested?"

"Finn, honey, leave the bird alone." Mia waved her son closer and turned her gaze back to Hunter. "Yeah, some designer. I told her where to find the house so she could take a look. But I think she's looking to buy immediately, so I really need Joe to call me back."

The prerecorded announcement interrupted over the speakers. "On behalf of everyone at Jonathon Island, we'd like to thank you for coming to the island . . ."

Mia began ushering the children onto the ferry. "Come on, kids, time to go." When Hunter made no move to follow, she paused, turning back toward him. "You're not coming?"

"My first meeting's not until two o'clock. I'll catch the next one."

The ferry pulled away, and Hunter turned toward home. No way he was letting someone take his house.

Two

DAISY'S BREATH FOGGED THE AIR AS she continued hiking the long road encircling the island. Her frozen hand clutched her now ice-cold coffee cup as though there was still a drop of warmth and it just needed to be squeezed out. In her other hand, her fingers were turning red with the cold as she held her phone, following the GPS toward her destination.

"It's not a sure thing," Mia had told her as she'd tapped the location into Daisy's Google Maps. "But I know Joe's been toying with the idea of selling for a while. And nobody nearby will touch the place, so you could probably get a bargain price for it."

She handed the phone back over. "Anyway, it can't hurt for you to at least see the house. Nobody's lived there in *years*." She'd drawn the word out, planting a seed of doubt as to Daisy's chances of reselling the place once it was done. Well, that and the little tidbit about nobody being willing to touch the place. But before she'd had a chance to inquire further, Mia was pointing her toward the road and pushing her on her way with promises to call and schedule a tour later.

And so here she was, hiking up the sloping hill that split off from the main road just behind the massive hotel, her weathered boots beating against the pavement.

A few locals on bikes waved politely as they whizzed by.

An actual *horse* clopped past. And riding it was none other than the world-famous singer, Eli Noble. Daisy'd tried to play it cool as he passed, giving her a polite nod.

A wooden fence curved along the path, and trees rose on either side until they dissipated and gave way to the view beyond. Daisy stopped, her lips parting in surprise. The road overlooked the shores of Lake Huron, and it seemed to glitter for miles. The bright morning sun scattered gold among the wave as it finished its ascent. The wind carried the scent of fresh water and pine, and for once, the cold didn't bite.

Daisy let out a soft breath, unable to take it all in in one glance.

Her cell phone pinged, her GPS indicating she'd reached her destination.

Daisy turned around.

"You'll know it when you see it," Mia had told her.

She was right.

On the hill behind her stood a well-aged two-story Queen Anne–style Victorian house. The ground level boasted a deep apron porch with stone-worked balustrades, and on the right, a weathered door overlooked the overgrown lawn, its stone walkway nearly lost to time. To the left stood a stunning three-story turret, its oval roof rising above the golds and reds of the tree line.

At first glance she may not have realized there was anything wrong with the house. Until she caught sight of the scorch marks that clawed their way out beneath the turret windows, a thick layer of grime preventing a view of the inside.

Daisy felt a squeeze in her chest. She hadn't planned to take on a project this big. A cute little bungalow with a bad porch, maybe? A sweet starter home in need of a new kitchen, sure. But nothing like this. This house would take time, precision, planning, and most importantly, funds.

The wind shifted, pulling her in, and Daisy thought of Augo's words earlier that morning. *You want to make God laugh? Just tell Him your plans.*

She couldn't go forward with this idea. Could she?

A tumble of leaves brushed across the porch, catching beneath the stunning bay window of what looked like a parlor. It really was a beautiful house, unlike anything she'd find back in LA.

Daisy pulled out her phone, and a moment later, Robin's face appeared on the screen. Her friend was wearing her power outfit—a black jumpsuit accentuating her golden pixie-cut hair and green eyes. "Hey, babe! What's up?"

"I'm about to go off the rails and it's really freaking me out and I need you to talk me out of it," Daisy said, angling the screen to avoid the glare of the sun off the water.

"Oh boy, here we go," Robin said.

Daisy turned the screen toward the house, the wind

tugging at one of the dangling shutters. "I found this amazing one-of-a-kind historic house that neeeeds me." The words came out like a child asking to keep the baby bird they found in the yard.

Robin's mouth was gaping, her eyes taking in the massive project as mental calculations scrolled through her expression.

"Babe . . . I don't think—"

"Before you tell me I can't afford it," Daisy interrupted, ignoring the fact that she'd called her friend to talk her out of the project, not the other way around, "I think we could pitch a YouTube show to some of my original sponsors. You know, the ones from pre–*Double Decker* days." Back before everything had gotten . . . complicated.

Robin pressed her lips together, thinking. Daisy watched her friend's expression light up, a slow grin spreading across her face. "That could work."

"Right? It'll be just like the old days." The days when they'd spent nights and weekends and every free moment building up Daisy's YouTube career, filming affordable DIY projects and how-to videos and designer collabs, working toward the goal of getting picked up for a design series on HGTV. And they'd done just that.

"Anyway," she went on, "I know we can do it again. I've already got a serious following. If we show the network that there is a demand for my content, I just know we'll get picked up again, and we'll be back on top in no time."

Robin shrugged. "Can't hurt to try."

"That's the spirit!" she cheered. "There's a lot of details to nail down still, but I'm gonna get a look around and see if I can't muster up some footage for proof of concept. Why don't you put together a list of potential sponsors in the meantime?"

"You got it," her friend said, already scribbling a hectic to-do list across the whiteboard behind her desk. "And send me your videos. I can be our editor until we can afford to hire someone."

"Sounds good. Love you!"

"Love you," Robin replied.

The call ended, and Daisy turned back to the house. She sucked in a deep breath.

Here goes everything.

"What's up, friends! I'm here on Jonathon Island, where we're embarking on a journey to uncover the beauty in the discarded!" Daisy held her arms out wide, showing off the disheveled house to her phone, which was propped against a pile of rocks on the yard's stone wall.

A gust of wind knocked it over, and Daisy let her arms flop to her sides. "That's okay. We'll fine-tune it later."

She strode through the dewy grass to retrieve her phone, flipping through the videos. She let out a sigh. She'd never get enough footage out here in the yard.

She cast a glance over her shoulder, her eyes climbing the porch to the second floor and over the picturesque turret.

Mia *had* said nobody'd lived there for years. It wasn't like she'd be intruding if she took a teensy look around . . .

Daisy crept up the front steps, the wood groaning beneath her feet. She raised a hand to the glass panels of the front door and peered inside, halfway expecting someone to jump out at her.

The entryway was still.

Daisy slipped the phone from her pocket again and snapped a pic of the porch.

"For the 'before,'" she explained to no one in particular. "Actually, I should probably grab a quick 'before' shot of the entryway, before it gets footprints all over it."

That was reasonable, right?

She tried the brass doorknob and let out a breath of disappointment to find it locked. Maybe it was for the best. She wouldn't be tempted to—

The door creaked open.

Well . . .

She pressed a fingertip to the door and pushed it the rest of the way.

She really should just wait for a formal tour. It wasn't her house . . . *yet*.

Daisy shot a glance over her shoulder.

"Oh, for Pete's sake," she mumbled to herself. "Just go in already."

She stepped over the threshold.

Her eyes took a moment to adjust, the edges of the foyer steeped in darkness. Dust floated in the light cascading from the open door. The floor, aged and faded, creaked as she crept farther in.

Across from the door, a wide staircase led to the second story, the banister of handcrafted oak worn and nicked around the edges. Daisy noted a few missing spindles. To the left, the hall opened to a parlor with coffered ceilings of the same wood.

"This place is incredible," she breathed. Her followers would love—an idea cut through her mind. What better way to show potential sponsors proof of concept than to get people begging for the YouTube show?

She tapped her screen and opened her social media app, turning the camera toward herself. Daisy's finger hovered over the *Go live* button. For a girl who'd spent the majority of her life following a blueprint, she sure was making a lot of decisions on the fly lately.

She tapped the screen. Desperate times and all . . .

"Hi, friends! It's Daisy!" She waved at the camera. "I'm working on a brand-new project that I'll be super excited to share with you a little later, but I thought I'd give a little sneak peek to all the followers who keep up with me."

Comments started scrolling across the bottom of the screen.

@CraftyHome: Can't wait!

@TheDIYDogMom: Tell me more!!!

@Anonymousquirrel: I love your designs. 🖤

"Aww, you guys are so sweet!" Daisy grinned. "I'm working on a new project, so I thought I'd do a little house tour of just one of the properties I'm considering for it. Let's take a look."

Angling the camera up so viewers could see both her face and the surrounding rooms, she wandered deeper into the house.

Her hand ran over the wood paneling as she entered

the parlor, her viewer count already ticking toward three hundred. "Take a look at this parlor. I love the attention to detail. There's just something beautiful about the story these old houses tell." She chuckled and flashed a warm smile at the camera.

All things considered, the house wasn't in that bad a shape. The original hardwood floors were a little worn by use. There was some water damage around the antique windows. But no animal nests. No rotting floors. It almost made her wonder why it was vacant. That was, until she spotted the scorch marks at the other end of the room.

Oh.

Tentatively, she crossed to the glass-paned door framed by soot. Above it, an empty hole gaped in the wall where a transom should have been. Daisy gripped the antique handle, the tarnished brass cold against her fingers, and opened the door to find a stunning, rounded sunroom: the bottom level of the turret.

She gasped.

"You guys have to see this!" She rotated the camera so it was looking into the space. The footage captured the faint blue of the walls, complementing them against the sparkling view of Lake Huron. Even with the thick layer of—what was that? Soot?—on the windows, sunlight still managed to pour inside.

Grinning, Daisy stepped inside, taking it all in. "This room is so much bigger than I expected." The space had obviously been expanded at some point.

Despite the peeling wallpaper and soot-stained walls, the missing stones around the fireplace, and the heavy wooden mantel hanging at a dangerous angle, ready to fall at any moment, the room was nothing short of spectacular. Daisy could easily imagine it filled with the love and laughter of a large family.

More comments rolled in, the viewers nearing a thousand.

@DreamingDelia: It's amazing.

@CraftyHome: WOOOW

@Kelsiewiththekids: Needs the Decker touch.

Giving the precarious fireplace a wide birth, Daisy started toward the next doorway to her left. She turned the camera back to face her. "Should we keep going?"

@TheGreeneHouse: Oh. My goodness. YES

@PosieDarling: Pleeeease

She reached for the handle, and her heart jumped into her throat.

It was locked.

"Okay, not a problem." She retreated the way she'd entered. The crystal doorknob turned, but the door wouldn't budge.

She was trapped.

Hunter's breath came out in foggy huffs as he strode purposefully up the familiar road, his mind playing out the argument he'd have with his dad just as soon as the man picked up his phone. What was he thinking, trying to sell the house?

Hunter's long strides ate up the pavement as he emerged from the covered tree line onto Sunset Cove.

Ahead of him, the lake spread against the horizon, the blue of the water merging with that of the sky. The family home loomed ahead with its Victorian gables and wraparound porch. The familiar sight usually brought him comfort. Today, it only fueled his anger. The front door hung open. Apparently, the unwelcome party had taken the liberty of going inside.

He wasted no time, tromping across the overgrown lawn and onto the porch. His heavy boots thundered up the steps toward the open door.

He entered the house and paused, his eyes scanning the dark foyer before a muffled thump caught his attention. It was quickly followed by a frustrated cry. Hunter frowned; his eyes caught the footprints in the thick layer of dust that covered the hardwood floors and followed them toward the parlor. The sound came again, this time accompanied by a voice.

"Hello? Is someone there?" The voice came from the sunroom.

Hunter jogged over, peering through the frosted panes of the glass door. Inside, he could make out a female figure, her hands pressed against the door.

"You all right in there?" Hunter called out, his anger momentarily forgotten at the sound of her voice, the edge of frayed nerves in her words.

"Oh, thank goodness!" Her voice gushed with relief. "The door is jammed. I can't get it open."

Hunter let out a sigh. "Hang on." He knelt to examine the antique doorknob, noting the slight misalignment that had been known to make it stick. "I see the problem . . ."

"But?"

"I have to step away to get the supplies to fix it." Hunter brushed his dusty hands off on his pants as he rose. "Will you be okay for a couple more minutes?"

He watched the outline of her shoulders slump and felt a pang of sympathy for her. She hadn't known what she was getting herself into when she'd stepped into the Barrett house.

"I'll be okay," she said quietly.

Hunter nodded, as though she could see it, and turned on his heels. His steel-toed boots thumped against the hardwood floor as he made his way through the maze of a house. He passed back through the sitting room, taking a left at the stairs to the hallway behind them. Memories rushed over him as he entered the old kitchen at the back of the house, memories of his childhood, his brothers laughing as they tracked backyard mud over the tile, his mother swatting a towel after them with a tired smile on her face. Her hand curling protectively around her belly—he pushed the memory aside, turning away as he strode toward the door on the opposite wall.

Morning light washed over him, his eyes squinting against the sun.

The backyard was a jungle. Vines and bushes clawed at the high stone walls around the back side of the property.

Weeds nearly as tall as his six-foot frame peppered the expanse of green grass and wildflowers. On the other end of the yard sat an old two-stall stable, which his father had converted to a workshop before Hunter was even born.

He picked his way across and entered the old workshop, emerging a moment later with the supplies he needed.

When he returned to the sunroom, the figure was gone, though a long shadow seeped out at the bottom of the door. Hunter smirked as he knelt to work. "You still there?"

"Oh, I'm here," she replied, her voice steeped with playful sarcasm.

He let out a sideways chuckle. "Good. I was afraid you'd run off before I'd get the chance to rescue you."

"My hero," the woman said. "I don't suppose you happen to be a firefighter or police officer or someone else who specializes in breaking down doors?"

Hunter glanced at her shadow, grinning despite himself. "You're in luck. I'm a contractor. Doors are kind of my thing."

"Hear that? A contractor, just what a girl like me needs."

He laughed, working on the mechanism. "You know, most people wait until after they've seen my face to start flirting."

"Who says I'm flirting? Maybe I just really, really want out of this room."

"Fair enough. Although I have to warn you, I've been told I'm devastatingly handsome. You might swoon when that door opens."

"I'll try to contain myself," she replied dryly.

With a final twist and a firm push, the door swung open. "There we go! You're free to—"

Hunter's words died in his throat as he found himself face-to-face with a ghost from his past. Her honey-brown hair was longer, her short, choppy bob now long enough to be pulled back into a peppy ponytail. Her clothes were different. Her makeup was different. But those eyes were unmistakable.

"Daisy," he breathed.

Her playful smile faltered, replaced by a look of shock that must have mirrored his own. "Hunter?"

For a moment, neither of them seemed able to move, memories flooding the space between them, holding them captive.

His chest tightened.

A flicker of movement over her shoulder caught his attention, and his gaze shifted to the wall behind her, where a phone was propped up against the windowsill. He caught sight of himself, his wide frame filling the doorway. His attention snapped back to the woman trespassing in his house, and he nodded toward the phone. "Turn it off."

Daisy's eyes flashed with confusion, her brows drawing together as she glanced back over her shoulder. "Oh! Sorry!"

She hurried across the room. "Okay, friends, I think that's enough of an adventure for today . . . maybe even enough for the next couple of days. Be on the lookout for new postings on my channel. Until next time, love ya!"

She tapped a button, and the stream ended.

"I am *so* sorry," she said, turning back to him. "I wasn't trying to trespass, I just—"

"What are you doing here?" He cut her off.

Daisy froze, her lips parting as though in shock. "What am *I* doing here? I've got the same question about *you*."

"I live here."

Daisy's gaze darted around the obviously unoccupied house.

Hunter gave an exasperated sigh. "On Jonathon Island. But you knew that."

She frowned. "No . . . I didn't. You told me you lived in Michigan. Not a magical Hallmark wonderland." Hunter rolled his eyes at that. "I wanna buy the house."

He crossed his arms over his chest. "It's not for sale."

She stepped back, cocking her head, the dirty sunlight spotlighting her as her demeanor changed. She rested a hand on her hip. "Really?"

"Really."

"Because I just talked to a realtor who said some guy named *Joe* was selling it. Last time I checked, your name's not Joe." Her hair swished behind her as she tilted her head in mock confusion.

Hunter let out a growl of frustration. "Joe is my dad, and it's not his house to sell."

At that, Daisy blinked, doubt sinking into that ever-present light in her eyes.

"Now, if you'll excuse me." He started toward the door. "I need to make the next ferry. I'd say it was nice seeing you again, but . . ."

He'd made it nearly to the door when the sound of her soft footsteps pattered after him. "Hold on! Hunter, wait!"

He stepped out onto the porch and continued down the path. The sooner he could put this whole thing behind him, the better.

"Hunter!"

Daisy caught up to him at the street, her hand hooking his elbow. "Please, just hear me out."

Against his better judgment, he stopped, his jaw pulsing as he turned toward her.

Winded, Daisy looked as though she'd run a marathon somewhere between the house and the street. The long hair that framed her face was swept back, showing off the flush in her cheeks. "Sheesh, you're fast," she said, dropping her hands to her knees as she sucked in another breath.

Hunter gave her his best apathetic expression. "What?"

Rising back to her full five foot three, she pasted on that Daisy Decker smile. "I'm sorry about trespassing. I don't have an excuse except that it's a gorgeous house and I am so in love with it." Her words came out in a breathless string as she grinned, pushing a strand of hair behind her ear in that familiar way that he'd only just managed to forget. "But I don't need to buy the house. I just want to remodel it. Restore it."

Change it, she meant. Hunter could read between the lines. This was his home. His family. No way.

Drawing in every ounce of his patience, he stepped into her space.

"Understand this, Daisy." He ducked his head to meet

her eyes as he enunciated every word. "You. Are. Never. Touching. That. House."

Daisy blinked, her doe eyes wide as her lips parted in surprise.

Hunter straightened, satisfied his words were sinking in.

"I don't remember you being this much of a grouch!" she shouted as he turned, leaving her behind.

"That's funny. I hardly remember you at all," he lied over his shoulder as he stomped back down the hill.

Three

F OR A DAY THAT HAD STARTED SO WELL, it hadn't taken long for things to spin out of control. The morning's events were still replaying in his head as Hunter pulled into the parking lot of Barrett Construction in Port Joseph, having picked up his car from long-term parking near the ferry. He didn't know what to be more upset about … His mother's unsolicited wedding invite, his father trying to sell the family home, or the reappearance of the woman he'd spent years trying to forget.

He gathered himself and stepped out of the truck, carrying his jacket. This far onto the mainland, the air off the lake didn't quite have the same chilling effect that kept the island a good ten degrees cooler year-round.

Hunter pushed through the glass doors, the familiar scent of coffee and sawdust doing little to calm his frayed nerves as he made his way toward his dad's office.

"Morning, Hunter," Dawn said, catching Hunter's attention from behind the administration desk with a hand over the receiver of her phone. Her desk was piled high with forms and notes, and a coffee cup sat forgotten beside the computer with a sticky note scribbled on in teal ink. She grabbed a stack of files and plopped them down on top of the reception desk. "Can you look at these when you get a chance?"

"Will do," Hunter said, sliding the pile into his palm. He nodded toward the scattered mess on her desk. "That kind of day already, it seems." Good to know it wasn't just him.

Dawn shoved out a breath. "Where do I start?" She rolled her eyes dramatically. "I've been on hold all morning with the permit office. The inspection for the Wilkinsons' project has been rescheduled—"

"What—why?" Hunter flipped through the pile with furrowed brows.

Dawn shook her head. "Your father stopped by and noticed that the window trim was half an inch wider than the approved specs." Of course he had. "Then there's the issue with the supplier for the Morton renovation. They're saying the order is delayed by at least three weeks because of some custom moldings we ordered?"

The unnecessary custom moldings Hunter had spoken at length about with his father. They were supposed to have been edited out of the design. Hunter ran a hand over his face. "All right, I'll call them and see if I can expedite it. What else?"

"Two of our best crew members called in sick, and we're short-staffed on the Riverfront project because we keep sending portions of the framing back to be redone," Dawn continued.

"Let me guess—"

"Your father says the nail spacing was off from the blueprints. We're going to be behind." Dawn continued, "Oh, and Mrs. Henderson is threatening to sue over the color of her kitchen cabinets."

"The color *she* chose and signed off on three separate times?" Hunter asked incredulously.

Dawn nodded, a wry smile on her face. "The very same."

Hunter let out a long breath, his eyes drifting shut. At least that was a problem that didn't require him to babysit his own father to keep him from derailing the entire business over minute details. "Okay, I'll handle the inspection issue first, see if I can call in a favor and get us rescheduled and back on track. Can you reach out to David over at Midwest Reno, see if he's willing to loan us some guys? If he gives you any flak, remind him of the carpentry job I did for him last minute a month back. And schedule a meeting with Mrs. Henderson for this afternoon. I'll smooth things over. Oh, and I asked Waylen to help out with Riverfront tomorrow, so add him to the crew count. He'll make sure they stick to the specs."

Dawn's shoulders visibly relaxed. "What would we do without you, Hunter? This place would fall apart in a week."

Warmth washed over him despite the heavy weight in his chest. He was good at his job. And he enjoyed the work. But sometimes it felt like he was single-handedly keeping the company afloat while his father obsessed over every little detail.

"Is my dad in?" Hunter asked, glancing toward the office at the back of the building.

Dawn's expression turned hesitant. "He is, but he's in a meeting."

Hunter frowned. "Did he say with whom?"

Before she could answer, the door to his dad's office opened, and Seb Jonathon, the mayor of Jonathon Island, with his graying hair and normally positive demeanor, stepped out, his expression sour as he stormed down the hall.

Apparently, Hunter and Dawn weren't the only people having a rough day.

"Seb," Hunter said in surprise.

Seb was so deep inside his head, he hardly noticed Hunter standing at the desk. He did a double-take, Hunter's greeting finally seeming to click. "Hunter! How you doin'?"

Hunter tilted his head, his brows raised. "It's been one of those days."

Seb chuckled half-heartedly. He glanced back over his shoulder and nodded in the direction of the office. "Maybe you could talk some sense into him?"

If only that had ever worked . . .

"I've got a great opportunity for the company," Seb explained. "An opportunity to get the business back onto the island, where you belong."

Hunter's brows shot upward. "Really?"

"Really," Seb said. "Thanks to the revitalization plan,

we've got a lot of new business owners on the island, living in houses that have been abandoned for a good deal of time. But aside from that, Liam has been looking for specialty contractors for the Grand to restore some of the hotel's more iconic features. We need a Barrett out there."

Hunter's chest squeezed at the opportunity.

Again, Seb nodded toward Joe's office, a look of disappointment seeping through the age-old responsibility lines of his face. "Talk to him. I know there are a lot of people who'd like him back, even if he doesn't believe it."

Before Hunter could ask for more, Seb clapped him on the shoulder and pushed past to the exit.

Hunter turned back to Dawn, who shared his look of confusion. She gave a sudden jolt and uncovered the phone receiver. "Yes, I'm still here . . ." Her words trailed off as the call resumed, and Hunter left her to it.

His father's office door was cracked, and Joe Barrett sat behind his desk, looking years older than he should. His broad shoulders slumped back against his chair with one hand threaded through his thinly combed, graying hair as he closed his eyes. Hunter could remember a time when his father used to look energized coming home from work, like the work had filled him rather than draining him dry. Hunter hesitated, his hand on the knob.

Even if he could convince his dad to take Seb's offer, if they sold the house, there'd be nothing left to go back to.

With a swift motion, he opened the door.

His dad dropped his hand from his face. "Hey, Hunter."

Hunter nodded over his shoulder, toward the lobby

where Seb Jonathon had just been standing. "Why didn't you hear Seb out, Dad?"

His dad shot him a look of dismay. "Not you too . . ."

Hunter rushed forward. "Come on, Dad. Moving the business back to the island is a good idea."

"We don't have the capacity, Hunt. In case you didn't notice." He grabbed a haphazard handful of papers and let them fall back to the desk. "We're drowning here."

"Only because you can't trust us enough to get work done. We should be doing jobs that we can really put our stamp on," Hunter replied. "Something we can slow down and put all our attention on, take the time to get perfect. I'm sorry, I know you're afraid to mess up again, especially back on Jonathon, but—"

"The answer is no." His father ran a hand through his thinning hair.

"Dad . . ."

"I'm not going back to the island, Hunt. It's not happening."

A tense silence filled the air, seeping into Hunter's lungs, making it hard to breathe. "Fine."

His father stared at him for a long moment and let out a heavy breath. He glanced at his watch. "It's a little late. Where've you been?"

Oh, no. They were far from done arguing.

"How long have you been planning to sell the house?" Hunter asked, cutting to the chase.

A flash of surprise crossed his face, and then his dad let out an exhausted breath, shaking his head. "I talked to Mia about it a couple of months ago—"

"A couple of *months*?" Hunter reeled back. "Don't you think that's something that you should have talked to your sons about?"

His dad picked up a pencil, fidgeting with it as he avoided Hunter's eye. "I was going to talk to you boys, trust me. I just asked her to put some feelers out. See if there was anybody asking."

"And?"

His eyes flashed back to Hunter, his shoulders sagging slightly. "And I've got a few people I'm talking to."

Talking to? That sounded like a lot more than putting out some feelers.

"You've got to be kidding me, Dad." Hunter ran a hand over the back of his neck. "I want to see the trust documents—"

"Hunter—"

"I want to see them. You can't sell the house; it's not yours to sell." He could feel his chest tightening, his temper rising at the betrayal. It was supposed to be the Barrett family home. Forever. A home that would be passed down from generation to generation. Giving them all a place to stay tethered. The Barrett house was family. And you didn't abandon family when things fell apart, or because of a little "bad luck."

His dad stared at him for a long moment, as though trying to decide if he was serious. He finally huffed out a breath, shaking his head as he opened his filing cabinet. He rifled around for a minute and then slapped a thick manila folder onto the desk. "Have at it."

The sun dipped beneath the horizon, pulling the blue from the sky as evening fell on Port Joseph. Hunter sat in the bed of his truck, the cold glass of the window behind him soothing against his neck. The distant horn of the approaching ferry barely registered as he stared at the envelope in his hands.

With a deep breath, he opened it and began to read.

THE BARRETT HOUSE IS HELD WITHIN THE BARRETT FAMILY LIVING TRUST, WITH THE OLDEST GENERATION—that would be his dad—ACTING AS TRUSTEE... Followed by a bunch of legal jargon. Hunter skipped to the section about selling the house.

THE PROPERTY HOLDER HAS THE RIGHT TO SELL THE PROPERTY, WITH THE PROCEEDS TO BE DISTRIBUTED AMONG FAMILY MEMBERS OR USED FOR OTHER PURPOSES SPECIFIED BY THE TRUST, ONLY IF (ANY OF THE FOLLOWING):

- THE NEXT GENERATION HASN'T MET THE CONDITIONS OUTLINED IN SECTION II OF THE TRUST BY THE END OF THEIR THIRTIETH YEAR.
- THE UPKEEP OF THE PROPERTY BECOMES FINANCIALLY UNFEASIBLE FOR THE TRUST.
- THERE ARE NO ELIGIBLE HEIRS IN THE NEXT GENERATION.

Hunter's pulse quickened. By the end of his thirtieth year. He'd be turning thirty-one in a matter of weeks.

There was still time. He flipped to Section II and scanned the conditions.

Trust stipulates that the house must be passed down to the next generation—i.e., himself and his brothers—when they get married, so long as the following conditions are met:

- The next generation member must be at least twenty-five years old—at least he had that one in the bag.
- They must demonstrate financial stability and the ability to maintain the property—and he could check that one off the list.

Hunter read the final condition and felt all warmth seep out of him.

- They must be married or engaged to be married within six months of receiving the deed to the house.

Of course. Married. Because who wouldn't want to marry into the Bad Luck Barrett Family?

Daisy leaned against the cherrywood bar at Martha's, a diner she had learned was the local favorite not only for food but also for gathering, loitering, and all-around small-town living. A handful of townsfolk occupied several booths along the green-tiled wall opposite the bar, including Augo, who sat with another older gentleman. The two of them made a show of heckling every person who stepped inside the diner. It seemed to be the only rowdy spot on the whole island.

"You boys settle down, or I'll make you pay your tab," Vera, the waitress who'd served Daisy not once but all three times she'd eaten there since yesterday morning, said.

"You don't scare me!" called Augo with a chuckle.

"She scares me!" That from Augo's friend, sitting across from him.

Vera's smile settled easily into the lines of her face. "At least Roger has some sense to him."

Daisy chuckled to herself at their conversation and took another bite of her meatloaf slider. It was easily the best thing she'd had in months, maybe even years.

With her free hand, she scrolled through the comments on the surprisingly successful livestream. Who knew getting trapped inside that old house would capture the attention of so many people?

@ParkzFam: That house is GORGEOUS! Can't wait to see what you do with it!

@VintageGirlie: Those original hardwood floors 😍 Please tell me you're keeping them!

@User8978: That sunroom is to die for. I need one just like it!

The overwhelmingly positive response should have lifted her spirits. But she was back where she'd started. No house. No prospects. No career. Just a failure with an agent. That project should have been exactly what she needed to restart her HGTV career and prove to the network execs that she still had what it took to captivate an audience.

She winced against the sting in her throat as she took in the amount of comments asking about Logan.

@NorthshoreSandi: Where's Logan? Is it true you two broke up?

@Nami8853: I was rooting for you guys. 💔

@bluebird37: Is it true you caught him cheating?

@GabbyGabi: I heard it was the other way around. 😲

Apparently, stories were already spinning about their breakup. It was no surprise.

Everything had happened so quickly she hadn't had time to process the breakup. She'd really thought they were the real thing . . . She and Logan. Thought that he'd been gearing up to propose.

She should be heartbroken.

She should be burning pictures and slashing tires, or whatever it was you did to cheaters nowadays.

But if she was being completely honest with herself, the only thing she really felt was relief.

What did that say about her?

She popped a fry into her mouth and scrolled further, letting the comments distract her.

@CraftyKatie: Forget about Logan, can we talk about that contractor? The chemistry between

you two was 🔥 🔥 🔥

Daisy's brow furrowed. Did they mean *Hunter*?

@Malawimamma: The way that guy looked at you when he fixed the door . . . girl, love at first sight!

@Kelsiewiththekid: Please tell me Cutie Contractor is going to be a regular on this renovation!

@PosieDarling: I ship it already! Daisy + Mystery Man 4ever!

Heat crept up Daisy's neck. She hadn't realized the camera had captured that moment. Her mind flashed back to Hunter's face when he'd opened the door, the shock and . . . something else in his eyes. Something that had made her chest flutter.

What her followers hadn't seen was that "cutie contractor" turn into the world's biggest jerk about two seconds later.

Daisy rolled her eyes and set the phone down. "Sorry, guys, that's one ship that'll never set sail." They'd already tested those waters. No, no matter how cute he was, with his chocolate-brown hair and dark eyes, those long lashes that had made her melt time and time again, she wasn't going to fall for Hunter Barrett again. But at least she could appreciate the little boost in engagement she'd gotten thanks to him.

She reached for her drink just as Vera swooped in, snatching it up onto her tray before setting down a replacement. "Pardon my reach, sweetie." Her eyes hitched on Daisy's open screen. "Is that the Barrett house?"

"Hmm?" Daisy replied, still caught on thoughts of Hunter. "Oh, yeah . . . I was touring it this morning."

Vera's brows rose. "Oh really?"

"Yeah." Daisy ran her hands over the fresh condensation on her glass. "The realtor I was with said it might be for sale." She watched the water bead up and fall. "Turns out she was wrong."

"You should count yourself lucky," came a shout from across the room. Daisy jumped, not realizing the old coots had been listening to the conversation. Roger gave a pursed-lipped nod. "House is bad luck!"

Vera shot him a look of disapproval, her red lips pressing into a tight line. "It is not."

"Sure it is." Roger gestured to his friend across the booth. "Augo, tell 'em."

Augo glanced between his friends, the tiebreaker. "Well, I don't like to gossip . . . but they do call it the Bad Luck Barrett House for a reason."

Daisy's brows shot up. "The *Bad Luck* Barrett House?"

"Sure!" Roger said, as though confirming the sky is blue. "There's not a person on the island who hasn't heard one thing or another about something bad that happened to that house." He took a long drink of his beer, savoring his rapt audience of one: Daisy. "I heard, back in the thirties, they had a party at the house with guests from the Grand." Roger leaned out of the booth. "Chandelier fell right out of the ceiling and almost killed Franklin D. Roosevelt."

"Oh stop!" Vera said, waving the story away. "Franklin D. Roosevelt never stayed on island."

"You don't know that!" Roger's eyes were alight with mischief. He turned toward Augo, dragging his friend back into the conversation.

"I don't know about FDR," Augo said carefully, "but I do know the house has had some rough times."

"Been hit by lightning." Roger lifted up two bony fingers. "Twice."

"Twice?" Daisy echoed, horrified.

Vera set her tray down on the bar top and slid onto the green leather barstool beside Daisy. "Don't let that scare you away," she said gently, a smile sliding into the corner of her mouth. "It might be called the Bad Luck Barrett House now, but it *used* to be called the Honeymoon House."

Daisy blinked in surprise. "Well, that sounds a lot nicer."

"Doesn't it?" Vera said warmly. "It's been passed down from generation to generation. Gifted from father to his son on his wedding day." She shot the boys a scathing look and returned her attention. "That's how Joe Barrett got it. It's a shame he wants to sell it."

Daisy felt a pang of guilt. That was such a beautiful notion. A family home, filled with history and love. She could see why Hunter didn't want to lose it.

"Probably *why* he wants to sell it too." Roger cut into her thoughts. "Not one good thing happened to that family since the day Joe and Lisa said 'I do.'"

Vera's expression shifted from warm to serious in a heartbeat. "That's enough."

Augo and Roger straightened like a pair of children being reprimanded by a parent.

Daisy cleared her throat, sensing the conversation being shut down. "Well, thank you all for . . . all that." Nailed it. Way to make things less awkward. "I think I'll be heading back to California tomorrow, so I should probably head out. Throw my things together."

She paid for her meal quickly, before she could get roped into another controversial conversation, and stepped out of the diner.

A deep knot burrowed into her chest. She'd really thought . . . when she saw that house . . . maybe God really did have plans for her. But then again, when it came to things that mattered—her job, her heart—she really couldn't afford to leave them up to the Big Guy anyway. It was a blueprint for failure. So maybe it was for the best. The house was beautiful, but it needed a lot of work.

"Maybe it's time to cut my losses," she muttered to herself. "Start fresh back in California."

She glanced toward the docks down the way, wondering what time the first ferry departed in the morning. A smart Daisy would have simply left after the tense confrontation with Hunter, but she wasn't ready to face the world yet. Not without a plan. So she'd decided to stay one more night. She'd get a fresh start in the morning.

Daisy turned off Main Street, the glow of the little town hidden as she entered the street heading toward the dock. The sun had set on the island, scattering stars in its wake, and Daisy gaped up at them in awe. She'd never seen so many stars, not even growing up in Illinois. There must be something special about Jonathon Island to make them shine like that.

She stepped onto the long boardwalk leading up to the ferry. The wood thumped beneath her boots as she passed below vintage lampposts, their lights dripping into the calm water. The nip in the air that had chilled her to the bone that morning had faded to a temperate fall breeze.

Reaching the empty ticket window, Daisy's eyes glanced off the posted schedule, wandering to the sound of churning water.

Fifty yards out, the 10:00 p.m. ferry was pulling up to the dock, its hull breaking through the lapping waves.

The ferry drifted to a stop along the pier, and one of the workers hopped over, hurrying to secure the vessel. A moment later, a ramp extended from the ferry to the dock, and the last passengers made their way off the boat.

Her eye caught on a familiar figure as he stepped off the ramp. His dark hair hung over his eyes, shoulders slumped as though carrying an invisible weight. He looked exhausted. His head lifted, and his eyes met hers. Hunter paused. His weary gaze hardened, the lines of his jaw tightening. Clearly, she was still unwelcome.

His voice blended with the depths of the water behind him. "What are you still doing here?"

Daisy hesitated. Stepped toward him. "Hunter . . . I'm really sorry about the house. I didn't mean to cause trouble."

Hunter rolled his eyes. "That's a first for you."

Daisy's polite expression soured. "Excuse me?"

He pushed past her, his heavy steps thrumming the boardwalk. "What do you want, Daisy?"

She couldn't believe him right now. Here she was trying to make him feel better—for what reason, she couldn't for the life of her understand—and he was treating her . . . well . . . like an *ex*. Which was crazy, because he had ghosted her. Not the other way around. "What I *wanted* was to try to make you feel better. But *now*, I want to know what your problem is."

He spun back. "*My* problem?"

"Yes, *your* problem," she snapped, hand on her hip. "At first, I thought you were just mad that I broke into your house. But apparently, it's me, specifically, that you're upset about."

He looked at her through incredulous eyes. "You don't remember, do you?"

"Remember what?" She flopped her arms in the air in a dramatic shrug. "Remember the way you kissed me and then completely dropped out of my life? I remember that. But for some reason, I feel like I should be the one upset about that."

"I kissed you?" He laughed. "As if I'd ever want to do that. No. *You* kissed me. And then you stole my designs. You and your *partner.* Or don't you remember that as part of the story of Daisy Decker's Big Break?"

Daisy's jaw dropped. Stunned. "That's not true—"

"It's fine. I'm over it. But you'll excuse me if I'm not thrilled to see you." Hunter let out a bitter laugh, running a hand through his disheveled hair. "It figures that you'll get what you want anyway," he said, his voice rough with exhaustion. "You always do."

Daisy blinked. "What do you mean?"

"The house. He's gonna sell it," he said, wincing as the words left his lips. "There's nothing I can do. I've spent the past twelve hours poring through trust documents and legal sites, and there's nothing I can do." He dropped his shoulders, running a hand over the back of his neck. "So, I guess start pulling your earnest money together, because in a few weeks, when I hit my thirty-first birthday, the Barrett house goes on the market."

The defeat in his voice struck Daisy hard. Despite everything, she felt for him. "That's . . . that's not what I wanted at all . . . Is there anything that can be—"

He cut her off with a sharp shake of his head. "No. There's not anything any of us can do. Not unless you know someone who wants to marry me within the next six months."

"Sorry—did you say *marry* you?"

"Yes. Marry me." He pressed his lips together, his jaw tight. "Per the trust, I don't inherit the house unless I'm engaged and planning to be married within the next six months when my thirty-first birthday hits."

Daisy frowned. "So, just engaged. Not married."

Hunter went on as though she wasn't even there, his thoughts tumbling out freely. "If I could just . . . hold things off a little while . . ."

Daisy's chest squeezed, a terrifying plan creeping into her mind. Maybe there was a way they could both get what they wanted. She pressed her lips together, hesitating even to suggest it. But . . . "I'll marry you, Hunter Barrett."

Four

Those were the words that had kept him awake all night, tossing and turning as his mind replayed them over and over again, until he'd started to wonder if he'd dreamed up the whole conversation.

When the first signs of sunlight warmed the sky, Hunter gave up on sleep.

Long shadows filled the living room as he crept through the open-concept kitchen/dining area/living room. For all his attempts to be quiet, he couldn't do anything about the loud snoring rumbling through the floor from his brother's room. Hunter shook his head. They were lucky the owners of the bakery downstairs hadn't started fixing the place up yet. They hadn't had a chance to get tired of Waylen's loud existence.

Hunter snatched his running shoes from the entryway, slipped them on quickly, and stepped outside.

He welcomed the brisk air, making his way down the second-story landing hidden in the narrow cross street that ran behind Main Street.

The streetlights were still glowing when he started jogging.

Hunter had always loved the escape that running offered. He loved the familiar wooded paths worn into the island, the way wrinkles turn into smile lines. He loved the smell of aspen and pine and the sight of driftwood on the beach. It was there that he'd always found clarity in the past . . . but today, he found himself turning not onto his usual path but up the hill. On the road leading home.

He crested the hill and found the old house waiting for him, the front windows reflecting the glow of the horizon. Hunter slowed, paused, his breath coming out in shallow puffs as he stopped at the stonework wall edging the property.

The early morning was stark against the burnt orange that surrounded the house, and he thought of his mother's early mornings spent sipping coffee on the steps of the porch as she sent his brothers and him off to school. He made his way that direction, kicking up dew on his trek to the porch. Finally, he settled onto the top step of the porch and looked out over the lake.

I'll marry you.

What had she been thinking?

The moment flashed back to him.

"What?" he'd asked, his brows furrowed.

"I'll . . . I'll marry you," she repeated, her face flushed, lips parted as she pulled in a nervous breath. "I mean, not for real," she said hurriedly. "Just . . . like, until you get ownership of the house. Or change the trust. Or whatever you need to do to keep it."

In that moment, she'd looked so sincere, so concerned with his hurt. The breeze had tousled her hair, carrying her familiar scent—honey and coffee, and uniquely Daisy.

Hunter winced, remembering the only words he could think to say at the time before walking away. "I . . . don't have time for this."

He'd managed to think up a hundred better responses in the night, the most important of which was, why? Why would she do that?

A sliver of sunlight crested the horizon, throwing a blanket of gold over the frigid water. It reminded him of his brother's sunrise kayaking outings. He could use Miles's guidance right about now.

Hunter debated for a moment before slipping his phone from his pocket and opening his brother's contact.

Miles answered on the first ring. "Morning, sunshine! What are you doing up this early?"

Hunter couldn't help but smile. "I think I could ask you the same thing. Don't you ever sleep?"

His brother scoffed, as if insulted by the insinuation that he needed rest. "Sleep? With all this beauty around? Nah, if the sun's awake, I'm awake."

"I knew you were a hippie." Hunter chuckled. He could imagine his brother, perched on the windowsill of his Chicago apartment, a lean arm draped over his knee as he peered out at Lake Michigan, his dark eyes soaking up the light. It had been a while since he'd seen Miles, but there were some things that just didn't change.

Miles hooted a laugh that sent Hunter grinning, exhaustion leaking chuckles from him.

"All right, all right, you caught me," his brother said, his voice settling down. "But that doesn't explain what *you* are doing up this early. What's going on?"

Hunter let out a deep breath and leaned his back against the stair railing. "I need someone to process with."

"Okay, shoot."

"All right," Hunter started, running a hand over the back of his neck. "But what I'm about to tell you is strictly confidential."

"Top secret, you got it."

"I mean it, Miles. Waylen can't keep a secret to save his life. Jude and Evan wouldn't take it seriously. You cannot tell a soul."

"You're good, Hunt." His voice turned serious. "I won't tell anyone . . . But you are freaking me out a little bit. What's going on?"

Hunter took a deep breath. "You remember Daisy."

"Daisy . . . As in, the girl you used to talk about incessantly for four years after every single conference you attended? And then never mentioned again after you very suspiciously stopped attending said conferences?"

Hunter dragged a hand over his face. "Yeah. That one."

"Never heard of her."

"Miles."

"Sorry. Yes, I remember her."

"Well, there's a little bit more to the story than that." He braced himself for a snarky quip.

"Okay, so tell me about it," his brother said, no quip. Huh.

Hunter's eyes traced the horizon, watching the sun rise as he told the story of Daisy.

"So, you know we met at these Midwest construction and design conferences. I was trying to expand the business. She was building her design portfolio and running a YouTube channel with her partner, Logan.

"The first time we met, I swear, I knew she would wreck me. And I leaned right into it. I thought to myself, 'Hey, we'll probably never see each other again. What's a little shameless flirting?' She was very charming while shutting me down. Which is fortunate, because as it turns out, the Midwest construction world is pretty small."

"This is ringing a bell," Miles joked.

Hunter ignored him, continuing the story. He had to get it out. To lay out all the variables in the equation of why Daisy Decker would offer to help him. The answer had to be there. "We started seeing each other at every convention. She and Logan and me. And we all became friends. We started looking forward to seeing each other at these events, swapping notes, sharing ideas. And then Daisy and I started talking outside of them too.

"I always thought there was something between us, but I don't think either of us wanted to mess up the good thing we had going. We were long-distance, and there was Logan . . ."

Even now, Hunter felt the burn of humiliation at just how naive he'd been.

"Anyway, at the Chicago convention, there was a huge design contest. The winner would get to pitch a show idea to a couple of HGTV showrunners. Like usual, the three of us were inseparable. And there was this electricity in the air. Like the whole world was riding on this shot. So Daisy and Logan suggested that we do a little brainstorming."

He ran a hand over the back of his neck, mentally preparing himself for what came next.

"I already had my design in the bag, but I was happy to help them. We were friends, and they didn't have anything sketched out. We all hung out in my hotel room. And then Logan decided to turn in early, and Daisy and I stayed up talking. And . . ."

The memory of that night filled his mind, Daisy's easy smile as his gaze dropped to her lips, her cheeks turning the lightest shade of pink when he brushed a lock of hair away from her face and leaned in . . . Like he'd said. He'd always known she would wreck him.

"It felt like everything was finally falling into place, you know? But then the next day, when it came time to submit my design, it was gone. And then Daisy and Logan won the contest . . . with my design."

He could almost feel his brother's pitying expression, and it burned in his throat.

"Hunt . . . that's . . ."

"Yeah, well . . ." Hunter replied, letting his brother off the hook from trying to make him feel better. "Daisy and I never spoke again. She got the show, and it came out shortly after that she and Logan were dating . . . I realized Dad was right anyway. Those conventions were a waste of money."

There was a long pause before Miles spoke. "So, what's got you losing sleep over this now?"

"This is the part you can't tell anyone," he said, the words scraping his throat.

"Okay . . . ?" Miles replied hesitantly.

"Dad wants to sell the house. And the rules of the trust say I can't inherit it unless I'm engaged when my thirty-first birthday rolls around."

"I'm sorry . . . I'm lost. What's that got to do with Daisy?"

"She's here."

A beat. "On Jonathon Island?"

"Yes. On Jonathon Island." Hunter's gaze trailed the path she'd trampled in the overgrown grass the day before. That girl always left a mark.

Miles cut into his thoughts, pulling him back to the conversation. "I still don't see how that's . . . Hang on . . ." His voice trailed off as he made the connection. "Hunt. Tell me you didn't propose to this girl."

"Actually, she proposed to me."

The house creaked under Miles's heavy silence.

"She's here looking for a new reno project," Hunter went on. "And I let the details of the trust slip. I was upset. And then she offered to marry me—"

"Marry you! Hunter—"

"Fake engage me."

"Not better."

"A fake engagement, just long enough to help me keep the house until I can figure something out." Even saying it out loud, he knew he was tiptoeing around the moral dilemma of the offer. It was fraud. Another good reason he was talking to Miles about this and not Waylen, the cop . . .

Miles was quiet for a long time, obviously having reached the same conclusion. "Listen, Hunt. I know you love that house, but . . ."

Hunter stilled, his jaw working as he stared out at the lake. "I won't walk away from family, Miles. Not from the good parts, and not from the broken parts either."

"The house isn't our family, Hunt."

"Isn't it?" Hunter's voice grew rough. "Every crack, every broken window, every scorch mark . . . it's all part of our story. And maybe it's not perfect, but you don't just give up on it because it's got a little bad luck." He ran a hand over his face. "You stay. You fix what's broken. Because that's what family does."

"Even when it's falling apart?" Miles asked quietly.

"Especially then." Hunter's chest tightened.

"Hunt . . ." Miles's voice softened with understanding. "It's not your job to hold everything together."

Hunter stayed quiet, the rebuttal dry on his lips. Yes, it was.

His brother let out a loud breath. "You know, I've been doing these early-morning kayak outings, and one of my favorite things about them is how quiet it is. Out there on the lake, I can just think. And lately I've been using the quiet as a time to talk to God . . . I'm a little new to it. Not super sure what to do outside of what we learned in church as kids. But I digress . . . I don't have a good answer for you. But I think if you give Him a chance to come through for you, you might be surprised."

It wasn't the clear answer Hunter had been hoping for.

He hadn't prayed outside of church in . . . had it really been years? It wasn't that he didn't believe. He just didn't have a deep relationship with the Big Guy. What was the point if He wasn't going to stick around when you needed Him?

Miles cut into his thoughts. "Listen, Hunt. I'm leading a tour in a few hours, so I gotta prep and hit the road. But . . . just think about it. I'll catch you in a couple days."

Hunter sighed, heaving himself to his feet. "Yeah, okay. See you."

The call ended, and he was left on the steps of the house, no closer to working out an answer.

Hunter envied Miles's newfound faith. The Barrett boys were all raised in the church, but Miles had found something greater than the motions. For Hunter, however, he needed a faith he could keep at arm's length. Something safe and predictable.

And yet, as he stood there, his family's legacy slipping through his fingers, he couldn't help but wonder what it was like to have faith like that. The kind that could move mountains—or save houses.

He glanced up at the worn plaque that hung above the door to the house, the verse etched into the wood by the craftsman who'd built it. *For I know the plan I have for you . . .*

With a sigh, he turned away. Prayer might work for

Miles, but Hunter needed something more tangible. He needed a plan.

Before he could talk himself out of it, he pulled his phone back out. He scrolled down the contact list to "Do Not Call Her" and typed a message:

She could not believe she'd *proposed* to Hunter Barrett. Like some crazed, desperate lunatic. Daisy groaned and rolled over, stuffing her face into her pillow. It was no use; no amount of smothering was going to erase the humiliation.

I . . . don't have time for this. "For your crazy" was what he meant.

"Ugh, I'm a mess," she breathed as she slumped from the bed. Sitting up, she grabbed her phone from the bedside table and tapped the screen.

Black.

"Figures." She'd been so upset when she made it back to her hotel room the previous night, all she'd wanted was to wash the day away with a hot shower and go to bed. She'd forgotten to charge her phone. "I guess that rules out booking myself a flight back to reality." At least until it had a chance to charge.

Daisy let out a sigh, dropping the phone into her lap. Her gaze lifted to the window as she remembered the coffee shop from the previous morning. "Might as well get some caffeine while I'm at it."

Thirty minutes later, Daisy stepped into the quaint coffee shop and instantly felt the kind of comfort only coffee shops and bookstores could give.

Her eyes swept across the room, taking in the rustic charm of the weathered wooden tables and black metal chairs. Soft morning light filtered through the large windows, casting a bright glow on the pastel teal display case and the walls adorned with vintage coffee signs and local artwork.

The coffee shop was quiet this late in the morning, only a handful of locals bustling in and out.

Daisy stepped up to the counter, eyeing the menu hanging against the subway-tiled wall behind the register.

A woman with bright-red hair stepped up to greet her. "Morning. What can I get for you?"

"Well, I was going to get a regular black coffee." Daisy pointed up at the regular menu, and then her finger darted to the next sign over, the one decorated with chalk pumpkins, leaves, and acorns. "But then I saw the seasonal menu."

The barista grinned, turning to glance at the menu with her. "We do like to keep it fun around here."

"Clearly," Daisy agreed. "Can I try the caramel apple macchiato? I could use some cozy fall vibes right about now."

"Absolutely." The barista rang up her order, and Daisy pulled out her card to pay, but before she could hand it over, another arm reached across her, slipping a ten across the counter.

"I'm buying," an older woman said. "And my usual, if you don't mind, Jill?"

Daisy turned to find her favorite waitress, Vera, standing behind her. "Morning, sweetie," she said. "Thought you'd be headed back to California by now."

Jill peeked over the espresso station. "You two know each other?"

"Oh, sure," Vera replied. "Daisy's been a regular down at Martha's the last couple of days—" She turned to Daisy. "It *is* Daisy, right?"

"It is," she replied with a polite smile. "And thank you for the coffee. That was sweet of you." And then she remembered Vera's question. "And I was just about to book a ticket, just as soon as my phone is charged."

Daisy glanced around the room.

"There's an outlet next to that booth there," Jill provided, sliding Daisy's drink across the counter along with Vera's.

Daisy picked up the cup, savoring the heat against her fingers. She glanced at the older woman. "Want to join me? It'll probably be a couple minutes before my phone has enough juice."

Vera's smile swelled at the invitation. "I would love that."

They sat down across from one another.

"So," Vera said, nestling against the gray-green cushion that ran along the wall. "If you don't mind me asking, what made you travel all the way from California just to look at the old Barrett house?"

Daisy warmed her hands around her mug. "Oh, it wasn't the Barrett house that got my attention. It was the dollar house program. I heard about it on the news coverage of Asher Quinn's concert. What they'd neglected to say in the news coverage was that all the one-dollar houses were gone."

"Oh! That's too bad."

"It's okay. Turns out I don't think it would have worked out anyway. I would have needed to open a business here too."

Vera smiled. "I didn't know you were a business owner."

"I'm not." Daisy laughed. "I mean, I was. I had a home-design firm once. But about five years ago, I started hosting this show on HGTV."

Recognition lit in the older woman's eyes. "*Double Decker*! The curb-appeal show, where you build the beautiful porches and reface houses and such."

Daisy shrugged, lifting her palms. "That's me."

"I knew I recognized you from somewhere," Vera said excitedly. "I really enjoy that show. Such beautiful landscapes. I loved the one where you incorporated that family's old gazebo into the deck rebuild. It was very touching."

Daisy smiled politely. "Thank you."

She'd enjoyed that build as well. And she'd had to fight tooth and nail off camera to keep that little piece of history. Logan had wanted to tear it down.

"It takes so much talent to do what you do," Vera said,

a touch of awe in her voice. "How did you get started in the business?"

Daisy cupped her drink and took a quick sip, savoring the bitter mixed with hints of caramel and crisp apple. It reminded her of corn mazes and yellow fields dotted with burnt-orange pumpkins. It had been a long time since she'd spent a fall in the Upper Midwest.

"Well, I grew up in the outskirts of Chicago, in an old neighborhood with a lot of young families. 'Starter homes' we call them in the reno business."

Vera sipped her coffee, nodded for her to go on.

"My mom and I lived in this cute little worker's cottage. It was blue with green trim," she continued. "It had all this personality. Sunburst gables. A covered porch with dentil molding. The bay window looking out over the garden my mom spent entire summers caring for . . ." She trailed off, realizing just how much design jargon she was using. She glanced up at Vera and found her grinning, her eyes alight, listening to her. Daisy laughed, shrugging. "It was a cute house. But the inside was a disaster. My parents had bought the place with plans to hire contractors to fix it up, but"—she sighed—"then I came along, and suddenly they didn't have the budget anymore.

"Anyway, my parents split when I was in middle school. A couple months went by, and then one day, my mom just shows up with all these supplies. Paint. Tarps." She let out a laughing breath. "She even got us matching overalls . . . That summer, we worked every night, painting and patching, and making every nook and cranny of that place just as much of a home on the inside as it was on the outside."

Daisy took another sip of her drink.

"Wow," Vera said, her voice reminding Daisy of a proud grandparent. "Your mother sounds like a strong woman."

"She is," Daisy easily agreed. "She's amazing."

"I bet she's very proud of you."

An overwhelming sense of homesickness washed over her. She wondered if her mom had heard the rumors already making the rounds. *Diva Daisy Decker storms off set.*

"I haven't talked to her in a while." Not aside from the usual "mom texts." *Thinking about you today. Hope you're doing well, sweetie.* Or the occasional *Just checking in.* She was saving her next phone call for a day with good news. Daisy ran her fingers over her neck. "Hard to find the time when you're in showbiz."

She should call. It wasn't like her mom would be disappointed in her. She'd never been disappointed in her. But she just . . . couldn't. Not yet. Not until there was a tangible plan to pull her from this catastrophic failure.

The sound of coffee grinding pulled her attention back to the present as Jill set a fresh batch of baked goods into the display case across the shop.

Vera took another sip of the drink and set it down. "And what about your cohost? Is he looking at houses as well?"

Daisy dropped her gaze to her fingers, picking at the corrugated paper sleeve of her cup. "Um, actually, I don't know what he's doing these days." She ripped a piece off and added it to the small pile growing in front of her. Cleared her throat. "They fired me from the show."

Well, that wasn't exactly true. But they might as well have.

"That's terrible," Vera gasped. "You were the heart of that show."

Daisy cracked an honest smile. Vera had no idea how badly Daisy had needed to hear that, her costar's voice fighting against it in her head. *You wouldn't even have this show if it weren't for me.*

"And you and—what was his name—"

"Logan," Jill provided from behind the counter, and both Daisy and Vera turned to look at her. Jill straightened from where she'd been leaning over the counter to listen. She shrugged. "What? I keep up with things."

Vera turned back to Daisy. "Are you two still . . ."

Daisy plastered on a polite smile. She'd been prepared for the question. But it didn't make it any easier to answer. "No. We split up too."

Vera reached across the table, giving Daisy's elbow a comforting squeeze. "I'm sorry, love."

"It's okay—I'm okay." Surprisingly okay. "I'm on to better things."

Suddenly the barista was beside her. "For what it's worth, I always thought you were too good for him." She set down a small plate with what looked like a cherry tart. "You're sunlight. And he's fog."

Daisy blinked up at her in surprise.

Hold on. Was everyone in this place listening in on their conversation? She glanced around and was relieved to see most everyone else had left.

"Sorry, I didn't mean to eavesdrop," Jill said. "Old habits, you know." Her eyes drifted to the empty outlet on the wall, and she frowned. "Weren't you going to plug in your phone?"

The reminder hit Daisy like a splash of cold water. She still had to book her flight, pack, and catch a ferry back to the mainland.

"Oh my goodness, I completely forgot, thank you." She fumbled through her purse and fished out a charger, plugging it into the wall with her phone attached. The screen flickered to life a moment later, and a message popped onto the screen. Daisy picked up the phone, unlocked it to look at the text.

Hunter
Meet me at the house at ten. We need to talk.

Daisy's eyes darted to the clock on the wall. 11:15.

"Shoot!" She scrambled to her feet, nearly knocking the table over in the process. "I have to go. I'm so sorry. It was so nice talking to you, Vera. Thank you for the coffee!"

Vera laughed and waved a hand. "Go!"

Daisy pushed through the door to the street and ran.

Five

HUNTER GLANCED AT HIS PHONE FOR about the tenth time and slumped back against the old oak door, pulling his knees up to rest his elbows on them.

She wasn't coming.

He ran a hand through his hair, hanging his head between his arms. What had he expected? That she'd just show up after the way he'd treated her?

He exhaled a heavy breath.

The crunch of leaves on the road and footsteps in the grass caught his attention, and Hunter lifted his head.

Daisy Decker.

She was picking her way across the lawn. She wore a brown flannel over a matching brown shirt. Her black leggings, which were tucked into high tan socks and boots, caught against every bush, collecting burrs as she shimmied sideways down the path.

Rising to his feet, Hunter strode forward and leaned against the wooden post supporting the awning, watching her fight against a waist-high thistle that had caught on her.

"I was starting to think you weren't coming," he said, his tone carefully neutral.

Her gaze lifted and she stopped, her doe eyes wide. "I am *so* sorry. My phone was dead. I went to charge it at the coffee place, and then I got caught up in conversation—"

Hunter raised a hand, stopping the long string of explanation. "It's fine."

Daisy searched his eyes and then, as though accepting the statement, she released a breath. She finished picking her way through the grass and stopped at the bottom step of the landing. Her hands flitted nervously over her sleeves, pulling the cuffs down to her fingertips.

"Beautiful day for a"—she glanced toward the hill, still slightly breathless—"nice brisk hike—"

"Daisy?" He cut in.

"Yeah?" Her gaze snapped back to him, brows raised.

"I don't want to talk about the weather with you."

"Right."

He shouldered away from the post and stepped down the few steps between them. "In case you've forgotten, you proposed to me last night."

"Yeah." She laughed, dropping her gaze as she swept her hair behind her ear. "I'm sorry about that. I don't know what came over me. I swear I'm not a nut . . ."

Hunter rolled his eyes, cutting to the point. "What's the catch?"

And the doe eyes were back. Wide and blue and beautiful. "The catch?"

"Yeah." He stepped down another step, ducking his head to meet her. "We get engaged. I get the house. What do you get?"

Daisy's face flushed, embarrassment creeping into her cheeks. "Right. The catch."

Hunter nodded. Raised an eyebrow. Waited.

She licked her lips, eyes darting to the house. "I . . . need a house to renovate."

Hunter's jaw ticked. Of course. He crossed his arms over his chest. "There it is."

"So I can start up my YouTube channel again."

Hunter scoffed, closing his eyes as he shook his head. "Unbelievable."

"And I'd like you to be my contractor on the channel."

His eyes snapped back to her. "Excuse me?"

"Look!" She scrambled up the step, pulling out her pink-and-blue phone and tapping the screen. "These are the comments from the livestream the other day." She turned the screen toward him, scrolling through pages of swooning comments. Hunter struggled to wrap his head around what he was reading. The number of hearts and flame emojis was . . . unnerving, to say the least. "They loved you. I don't think I've ever had this kind of engagement. Even at the height of my YouTube career."

He stepped back, leaning on the handrail. "You want me to costar?"

Daisy grinned, a bright laugh bubbling out. "No. Just cameo."

He relaxed an ounce.

"You'll show up once an episode, let the viewers see what you're up to." She shrugged. "Flash a little muscle."

Hunter's brows shot up. "Flash a little mus—"

"Flirt a little," she said, her gaze carefully studying the sleeve of her flannel.

"Flirt—You'd like that, wouldn't you?" he huffed.

Her cheeks flared pink. "The viewers would."

He sniffed.

"Look, I know it sounds crazy," Daisy went on, "but this could be good for both of us. You get the house, I get content, and six-ish months from now, I'll either be out of your hair or we'll be married."

Was that a joke? Hunter didn't laugh.

She let out a breath, looking around awkwardly. "Okay then . . . no joking allowed."

Hunter studied her for a long moment, his jaw clenched. She would wreck him again. His eyes traveled up the banister behind her, settling on the old front door of the house. He exhaled a heavy breath. "Fine. Let's say I consider this ridiculous plan. What exactly did you have in mind for renovations?"

Daisy's face lit up, and she bounded up the remaining steps. "Okay, I have a lot of ideas. Can we do a walk-through?"

Hunter eyed the phone in her hand. "Off camera."

She blinked, and then his words clicked. "Oh, ha ha. Yes. Off camera this time. Promise." She shot him a warm smile and waved toward the door as if to say *After you!*

Hunter reluctantly opened the door and stepped aside,

allowing her to enter. As they walked through the foyer, Daisy's enthusiasm bubbled over. "We could open up this space, create a more welcoming entrance. It should be bright and inviting, so we replace doors—"

Hunter barked a laugh. "Absolutely not."

Daisy froze, her hands still splayed in the air as though painting the picture inside her head. She let her arms fall. "Okay. No problem."

She turned toward the stairs and gestured toward the faded floral stair runner. "I think it goes without saying that the matching carpet and wallpaper have to go." She stepped toward the heavy wooden banister. "This banister too. It's pretty, but it's too bulky for the space. Totally distracts from the room."

Hunter shook his head. "The carpet stays. The banister stays."

Daisy's brows pulled together. "The *carpet* stays?" She pointed at it as though he must be confused. "This carpet."

"It's vintage, Daisy. It was installed with the house."

Daisy gave him a look of complete disbelief, her rosy lips parted slightly. "Oh, I'm so sorry, I didn't realize you had so much attachment to a strip of carpeting so aged that you can't even tell it was once a lovely peach floral. From the 1960s—not the late 1800s. Which you would know if you had gone to design school like I did. Would you like to throw a little funeral for it? Pay your respects?"

Hunter remained unmoved.

Daisy clicked her tongue. "Okay."

As they walked through the house, Daisy continued her tirade of ideas. "We could move this door to the opposite wall and turn this drawing room into a pantry. Oh, and in the kitchen, imagine continuous granite counters and backsplash, add an overhang on the island for seating."

"No," Hunter said flatly to each suggestion. He wasn't going to inherit the house just to have it completely changed, wall to wall.

Daisy continued until they reached the sunroom, and Hunter quickly closed the door. "This room is off-limits," he said gruffly.

"What?" Daisy gaped at him. "Hunter, it's the focal point of the house. Every person who watches the show will be looking forward to the sunroom renovation."

"No."

Finally, Daisy's perpetual optimism seemed to crack. "Why did you call me out here if you were just going to shut me down?"

Hunter's jaw ticked. Why *had* he called her out here? It was obvious this was never going to work.

"Were you just looking to get the last word? To pay me back for supposedly stealing your career by getting my hopes up and shutting me down?"

Hunter felt his throat go dry. That wasn't what he'd intended at all.

Her eyes flashed as she continued, "Well, news flash. I have NO idea what you meant when you said I stole your designs. I never did that. But I wouldn't expect you to believe me."

"Good," Hunter replied coldly. "Because I don't."

"Good," she shot back.

"Good."

"Great," she said, her head tilting, her long hair sliding over her shoulder. "Now that that's out of the way, why don't you tell me what you *will* let me renovate?"

Hunter crossed his arms over his chest. Pretended to consider for a moment. And then, "The porch."

Daisy stared at him for a moment, her eyes widening in outrage, and then released a furious snarl before storming out of the house.

Hunter let out a satisfied chuckle, watching her storm out before following.

She was already halfway across the lawn, burrs snagging the hems of her flannel, clawing at her to stay. Her brows were pinched with frustration, her face flushed with pink.

Shoot. She was really leaving . . .

He rushed down the steps. "Hey! Where are you going?"

Her feet pounded the pavement. "To catch a ferry."

Hunter jogged after her, catching her by the elbow gently. "Daisy, wait."

She stopped but made no move to turn. Her lips were pressed together. Her jaw locked tight. Hunter felt a pang of guilt for giving her such a hard time. She was trying to help him, after all.

"I'm sorry, I . . . I'm not ready to give you free rein over the whole house." He ducked into her line of vision, but she refused to meet his eye. "But . . . maybe we can start with the porch and see how it goes. If it turns out well, we can discuss expanding the project."

Her gaze flicked toward him, her eyes calculating,

searching, and he had the sense he was being measured up. Against what, he wasn't sure.

"The porch . . . and the foyer," she said finally.

Hunter winced.

Daisy shrugged. "That's fine. I'll just wait it out. House goes on the market in, what did you say, a few weeks?"

Hunter raked a hand through his hair. She was bluffing. She couldn't afford it . . . could she? He straightened, really seeing her for the first time since she'd arrived on the island. And he couldn't help but feel a grudging admiration for her determination. She might be infuriatingly sunny, but she certainly wasn't backing down.

And it wasn't like he had any other options. For now. He'd work something out. They wouldn't have to lie for long.

Disbelieving what he was about to do, he extended a hand. "Fine. But it's only temporary. Just until I can find a loophole or some other way around the rules of the truth. And I have final say on all design decisions."

Daisy's eyes lit up again, a bright smile gracing her lips as she took his hand. "So we're doing this."

"Apparently."

She stepped back, turning to look at the house. She took it in with a look that sparked something inside him he couldn't place.

A moment later, Daisy's grin faded into a more serious expression. "So, about the engagement . . ."

Hunter's pulse quickened. "What about it?"

"Well, if we're going to do this, I'll need a place to stay."

Hunter's eyebrows shot up as he glanced meaningfully

toward the dusty, dilapidated exterior of the Barrett house. Daisy followed his gaze and quickly shook her head.

"Very funny." She gave a mock laugh, wrinkling her nose. "I need running water and heat. Heat is very important."

Hunter rolled his eyes. "Fine. I know someone with a sublet available. We can go talk to them right now."

He started toward the town, but Daisy hesitated. "That . . . brings up the second issue."

Hunter frowned. "What's that?"

"When do we start?" she asked, brushing her hair behind her ear again, suddenly shy. "I mean, do we walk into town hand in hand, or are we more of a zero PDA kind of couple? Or do you not want the town to know? Any of which are fine with me. It's your engagement . . ." Her words drifted off as she glanced back up at him.

The balls of her cheeks grew pink the longer she spoke. He'd almost forgotten that endearing way she rambled when she was nervous.

Hunter grimaced, running a hand over the back of his neck. "Right. I guess we should probably get on the same page." He glanced toward the town, splayed out at the bottom of the hill. This was a terrible idea. A terrible, horrible idea. But he couldn't lose the house. He wouldn't abandon it. Might as well rip the Band-Aid off. "Let's start today. Now."

"Now?" Daisy's eyes shot up. "Don't you think we should plan this out a little more?"

"I think if I plan this out, I'll come to my senses." Hunter sucked in a breath. "We start now."

Daisy hadn't really expected the charade of their engagement to start *immediately*. After all, any sane person would assume they would ease into it. Drop some hints around town. Introduce her to his family, make a whole whirlwind romance escapade out of it. It would take planning to get it right. To make people believe in their love story.

So when Hunter's fingertips slid into the space of her palm, curling between her fingers with ease as they reached the outskirts of town, she'd tried, and failed, not to flinch in surprise.

"Relax," he said gruffly, nodding toward one of the houses lining the street, and more specifically, the older woman flitting around her front yard, raking leaves into neat little piles.

"What are you doing?" she hissed through smiling teeth.

Hunter tilted his head close to Daisy's, his voice dropping low. "Martha Kelley. Owner of Martha's on Main and all-around busybody. We want people to start talking about us? She'll get the rumor mill going."

Daisy's eyes widened as they passed the woman. She'd eaten at Martha's several times already, but apparently their paths had simply missed each other. The woman paused her raking, her eyes pausing on their clasped hands. Her gaze narrowed, like a hawk zeroing in on its prey.

"Afternoon, Martha," Hunter called, raising his unoccupied hand to wave at her.

Martha blinked without response and then scurried off into the house, taking her rake in with her.

"Oh yeah, that'll get the job done," Hunter said, a smug smirk tugging at his lips. He quickly dropped her hand, and the cold rushed in to take its place.

At midday, the sun shone brightly over the town, making the colorful awnings pop as she and Hunter strolled down Main Street. It really was a storybook town. *The American Dream: Island Edition*. Daisy found herself craning over her shoulder to examine the colorful storefronts while trying to keep up with Hunter's long strides.

"So, the town really gave away those storefronts along with every dollar house?" she asked as they passed an adorable little studio with yellow-striped walls and a For Lease sign in the window.

Hunter shot her a glance over his shoulder. "Yeah."

"It's a brave move, that's for sure," she said as they passed a grayish-colored horse parked outside the Jonathon Island bank, flicking its white tail lazily down its legs. "Where's yours?"

"My horse?" he asked, his brows pulling together.

"Your storefront. You're a contractor, right?"

"It's on the mainland." Hunter pointed toward the lake. "We don't do business on the island." The way he said it made her wonder if that was a policy . . . or a choice.

"Why's that?"

Hunter sighed, his jaw tightening. "We don't have to talk, you know."

Daisy grinned, undeterred. "Ah, but then how will I get to know my"—she dropped her voice into a whisper—"fake fiancé?"

Rolling his eyes, he shot her a sideways glance. "You already know me."

"Correction," she said, skipping a little to catch up to him. "I *did* know you. But that was another time. Another version of whatever *you* this is."

Hunter's lips pulled into a tight line as they crossed the street. "The company policy is to focus on mainland projects," he replied, a hint of frustration in his voice. "They're less risky and more cost-effective."

"Hmm," Daisy mused. "Is that why you're so charming? Saving all that personality for your fancy mainland clients?"

Hunter shot her a look. "I'm plenty charming."

"Oh, of course." Daisy nodded solemnly. "Nothing says 'Prince Charming' quite like brooding and monosyllabic answers."

A reluctant smirk tugged at the corner of Hunter's mouth. "I'll have you know, girls like the brooding. It's part of the look."

Daisy laughed. "I'm sure they do. Let me guess, you also have a leather jacket and a motorcycle hidden away somewhere."

"Wouldn't you like to know," Hunter replied, his tone lighter than before.

"Actually, yes, I would," Daisy said, bumping his shoulder playfully. "That's kind of the point of asking questions."

Hunter rolled his eyes, but for a moment, Daisy caught

a glimpse of the man she once knew. He exhaled heavily. "You're relentless, aren't you?"

"It's part of *my* charm." She grinned. "Someone has to balance out all your brooding."

"Lucky me," Hunter deadpanned, but there was no real bite to his words.

Daisy beamed up at him. "See? We're bonding already. By the time we get to wherever it is you're taking me, we'll be the picture of love."

Hunter snorted, and then, just as quickly as their little banter had begun, he shut it back down. "We're here."

Daisy blinked and looked around.

They were in front of the coffee shop again.

"After you," he said, hesitating for a split second before pressing his hand to the small of her back as he led her inside. Daisy's stomach gave a flutter that she chalked up to surprise. Apparently, the show had begun.

Jill raised her head as the door fell shut. "How you doing, Hunter?" And then her eyes found Daisy. "Back so soon?"

Hunter stopped, glancing back at Daisy with obvious confusion. "You know each other?"

She gave him a look, crossing her arms over her chest. "Did you really think I'd go three days on the island without getting coffee once?"

Hunter's eyes narrowed at her snark, and Jill cut in. "The real question is, how do *you* two know each other?"

Daisy lifted her gaze to meet his. *Last chance to ditch this crazy idea.*

He swallowed, one final battle waging behind his eyes.

And then his arm lifted to wrap around her waist, his warmth enveloping her as he pulled her in. "You want to tell her?" he asked, his eyes sweeping lovingly over her cheeks, her lips, her eyes.

Oh, heavens. Daisy's cheeks flushed, her heart giving a pitiful leap. Where in the heck had that look of his come from?

She tore her gaze from his and tried to catch her breath. Focus, Daisy. "We're getting married!" There, she said it.

Jill's polite smile faltered, her mouth falling open. "What?" And then, after the words had a moment to process, "Oh my goodness! Hunter!" She threw her arms around both of them.

"Oh," Daisy said, not sure how to accept the hug wrapped haphazardly around her neck. She gave Jill's elbow a polite pat.

After she'd juiced every bit of love out of them, Jill stepped back, although her hands remained on their shoulders. Her gaze darted to Daisy. "You know, I thought maybe you and your cohost had been separated this last season. Why didn't you tell me this morning you were here with Hunter?"

Daisy felt her smile falter. See, this was why they should have planned this out a little. "I—"

"We didn't exactly plan it out," Hunter cut in. "Daisy and I met years ago, and we missed our shot. So when she showed up, I didn't want to let her get away again."

"Wow." Jill blinked. "It's a big decision, marriage. Don't get me wrong, it's very romantic, but . . ."

"Trust me, Jill. There's not a day in the last five years I haven't thought this through."

Daisy flushed.

"A whirlwind romance, then." Jill beamed, accepting the answer without question. "I could not be more excited for you two!"

Hunter smiled; it was bright and comforting. She remembered that smile. "Thank you, Jill." He stepped back to Daisy, wrapping his arm around her shoulder again. A gesture she would probably never get used to as warmth spread beneath his palm. "Daisy and I are planning to renovate the old house as soon as we can. But in the meantime, she'll need a place to live. Any chance the upstairs apartment is still available?"

Before Jill had a chance to respond, the door opened behind them, a gust of fall air breezing through, and in stepped another woman. She looked to be in her fifties, with silver-blonde shoulder-length hair. She wore a pair of surprisingly trendy straight-legged jeans, a navy striped sweater tucked in around her trim waist, her sage green jacket hanging open. She was the picture of sophisticated aging.

The woman's eyes touched on Hunter's arm around Daisy's shoulder, and she felt it drop away.

"Oh, Tara, hi," Jill said brightly. She gave Hunter's shoulder another squeeze and hurried back around the counter. "What can I get for you?"

The woman shot Hunter a strained smile, strolled past him to the counter, and set her purse down, fishing for her wallet. "Chai latte, please."

Jill rang up the order and quickly went to work. She glanced at Hunter over the counter while heating milk. "Daisy is more than welcome to stay in the apartment." She turned her gaze to Daisy. "I can take you up there in a few minutes."

"What's this?" Tara asked, turning toward them.

"Oh, sorry," Jill said, now combining the steamed milk with tea concentrate. "This is Daisy, Hunter's fiancée."

Tara blinked in surprise but recovered quickly, a gentle smile spreading across her face, not quite reaching the corners of her eyes. "That's wonderful, Hunter. Congratulations."

Hunter stiffened visibly. "Thank you, Mrs. Chamberlain."

Daisy got the feeling she was missing a crucial piece of information. What was going on here? Who was this lady? And why did she draw such a reaction from him?

Tara gave them another polite smile before retrieving her drink from the counter. "It was really nice seeing you, Hunter. You two take care." The bell rang on the door again as she stepped back onto the street.

"Okaay then . . ." Jill blew out a long breath. She gave Hunter a sad smile and then turned back to Daisy. "How would you like to see the apartment?"

"That would be great. Thank you."

"Great, let me grab the keys. I'll be right back." Jill ducked into the back, and Daisy rounded on Hunter.

"Are you okay?" she asked softly.

The moment her fingers touched him, Hunter stiffened. "I'm fine," he said, pulling away, his face set into perfect indifference.

Right. Fake engagement. Fake tolerance for her existence. Got it.

Jill popped back to the front, jingling keys. "Follow me!" she said and strode toward the back of the shop.

The apartment was cozy. A perfect little studio that overlooked Main Street and the lake behind that. The blue of the water met the sky, and Daisy didn't know which was which. If she'd had endless time and resources, she would have found a way to feature every nook and cranny of this little town in her show. As it was, she'd have to settle for the priceless heirloom Victorian.

"Thank you again, Jill. I'll try my best to stay out of your hair," she said, standing in the middle of the carpeted room. A small bed, already made up with a lacy white quilt and mismatching pillows, sat to her right, a desk and chair to her left, and that was it. "What can I pay you for rent?"

Jill scoffed. "I'll tell you what, business is slow this time of year. You keep buying coffee every morning, and we'll call it good." She gave Daisy a wink.

"I couldn't do that!" Daisy protested.

Jill waved her off. "It's really no problem. It was just sitting empty." She fished the keys off her key ring and cupped Daisy's hand as she pressed the key into her palm. "I have to get back, but there's an exterior exit just over there. It leads to the alley out back." She pointed toward the door in the far corner as she retreated in the opposite direction. "I'll leave Hunter to help you get settled in."

And then she was gone.

Hunter stood beside the small kitchenette, leaning against the wall with his arms crossed over his chest, his jaw working through waves of tension. That woman had really gotten to him.

Daisy wanted to reach out, the way she might have when they used to know each other, but that look in his eyes told her to keep her distance. She was an unwelcome guest inside his world right now. She stepped back, turning to look around.

"This place was a great idea, Hunter. Good thinking." She sat down on the desk chair and spun toward him. "What should—"

"I take it you can get yourself settled?" His voice had turned hoarse.

"Oh." What else had she been expecting? It wasn't like he actually wanted to be around her. "Yeah, I'm okay."

He shrugged away from the wall, his dark hair falling into his eyes. "I'll see you tomorrow."

"Tomorrow?"

He stopped at the exterior door. "Be ready at eight thirty."

"Ready for what?" she called after him.

"Church."

The quiet of the room swallowed her whole when the door shut behind him. Daisy let out a deep breath, the one she'd been holding since she got his text. And then she pulled out her phone and typed a message to Robin.

_______________Daisy

So . . . I might have proposed to Hunter . . . but
on the bright side, we got the house. Call me.
I'll tell you everything.

Six

IF JONATHON ISLAND'S CHARMING SET-
ting or endearing locals hadn't been enough to make
Daisy fall in love, her new apartment certainly was. Good
Day Coffee had been closed by the time she'd gotten all her
things from the inn and moved them to her new temporary
home the following evening, but this morning, the café was
awake and bustling, and Daisy had woken to the fresh scent
of coffee and a view of the sun on the lake.

"Morning!" Jill called over the surprising crowd gathered in the shop as Daisy stepped in at 8:25. A line at least
five deep curved toward the door. Behind the counter, Jill
and her teenage helper navigated each other gracefully as
they tried to keep up with the orders. Jill pointed toward
a cup of coffee at the end of the counter with Daisy's name
scrawled on the outside. "A little something for you."

"Wow, thank you," Daisy replied, taking the warm cup
in her hands.

"Oh, no," Jill called over the sound of the coffee grinder. "That's not from me." She nodded again, this time across the room to where Hunter sat waiting. His broad shoulders were clad in a well-worn leather jacket. His dark eyes connected with hers beneath slightly furrowed brows. His short, tousled brown hair softened his hard lines just slightly. As he stood to greet her, Daisy couldn't help but notice the way conversations around them faltered and the curious glances cast their way.

"Thank you," Daisy said, suddenly shy beneath the eyes of so many onlookers. "For the coffee."

"No problem," he replied.

Hunter's eyes darted over her head, as though noticing the commotion, the attention they'd drawn, for the first time. His dark gaze returned to her, and, to her surprise, his hand came up to her lower back, pulling her in as he pressed a soft kiss to the top of her head. The gesture was gentle, leaving Daisy with an unexpected flutter in her stomach. She jolted, nearly spilling her coffee.

Whoa, there. Give a fake fiancée some warning.

Hunter stepped back. "You ready to go?"

Daisy blinked up at him, all thought cleared from her mind save the fading feel of his arm around her and his breath against her hair. "What?"

A self-satisfied smirk slid onto Hunter's face. "Are you ready to head out?"

The fog lifted, and Daisy cleared her throat as she tried to regain her composure. "Ready."

His eyes crinkled. Apparently, he found her fluster very

amusing. "Great." He slipped an arm around her shoulder, his heat seeping through her flannel. "Let's go, then."

They stepped out of the coffee shop, leaving the crowd of unabashed gawkers behind, and Hunter immediately let his arm slip away, returning to the distance between them.

Talk about whiplash. This was going to be a whole lot more difficult than she'd thought.

"So . . . church?" she asked, glancing up at him expectantly.

Hunter's eyes remained fixed ahead. "Yup," he replied simply.

Great. Mr. Monosyllable was back.

He glanced down at her, and to her surprise, added, "Service doesn't start until nine, but we need to get there early to beat the crowd. Half the town is still back there in line for coffee." He jerked his thumb back toward the shop they'd just left. "And Jill shuts down for the service in five minutes."

It took a stunning fifteen-minute stroll up the boardwalk, the bright sun cutting through the chill, for the little church to come into view.

Daisy let out a gasp. "It's so beautiful."

The quaint building was easily a hundred years old, four walls of white and gray stone, with stunning arched stained-glass windows overlooking the lake. The entrance wrapped around the side of the building, letting church-goers enter at the center of the sanctuary. Worn wooden pews lined the room, looking toward a wood-carved pulpit in front of another massive stained-glass window. The light poured through it, painting the room in shades of blue and red and gold.

"You're gawking," Hunter said, giving her shoulder a nudge.

"Why aren't you?" Daisy breathed.

Hunter smirked. "Probably because I've sat inside this church every week since I was born."

"That's . . . really nice." Daisy gave Hunter a tight smile. She hadn't been to church in years. In her college years, she'd been a regular attendee at Hope Church in Chicago. But once she moved to LA and her show took off, she hadn't really had time in her schedule. A seed of guilt took root in her chest.

Hunter shrugged.

"Where is your family?" she asked, peering through the crowd for anyone with a family resemblance.

Hunter placed a hand on her back, heat seeping from his fingertips as he ushered her further inside. "You'll meet them later. Waylen's the only one who lives on island, but he's never been much for church."

"Don't you think it's odd to be flaunting our engagement when I haven't even"—she dropped her voice into a whisper—"haven't even met your family?"

Hunter paused, his brows knitting together. "I hardly think it's out of the realm of possibility that my long-distance celebrity fiancée hasn't met my family," he said low, dipping his head. "Besides, Waylen spent the night at Jude and Evan's place last night. I doubt the news will spread all the way to the mainland before Pastor Arnie is done with his sermon. Come on, we should sit before the coffee line catches up with us." Hunter gestured toward an open pew where a blonde and a brunette, both probably a few years younger than Daisy, scooted down, patting their empty seats.

Daisy shuffled into the pew, and the women both leaned forward, grinning.

"You must be the mysterious new woman in town," the brunette whispered.

Hunter rolled his eyes. "Ladies, this is Daisy . . . my fiancée." Both women let out an excited squeal that Hunter seemed to be trying his best to ignore as he continued introductions. "Daisy, this is Jordi Chamberlain"—the brunette—"and Holland White. Her brother, Jonah, is my oldest friend."

The blonde, Holland, frowned. "Oh, is that all? All this time, I thought *we* were friends."

Hunter leaned toward Daisy, speaking exaggeratedly low. "She's also a little dramatic—"

"Hunter Barrett." Holland smacked him on the arm before turning back to Daisy. "It's really nice to meet you, Daisy."

Daisy didn't get a chance to respond before a horde of middle-aged church women bustled up, closing around them in the aisle and surrounding pews.

"Well, if it isn't the happy couple!" the woman Hunter had pointed out as Martha Kelley exclaimed, her eyes not-so-subtly looking for a ring on Daisy's finger. "We're all just dying to hear how this came about. It's so . . . unexpected." Her eyes stopped scouring Daisy's fingers long enough to meet her eyes. "I'm Martha, by the way."

"Daisy," she replied, extending a hand.

Another woman chimed in, taking over the handshake when Martha finally let go. "When's the big day?"

Before Daisy could respond, a third woman leaned in, "And Hunter, why is this the first we are meeting her? Daisy, you are just beautiful."

Daisy felt her cheeks flush. "Oh, thank you."

"Now, now, ladies," Martha interrupted, her smile predatory. "I'm sure they'll make a lovely announcement when they're ready. Though it does seem to be a little out of the blue. I don't think Hunter's been in a relationship since, well . . ."

Hunter tensed beside Daisy, his jaw clenching.

Just as Daisy was about to stammer out a response, a familiar voice cut through the chatter.

"All right, that's enough interrogation," Vera said firmly, appearing beside them. "Why don't you all give these two some space? Service is about to start."

The women reluctantly dispersed, throwing curious glances over their shoulders. Vera found her own seat as well, but not before leaning close to say, "Don't think you'll get out of telling me everything later," with a wink.

Daisy let out a breath she hadn't realized she'd been holding and glanced over at Holland, who was chuckling quietly to herself.

A hush fell over the church as a few members of the congregation stepped up onto the small stage and worship began. A few minutes after that, the pastor stepped up to the pulpit. Though his red hair made it difficult for Daisy to determine his age, he looked to be in his mid-fifties.

He gave the congregation a warm smile, his eyes stopping briefly on Daisy, then Hunter.

In the front row, the woman from the coffee shop, the one who'd made Hunter so tense, sat in the front row, and Daisy realized with a start that she must be the pastor's wife. Daisy peeked over at Hunter to see if he'd noticed the woman, but his eyes were focused on the speaker.

"I don't know about you all," he began, his voice carrying easily through the church, "but I've got a laundry list of things to accomplish this week."

He pulled out a small notebook from his pocket, flipping it open with exaggerated movements. "Let's see here . . . I need to mow the lawn, pick up groceries, finish that report for the church board, clear the gutters, help Holland with her Bible study prep, meet with the youth group, fix that leaky faucet in the kitchen . . ."

As he continued, his list grew more elaborate, drawing chuckles from the congregation. ". . . repaint the garage, learn to speak fluent Italian, solve world hunger, and maybe, just maybe, find time to sleep."

He closed the notebook with a snap and a wry grin. "Sound familiar to anyone?"

Daisy found herself nodding along with several others in the church. She could practically feel the weight of her own to-do list pressing down on her shoulders, everything she needed to do if she was going to get her YouTube channel off the ground.

"In today's world, doesn't it seem like it's always go, go, go?" the pastor continued, his tone becoming more serious. "That we're always pushing for more, always striving to do something big with our lives, to succeed. It's like we're on this never-ending treadmill of achievement and productivity."

He paused, letting his words sink in. "Society tells us we are the sum of what we do in life. Our jobs, our accomplishments, our social media presence—it's all supposed to define who we are. But you know what? God is here to tell us that we're so much more than that." He leaned forward, his hands gripping the sides of the pulpit. "And thank goodness for that! Because if who we are was determined solely by the things we did, we'd all be in for a nasty surprise."

A ripple of laughter spread through the congregation. Daisy shifted in her seat, her shoulder brushing Hunter's.

"Think about it," Pastor Arnie said, his voice softening. "If our worth was based on our actions alone, on our successes and failures, our good deeds and our mistakes—where would that leave us? We'd all fall short. Every single one of us.

"Fortunately for us, God's grace is sufficient. He doesn't tally up our good works. He doesn't compare them against the saints, or the celebrities, or even our neighbors. He gives life we don't deserve out of a love we could never earn. Just because."

The pastor's eyes landed on Daisy, and she felt her breath hitch.

It wasn't a foreign concept to her. Sure, for God so loved the world . . . But when it came down to reality, people always expected something. And frankly, that was a little easier to handle. There were social transactions she could follow. But when you pulled works out of the equation of faith, you were left trusting in God's grace. Hoping that His love would still be there when you fell short.

No, thank you. Daisy was happy with her terms and conditions.

"Today we're going to continue our series on Ephesians with a glimpse at the message behind Ephesians 2:8-9. Let's open our Bibles . . ."

Daisy settled back and listened to the rest of the message, but the words were like writing in the sand, each carefully crafted point washed away by waves of doubt.

When the sermon was over, she and Hunter stepped out of the church into the midmorning sun.

Daisy lifted a hand to shade her eyes, turning to her pseudo-fiancé. "So, what's next?"

Hunter quirked an eyebrow. "Now you meet the rest of the Barrett Boys."

Hunter's truck pulled up to the modest ranch-style house on the outskirts of Port Joseph. He let out a tense breath, and Daisy noted the slight white of his knuckles against the wheel.

"Everything okay?" she asked when he strung a hand through his hair.

He gave a gruff nod and unbuckled. "I'm fine."

He hopped out of the truck and came around for her door. He extended a hand to help her out, but he seemed miles away as he led her to the door.

They stepped up to the welcome mat that read *Go on*

now, git! and Hunter suddenly turned to her, his expression serious. "We're Lions fans."

An amused smile tugged at her lips. "Okay?"

"But more importantly, we hate the Packers. You see even a flash of green and yellow on that screen, you should be booing and tossing popcorn. Got it?"

Daisy let out a laugh, and then, "You're serious?"

"Of course I am." Hunter's expression remained stoic. "You'll never convince them we're in love if you don't take this *very* seriously."

Before she could respond, the door swung open. A man who must have been Hunter's brother filled the doorway. He had the same chocolaty-brown hair, the same dark eyes, but where Hunter's were dark and guarded, his were easygoing and light.

"Better late than never. Kickoff's about to . . ." His words died off, and a goofy smile slid across his five-o'clock shadow. "Well, who'd you bring us, Hunt?"

Hunter brushed past his brother, pulling Daisy along into the house, which entered directly into the living room.

The room was arranged around the large TV, which pictured the Detroit Lions facing off against the Packers. Near an archway, leading to what looked like a dining area, a pair of men, who had to be twins, stood, blinking away matching looks of astonishment. Seated in an overstuffed armchair in the corner, an older man sat up, craning his neck to get a look at her.

If the other men were Hunter's brothers, based on resemblance, this man could only be his father. He rose from his chair, easily matching Hunter's height, with broad shoulders that spoke of years of physical labor. His face was weathered, etched with lines and creases that told stories of a hard life. His hair, likely once as dark as Hunter's, now thin, was a salt-and-pepper mix, cut short and slightly messy, as if he'd just run his hand through it.

"Daisy, I'd like you to meet my dad, Joe." He pointed toward his dad, who gave a polite nod. "And these are my brothers. This is Waylen." He gestured toward the man who'd answered the door. "That's Jude." He pointed to the slightly taller of the twins. He smiled, nodding and lifting a cheesy nacho in what looked like cheers. He, too, looked like Hunter, but taller, with a slight beard. "And lastly, Evan."

"Always last." Evan shook his head, his lips tilting in a crooked smile. It would have been difficult to tell the twins apart if not for Evan's neatly trimmed hair.

"Dad, Waylen, Jude, and Evan"—Hunter threaded his fingers through hers, pulling her into his shoulder—"I'd like you to meet my fiancée, Daisy."

Hunter leaned back on the couch, his arm draped around Daisy's shoulder in his best attempt to be casual as the Lions made another fifteen-yard pass down the field. To say he'd been surprised by how well they'd taken the news was an understatement. Even now, as they sat watching the game, Hunter felt like everything could come crashing down any moment.

"Oh, come on! Are you blind? That was clearly interference!" his dad bellowed, gesturing wildly at the screen. He was in rare form today, shouting at the TV with every flag, regardless of which player it had been thrown on or which team was penalized. It was clear who the real opponents were in his mind, and they were wearing stripes.

Jude and Evan had created a small smorgasbord of nachos, donuts, and drinks on the coffee table, and they were now lounging on the floor in front of the TV, chuckling at their dad's outbursts.

And Waylen stood at the side of the room, arms crossed, scowling at every play, regardless of which team had possession. Like father, like son. His initial reaction to the news had been a whooping bear hug tossed around Hunter's shoulders, but it had been quickly swallowed up by suspicion until Daisy told them the story of how she'd come to the island looking for a project for her show and had run into "the one who got away." Hunter wasn't oblivious to the fact that it wasn't exactly a believable story. But then again, Waylen had been there when Daisy had been in the picture. She'd been the whole picture. So maybe it wasn't so hard to believe after all.

"Touchdown!" Daisy cried, jumping to her feet along with Hunter's dad.

"Let's go!" Waylen shouted, thumping his chest as he cheered at the screen.

Hunter remained quiet, hyperaware of Daisy's presence as she settled back down beside him, her hand briefly squeezing his bicep. The touch sent his heart racing as he reminded himself once again that the whole thing was an act.

Daisy Decker was a character meant to make people love her. And he would not be fooled again.

"Halftime," Jude said, clapping as he hopped to his feet.

"You ready, Daisy?" Evan reached out a hand to help her up.

Hunter tensed, immediately knowing what was coming. "She doesn't have to, guys."

Waylen raised a brow. "I think you should let her decide for herself, lover boy."

Daisy looked between them, her beautiful doe eyes clearly curious. "Ready for what?"

Joe chuckled as he rose from his chair. "Halftime backyard football." He winked, reaching for her hand as though he already knew what she was going to say.

Her eyes lit up with that familiar excitement of hers. "I'm in!"

"Oh, this is gonna be good," Evan said, and he and Jude raced toward the back deck.

Twenty minutes later, Hunter crouched low, his eyes locked across the makeshift line of scrimmage. His opponent, five foot three, 120 pounds soaking wet, flashed a mischievous grin, and he rolled his eyes.

"Scared, Barrett?" Daisy taunted playfully, the scrunch in her nose as she gave him her best "game face" smothering any shot she had at intimidation.

"Quaking," he shot back.

Jude crouched beside her. "All right, you two, that's enough. There's no flirting in football."

Hunter nodded accusingly toward his fiancée. "Tell that to your teammate!"

She gaped in exaggerated outrage. "I don't know what you're implying here! I'm one hundred percent in the game."

"Yeah, yeah, just play," Evan said, crouched to Hunter's right.

On Daisy's other side, Waylen snatched up the ball, starting the play, and Daisy took off down the yard. Hunter backpedaled, keeping his eyes on her as she darted left, then right. He had to admit, she was quick, even in those ridiculous boots. Waylen, playing quarterback for their team, launched the ball in a perfect spiral.

Hunter saw it coming. He leaped, his fingers just grazing the ball as it sailed over his head. And Daisy snatched it out of the air with ease, spinning around to face him with a triumphant grin.

"Ohh! Another one for the dream team!" she called out, spiking the ball as she squared up against Hunter, the top of her head barely reaching his chin. "What's the matter, Barrett? Can't keep up with the pros?"

"As a reminder, we're all Barretts here!" Waylen called from the distance, but they ignored him.

"Just warming up, *Decker*," Hunter said, his eyes narrowing on hers. She wanted a challenge? So be it.

They returned to the line of scrimmage, Hunter crouching low beside his dad, who said, "Let's show them how it's done, son."

The play began. Daisy came charging.

Hunter grinned, grounding himself to dodge. Waited for her to get closer and then—

He slipped.

His boots slid against the grass as he and Daisy collided.

Daisy's arms wrapped around his waist as they tumbled to the ground. His arms enveloped her, his palm pressing her closer as they rolled through the grass and landed with a soft thud, Daisy half on top of him, their faces mere inches apart.

Daisy stared down at him, her eyes wide with shock, and for a moment, everything else faded away. All he could see was her. The pink tint to her cheeks, her breath in the cold fall air, every fleck of gold in her blue eyes . . . or were they green? His heart hammered in his chest, and he found himself unable to look away.

"Kiss her!" Jude's voice shattered the moment, loud and teasing.

Hunter shot his brother a scowl as Daisy stiffened in his arms.

He quickly loosened his grip, sliding out from under her.

From the corner of his eye, he saw his dad elbow Jude sharply.

"What?" he protested.

Hunter sat up, brushing the grass from his shirt, avoiding Daisy's gaze as he helped her to her feet. Her fingers were soft against his palm, and he quickly stepped back, putting a healthy dose of air between them. What on earth had happened to his brain during all that?

He reached to pull a twig from her hair and stopped himself. "You okay?"

"Yeah," she said with a shaky laugh.

"Let's take a time-out," his dad cut in. "I'm gonna grab us some drinks."

Thank goodness.

"I'll give you a hand," Hunter called out, leaving Daisy with his brothers as he caught up at the door.

The kitchen was warm in comparison to the brisk fall afternoon. Hunter's eyes took a moment to adjust to the dim lighting from the window, and he found his dad pulling a variety of drinks from the fridge.

"Jude's going to get himself in trouble someday if he doesn't watch what he says."

His dad chuckled over his shoulder. "Something tells me Daisy can take as much as she doles out."

Hunter felt a wry smile slide across his face. "Yeah, you're probably right."

His dad straightened, setting a handful of glasses on the counter. "She's amazing, Hunt. I'm happy for you."

"Thanks," Hunter said, running a hand over the back of his neck as a mix of pride and guilt washed over him. "She is pretty great." He took a deep breath. It was now or never. "Listen, about the house . . ."

His dad raised an arched brow and leaned a hip against the counter, his eyes seeming to see right through Hunter. "You want the house . . . now that you're *engaged*."

His gaze held a look that made Hunter wonder if he knew more than he was letting on. A look that said *I know you better than you think*. Hunter's heart leaped into his throat.

"The house is yours," he said, a smile breaking out across

his face as he slapped a hand on Hunter's shoulder. "Just so long as you two end up married."

And there it was. The unspoken meaning behind that look. If the engagement fell through, so did the house. Hunter's chest grew tight.

His dad tightened his grip on his shoulder. "At the end of the day, I just want you to be happy, son. And if you think this is God's path for you, then that's good enough for me."

The guilt that had washed over him earlier came coursing back, a torrent that sent heat up his throat.

Hunter nodded, swallowing hard.

"All right," his dad said, smacking his shoulder one more time for good measure, driving his point home. "Halftime's over. Let's get back to the game."

The evening sun was well below the horizon when they left the house, the stars winking down at them as they stepped onto the back of the ferry, headed home, the water churning white in their wake.

Daisy leaned against the railing, the wind catching in her honey-brown hair, and Hunter resisted the familiar urge to reach out and catch it in his hands.

She had been amazing today. She had laughed at every one of his dad's bad jokes, chimed in with Waylen's heckling of the refs. She'd smiled up at him, curling into his shoulder like a woman in love, and Hunter was almost sorry he'd be going back to work tomorrow with no excuse to keep up the charade.

Daisy reached up to tuck her windswept hair behind her ear.

"I really didn't steal your designs," she said quietly, catching him off guard.

"Hmm?" he replied, frowning.

She turned her gaze to meet his, her eyes starry and deep. "In Chicago. I had no idea."

Hunter pulled back, throwing the walls back up that he'd let fall throughout the day. He turned his gaze back to the water, unable to look at her anymore. "I don't want to do this right now, Daisy."

"Really, Hunter," she said, her eyes searing through him, her presence suddenly too close. He wanted to run. He eyed the deep water, wondering how long it would take him to swim to shore. "When Logan showed me the design, told me he'd had a burst of inspiration after our brainstorming session, my head wasn't . . . I wasn't all there." She paused, collecting her words. "I was too busy thinking about us . . . about our kiss."

Hunter's gaze snapped to hers, unable to stop himself.

"If I'd been paying just an ounce of attention . . . I would have seen that it was far too elaborate and innovative of a design to have been thought up in a few hours' time." Her lips pressed together, her eyes imploring. "But I see it now. And I'm sorry."

A flash of guilt crossed her face, and Hunter felt a piece of his resolve crumble away. He wanted to believe her. To believe that she was the kind of woman he could trust.

But he wasn't in the business of letting people in just so they could hurt him. Not anymore.

Hunter let out a heavy sigh and turned back to the

churning waters, dragging a hand through his hair. "It's fine, Daisy. Just forget about it."

"But—"

"When do you want to start working on the house?" he asked, changing the conversation. She'd kept up her part of the bargain so far. No sense in delaying his end.

Daisy hesitated, her gaze boring into him again. "I'd like to get going as soon as we can. What's tomorrow look like?"

He turned his head, flattening her with a look. "It looks like a Monday."

"Right. You've got work," she mused, biting the corner of her lip. "Any chance you want to work evenings?"

Hunter straightened as the island came into view. "Might as well get it over with."

Daisy smiled, though its usual brightness didn't quite reach her eyes. "Great. I'll get started on plans tonight."

"And I'll start digging into the trust." See if he could find them a way out before they actually wound up married.

Seven

EPISODE 1: NEW BEGINNINGS, UPLOADED (OCTOBER 1ST)

A view of Jonathon Island's Main Street fills the screen, panning from the picturesque lake to Good Day Coffee before transitioning to a shot of Daisy as she steps onto the screen.

Hi, friends! Daisy here." She smiles into the camera, her eyes gleaming with excitement. She is wearing her standard uniform: a white T-shirt under a bright set of lavender overalls with a daisy on the front pocket. Her hair is pulled into a high pony, a few long strands framing her face. "I'm here in the world's cutest little small town, Jonathon Island. And I have some exciting news!"

She steps back and the camera cuts to a wide shot of the Barrett house in the late afternoon light, flashing a montage of detail shots of the door, the stairs, the porch, before cutting back.

"You guessed it! This stunning Queen Anne–style Victorian is going to be the very first project on my new show, *House to Home*." She moves toward the house, the camera following her as she stops beside the front steps. "And I'm not doing it alone!"

Daisy gestures off camera once, twice, and then finally reaches out of screen, dragging back a reluctant Hunter a moment later. "This is Hunter. He's a design professional with tons of experience, and we're teaming up for this special project."

She glances expectantly at Hunter, who gives a solemn nod.

Turning back to the camera as though Hunter has just given the world's most engaging speech, Daisy continues, "So let's get started . . ."

Comments:

@VintageGirlie: That house is so pretty though. Can't wait to see what she does with it.

@RenovationRomantic: Cutie contractor is BAAAACK! Oh I'm so excited!

@TeaAndBooks: Where's Logan?

———

EPISODE 2: PORCH PERFECT, UPLOADED (OCTOBER 3RD)

The camera pans over the now slightly less

wild front lawn of the Barrett house, the foliage having been recently cut back. Daisy and Hunter can be seen seated on a picnic blanket surrounded by sketches and fabric swatches. Daisy, now in pink overalls, sits with her legs folded, her sweater discarded on the warm day, a piece of paper in her hand, and a carpenter's pencil behind her ear. Hunter sits beside her, leaning back with an elbow on his knee.

"When tackling a renovation project, it's crucial to start with a strong foundation. For us, that means beginning with the porch and staircase—the first things you see when approaching the house," Daisy's voice says over the footage.

Hunter leans closer, his shoulder brushing hers as he points to something on the page.

Daisy's voiceover continues, "Now that we've got a plan for the outside of the house, Hunter can get started ordering supplies and pulling a permit so we can tear up the decking on the porch and replace the turned columns, which are no longer structurally sound, with more modern, but still timeless, rounded double columns."

The camera cuts to a shot of Daisy walking up the interior staircase, her hands gliding expressively over the banister, as Hunter follows, a few steps below. "I think we need to do something really special with this banister, something that will really draw the eye up."

She turns to face him and slips, her foot catching on one of the carpeted treads. She reaches for the banister, teetering backward with a small gasp.

Hunter moves forward, his hands wrapping around her waist as he steadies her.

For a moment, they are both frozen, Daisy's hands clutching his shoulders, her eyes wide with shock . . . or . . .

"Careful," Hunter murmurs, stepping back.

The voiceover resumes, "Boy, am I glad to have that guy around . . ."

Comments:

@BookwormBarista: Did . . . did this just become a romance novel?

@DIYDreamer: The way he caught her! *Swoon*

@Kimmiwiththekats: Be right back, sending to my husband so I can conveniently fall down the stairs later.

@User8978: Love the double column idea.

———

EPISODE 3: JUST CALL ME DEMO DAISY, UPLOADED (OCTOBER 10TH)

The camera cuts to a shot of Hunter and Daisy standing together in the grass, looking at a blueprint as Daisy points at something on the house. Her voice fills the scene. "You know I always love to hit the ground running. That's what a solid plan is all about. And thankfully, that's exactly what we will be able to do after Hunter makes a few calls and gets our permit expedited. Turns out, the town revitalization council is just as excited to see this house come back to life as we are! And not a moment too soon, because we only have a few weeks before snow falls.

"Thanks to Hunter's local connections, we are also able to get our supplies lined up crazy fast. So don't expect this kind of timeline at home, folks." The shot pans to the road just as two horses crest the hill, a large wagon filled with lumber and supplies tugging along behind them. The camera zeros in on the rugged man leading the team of horses. "And if you think you recognize our delivery guy, you're right. That's Asher Quinn, or as you might know him, Eli Noble, famed musician . . . and also, apparently, horse guy."

The shot transitions with a time-lapse as the sun sets behind the house and rises again on the horizon before cutting to Hunter, leaning up against the porch, his sleeves rolled up despite the autumn evening air, a sledgehammer in his hands. Two steps up the landing behind him, Waylen sits with a crowbar across his knees.

Daisy steps into the shot. "Finally, it's demo day here at the house!" She lifts her arms, revealing another sledgehammer, this one in her own gloved hands. She backpedals, joining her team by the stairs. "As you know, Hunter and I have been working almost around the clock to get the porch done before it gets too cold. So Hunter brought along his brother today to help us out."

She turns and Waylen waves at the camera.

"Feel free to swoon, ladies," he says with a cheeky grin. "Unlike my brother here, I'm on the market."

Hunter's cheeks redden slightly, and he clears his throat, running a hand over the back of his neck.

"And with that burning question out of the way," Daisy cuts in, a hint of sarcasm to her voice, "let's get to work!"

Comments:

@Justthatgirl: There are TWO of them!

@MidwesOpe: Can someone tell me where this island is?

@DreamingDelia: Anybody notice the part where they said Hunter's taken? . . . think he and Daisy might be together?

———

EPISODE 4: JUST A COUPLE WEEKEND WARRIORS, UPLOADED (OCTOBER 17TH)

The episode opens with Daisy, sporting a set of burnt-orange corduroy overalls, her hair in a floppy bun on the top of her head. She sits on a pile of lumber, a hammer in one hand and leaning back on the other. Hunter stands in front of the pile, leaning back with a quirked smile on his lips as though they've just been sharing a laugh moments before the camera is rolling.

"Hey, fam! Daisy and Hunter here, and we want to start this episode off with a HUGE thank you for all the love and support the channel has been getting these past few weeks." She glances at her partner, who nods in agreement. "We still have a lot of work to do, but first, let's get you caught up!"

The camera cuts to a shot of the bare bones of the porch, the decking removed and discarded in a pile on the grass. Daisy's voiceover starts just as a team of men arrives, with Hunter in the lead as they begin rebuilding. "What a crazy weekend! We made some incredible progress on the porch, thanks to some extra helping hands. Hunter was able to wrangle a few of his friends down at Barrett Construction into helping us for the weekend."

A montage of shots fills the screen, showing different angles of work being done. Daisy can be seen among them with a nail gun in her hand.

The scene transitions to a time-lapse shot of the porch columns being removed, the workers moving in fast-forward as they lift, place, and secure the new columns, placing two side by side, where each one had been.

The scene ends, and Daisy and Hunter fill the screen, sitting on the top step of the newly finished, yet still-unpainted porch. The evening light casts blue shadows over their faces, the gold of the sun still dimly lighting the scene.

Hunter turns toward his costar, a quiet breath rising and falling in his chest. "You were right," he says.

Daisy gives him a coy look. "Oh really?"

His gaze drops to her lips for just a breath. "Really."

"About what?" She laughs.

He gestures toward the columns. "I was a skeptic."

"As usual," she chimes.

"But they look nice."

The shot pulls back to show the two of them, shoulders brushing, under the setting-sun sky.

UPLOAD COMPLETE.

DAISY SLUMPED BACK AT HER DESK, her shoulders sore from two weeks of nonstop work. Each day had been filled from sunup to sundown. Every morning, Daisy woke to a laundry list of items: post socials, upload all footage from the previous evening and send to Robin to edit, make a run to the mainland for building supplies, return in time to meet Hunter after work, work until the sun went down, wait for Robin to send her the edited video, post it. Sleep. Repeat.

But even with the seemingly endless cycle, she would rise and do it all again. Because the result was an overwhelming success. And every day, their subscriber count grew exponentially. People loved the show. They loved Hunter. They loved her.

And best of all, they'd overwhelmingly stopped asking about Logan.

Daisy had tried her best not to check up on Logan's socials. But she was only human. She'd spotted a few self-congratulatory posts referencing another good year for *Double Decker*. The posts had shown him alone, beside the last project they'd worked together, Logan holding a hammer. It was laughable. He'd become less and less involved in the actual renovation every season since they'd started. And there he was, taking the credit.

No, Daisy was better off not knowing. She'd keep her head down and come out ahead.

Her phone vibrated, and Daisy picked it up quickly, half hoping to see Hunter's name on the caller ID.

"Hey," she said, answering the video call.

Robin's face appeared on the screen, her short blonde hair framing her eyes. "I don't know about you, but I think I might be in love with your fake fiancé."

"Ha, you and every other woman in the Midwest, apparently," Daisy said, aiming for playful and missing the mark somewhere around . . . jealous? Oh, that couldn't be right. She'd put out the flame for Hunter years ago. Right after he'd stolen her heart and then ghosted her . . .

Robin cut into her thoughts. "Listen, there's something I want to run by you."

Daisy frowned, her curiosity piqued. "Okay?"

"Do you think you could get Mr. Tall, Dark, and Serious to let you renovate that sunroom?"

Daisy's mind flashed to the way he'd closed that door.

The way he'd reacted when he'd found her there that first day. "I don't know . . . Why?"

"Because we're going to submit the house for the *HOME* New Year's Virtual Parade of Houses," Robin said excitedly. "They've got a big contest going, with voting by fans. The winner gets featured in the January issue, as well as a large sum of money toward renovations, which I think could be a big step up for us."

Daisy perked up. "That would be huge!" She was already nearing the end of her savings and was not looking forward to the idea of taking out a line of credit. Winning that contest could be exactly what they needed to be back on top.

"I know!" Robin grinned into the screen. Behind her, the LA skyline was growing dark, tones of gold and red fading into blue. It was a beautiful sunset.

Daisy had missed those sunsets.

Her gaze drifted out the window, toward the stars reflecting off the lake. There was something to be said for starry nights too.

"Okay, so, we'll have to submit photos by December tenth. The contest will run through that whole month, so don't break off your engagement until you've at least finished the foyer and stairs . . . And if you can get that sunroom done, I really think it will set us apart."

"Noted," she said, giving her friend a *don't push it* look. Except that's exactly what she wanted to do. Daisy hung up the call and immediately pulled out her notebook, sketching the sunroom from memory.

There had to be a way out. Hunter's fingers threaded through his hair as he leaned over the Barrett Family Living Trust documents, going through them again. His eyes strained as he read the same line again, the letters seeming to blur the longer he looked at them. He pressed his thumb to his lips, wetting it slightly before turning the page.

"... the oldest generation acting as trustees ..." He leaned back, stretching his back as he closed his eyes in thought. From what he'd learned, a trustee might be able to go through a legal process to change a trust. But seeing as his dad had made it abundantly clear they'd be selling the house if Hunter and Daisy's wedding fell through, there wasn't much chance that his dad would be willing to change the trust. It seemed his dad, like everyone else, had given in to the idea that the house wasn't worth saving. Fat load of help having the oldest gen—

Realization dawned on him, and Hunter shot up, flipping through the pages again.

"It's not Dad," he muttered, smacking himself in the forehead. "It's Grandpa."

Hunter didn't have to think much for a plan to formulate inside his head. In a few short weeks, Hunter's grandfather would arrive for his annual Thanksgiving visit. Hunter just had to get him alone, tell him how much he wanted to preserve the house, to continue the tradition of passing it down, but he couldn't do that if some rich yuppies bought it and made it a summer home. The house was meant to be filled and loved.

It was part of the family, and he wouldn't abandon it.

It was worth the effort to save.

His grandpa would understand.

Hunter's phone pinged, a text from Daisy, no doubt wondering when he'd get back to the house. They had plans to start in on the foyer. He tapped his screen, and the clock showed 5:00 p.m.

Perfect timing.

He reached for his jacket and headed for the door.

The carpeted hall was quiet as he made his way to the lobby. As he passed by the open door of his father's office, his dad lifted his head. "Heading out already?"

Hunter gave his father a stern look. "It's closing time, Dad. I'm leaving, and so should you."

His dad simply grinned, waving away his son's prescription. "Tell Daisy I said to drag you over sometime. I'd love to see more of her."

Hunter gave a two-finger salute. "Will do."

No sooner had he bid his father goodbye than he heard a set of worried footsteps catching up to him in the lobby.

"Hunter! Wait up!"

He turned to see Dawn hurrying toward him with a stack of papers in her hand. Despite his rush to leave, a small smile tugged at the corners of his mouth. There was always something comforting about Dawn's presence. This place would have been sunk a long time ago without her.

"Are you—are you leaving?" she asked, slightly out of breath.

Hunter's good mood faded as he glanced at the papers piled up in her arms. He knew what was coming.

Dawn continued, her tone hinting at her concern. "I'm sorry to catch you as you're heading out the door, but you've been a little hard to catch these last few weeks. The Morton project is three days behind again, the Clark renovation hasn't even started, and the Wilkinson project was scheduled for an inspection but . . ."

But he'd missed the appointment. The one he'd called in special favors to get back on the schedule. Hunter ran a hand through his hair, guilt washing over him. He knew exactly what had caused them to fall so far behind, and she was waiting for him now, probably wearing another ridiculous pair of colored coveralls.

"I know it's not your job to stay late, but . . ." Dawn said, her voice trailing off.

He sucked in a heavy breath and let it out. "But I've stayed late every night for the last four years, and now our company is built on that assumption."

Dawn's lips pressed into an apologetic line.

"I'm sorry, Dawn," he said, genuinely sorry. "I never should have let it get this bad. I'll get on top of these first thing tomorrow, I promise."

But tonight . . .

Hunter stepped into the house, still feeling a pep in his step despite the nagging feeling that he shouldn't be here with her tonight. Not when there was so much work to be done at the office.

His boot creaked on the old flooring. The air carried the comforting smell of sawdust and fresh paint. He glanced around, looking for Daisy's vibrant presence, but the house was quiet.

"Daisy?" he called out, his voice echoing through the empty rooms. No answer.

Hunter sighed and leaned against the doorjamb, looking out at the newly finished porch. It was amazing how much had changed in just a few weeks. When this had all started, he'd wanted nothing to do with the renovations. The idea of Daisy, of all people, making changes to his family home had set his teeth on edge.

But now... Hunter shook his head, a wry smile playing on his lips. Now he actually found himself looking forward to their evenings together. To trying to guess what color overalls she'd be wearing. To the way she tried to pull him into every video, despite his firm protests. To the way she saw the house and what it could be. Not what it was.

His eyes wandered to the still largely untouched foyer. It wouldn't take long for her to leave her mark there. Already, she was planning to completely remove the banister and replace it with something unique and eye-catching. And he was certain it would be the perfect addition to the home.

Not that he'd tell her that. She'd get a big head, and it would be all over.

Hunter chuckled.

His phone buzzed in his pocket, and he pulled it out. Must be Daisy, probably running late. He answered without looking at the screen. "Yeah?"

"Hunter?" a woman's voice asked.

Hunter's spine stiffened. "Mom."

"Hi, Hunt," she said, her quiet voice ringing in his ears. "How are you?"

Hunter's lips parted, but no words came out. His lungs were suddenly dry and sticky. The house creaked restlessly, as though awaking to her voice, even after all these years.

It had been years since he'd spoken to his mother. And even longer since he'd seen her.

Hunter cleared his throat. "I'm good."

He couldn't see her, but he could imagine the sad smile tugging at her lips. "I'm glad to hear it . . ." Another awkward pause filled the air. "Well . . . I know you're busy. I just wanted to call and ask if you got my invitation."

The wedding invitation.

Hunter grimaced, ran a hand over the back of his neck. "I got it."

He couldn't help the ice in his voice.

And apparently, she couldn't help the hurt in hers. "Oh, okay . . . I really hope you can make it. I'd really like you to be there."

Hunter closed his eyes. "Um, I don't know, Mom. Work is really busy. It's a long drive . . ." A long drive to watch the mother who abandoned him marry a man he'd never met. Yeah . . . hard pass.

Another achingly long pause and then, "You're busy. I understand."

Hunter swallowed the ache in his throat. Aww, Mom. "We'll—we'll see. I'll try. I can't make any promises."

"Okay," she said, her voice damp. "You know, you're always welcome—"

"Listen, I gotta go, Mom. I'm working on this project . . ."

"Yes. Of course. I'm sorry to bother you." Hunter winced against the apology. "I hope to see you soon."

"Yeah." *Love you.* It was on the tip of his tongue. "Take care, Mom."

"Love you, Hunt."

The call ended and the house went quiet.

Eight

DAISY GLANCED AGAIN AT THE TIME as she hurried up the hill toward the Barrett house. 6:07 p.m. Oof. She really needed to get a bike. Or better yet, a horse. Daisy emerged from the wooded portion of the road, the overcast sky dyeing the lake a deep shade of blue, dark and cold. In her arms, she carried her notebook, full of the plans she'd drawn up for the house so far. The newest page held the sketch she'd been preoccupied with most of the day.

With the success of *House to Home* so far, she was sure she could convince Hunter to add the sunroom to the renovation. After all, it was just one room.

Daisy's boots crinkled against the tarp they'd laid on the freshly painted porch to keep it clean.

"Before you lecture me for being late," Daisy called as she stepped into the house, "I think you should know that I . . ."

Her words trailed off at the emptiness of the foyer.

It wasn't like Hunter to be late.

"Hunter?" she called, her voice carrying through the house.

She crossed the parlor, where their workstation—a table built from plywood and sawhorses—stood over a canvas tarp, protecting the floor. She set her notebook down and continued to the door at the other end, which was slightly ajar. Unlike the way Hunter had left it.

She pressed the door slightly, and it opened to reveal Hunter, sitting on the floor of the sunroom, his back against the rounded wall, arms resting on his knees. His dark hair hung over his eyes, casting them in a shadow— but not enough to obscure the weight of whatever was bothering him.

"Hey," she said, still standing at the threshold of the room. "Is everything okay?"

"I'm fine," he replied, his chest rising and falling in even breaths. His eyes lifted slowly, landing not on her but on the scorched mantel against the outside wall. "Do you know why they call it the Bad Luck Barrett House?"

"No," she lied, Roger's words from the diner weeks back coming to mind. *Not one good thing happened to that family since the day Joe and Lisa said "I do."* Daisy took a hesitant step into the room, quietly sitting down beside him. "Will you tell me?"

He flipped his phone in his fingers absentmindedly, his head resting against the wall. "When I was growing up, this house was the Barrett legacy. It held the history of every generation, all the way back to my great-great-grand-parents. It was just 'the Barrett house' when I was growing up.

"But it had its history. It's been struck by lightning, caught on fire, a collapsed roof line. Still, people didn't start calling it bad luck until my family lived here."

He slid one leg out, leaving the other for his elbow to rest on. His eyes traveled the walls, as though trying to decide which memory to tell. "My dad built this room, you know. For my mom. It used to end just here." He pointed to a spot in the floor where the direction of the floorboards changed, marking the outline of the circular turret structure. "She wanted a big family with lots of kids, and these old houses are so compartmental. She wanted somewhere we could all be together. So one year, as an anniversary gift, my dad opened it up and connected it to the old breakfast room. She loved this room . . . I used to see them dancing in here when I was a kid."

Hunter sucked in a breath, his eyes returning to his hands as though the room was too much to take in. "I was the youngest for a long time, until my mom finally managed to get pregnant again. I remember my parents were so excited. The whole town was. They decorated all of Main Street with blue and pink streamers the week my parents found out what they were having."

Daisy felt an ache in her chest. She knew what was coming, if only because she'd met his family . . . All but his oldest brother, Miles.

"And I was almost ten when they went in for the eight-month appointment and there was no more heartbeat,"

Hunter said, his voice growing hoarse. "My parents . . . they just never recovered."

"That's when they started calling it the Bad Luck Barrett House . . ." Daisy said, her voice close to a whisper.

Hunter shook his head. "They didn't start calling it that until the boardwalk collapsed."

Daisy frowned slightly, confused.

"My dad has a bad habit of throwing himself into his work as a way of avoiding life. So when things got rough between him and Mom, he picked up whatever projects he could get . . . even ones he wasn't prepared for."

"Like a lakeside boardwalk . . ." Daisy added as the information clicked.

Hunter glanced over at her, his shoulder brushing hers as he nodded slightly. "Anyway, my parents stuck it out for two years. During which time, Dad's company picked up the new boardwalk project, even though they specialized in carpentry and luxury renovations. They weren't ready for that kind of project. Dad should have brought in a specialist to consult, but he couldn't afford it. So he built it anyway, and he miscalculated the spacing for the lateral braces. About a year later, the boardwalk collapsed. Dad's construction company took a major hit. And to top it all off . . . the house was struck by lightning again."

Hunter let out a breath. "I remember that night like it was yesterday. Dad had been working late, spending most nights off island, sleeping in his truck so he could work twice the amount of jobs. I remember my mom sitting on the porch, watching the lightning over the lake."

He licked his lips and went on. "I didn't recognize it

back then, but she was exhausted. She didn't smile much anymore, but she was smiling that night. I went out to check on her, and she asked me to sit with her, and I remember thinking that it felt nice, just sitting and watching the storm.

"That night, I woke up to the loudest noise I'd ever heard. Felt like the house might just split down the middle. My mom came rushing in. Dragged me and my brothers out of bed and out of the house. I remember standing in the street, waiting for the fire truck to arrive while smoke billowed from the house. This room."

He sucked in a breath, the memory fading from his eyes. "Anyway, we stayed at the inn for a while, waiting for Dad to do repairs, but the damage was done."

Daisy winced, but Hunter's focus was back on the mantel, the focal point of his father's gift of love for his mother. To the literal ashes of his childhood. And suddenly, her plans to renovate the room felt . . . wrong.

"And that's when they started calling it the Bad Luck Barrett House," Daisy whispered.

"Mom couldn't handle it. She couldn't take the pitying looks, people walking on eggshells." Hunter flipped the phone between his fingers again. "So she packed up her bags and left. She told me it wasn't worth being a Bad Luck Barrett if it meant she'd have to keep putting her life back together." He drew the words out in loose imitation of the memory. "And just like that, our family fell apart."

Hunter let his other leg slide out, his hands falling with the great weight of hurt into his lap.

"Hunter?" she asked, tears aching in her throat for him. "Did something happen?"

A sad smile played on his lips. He lifted the phone. "My mom called . . ." He let out a breath. "She wants me to come to her wedding."

Through the window, a ray of light broke through the clouds, the warmth of it spilling into the room, reaching almost across, but not quite touching their feet.

"I haven't talked to her in years," he admitted. "Not since my high school graduation. To be fair, she hasn't reached out much either. She tried a few times, but . . ." He shook his head. Paused a moment before going on. "Still . . . I guess I was still holding out hope that she'd come back," he said, his voice thick.

Daisy felt the urge to reach out and take his hand. To pull him into her arms and hold him the way she wished she'd been held when her dad walked out. Because she knew where he was inside his head. She knew the nagging voice that told him he wasn't good enough.

"I'm really sorry, Hunter," was all she could say.

"It's okay." He closed his eyes and let his head fall back against the wall with an exhausted thump. "I don't suppose you know any good stunt doubles I could hire to go to a stuffy wedding?"

Daisy snorted a laugh. "I don't. But I know a fake fiancée who'd love to go with you."

He gave her shoulder a playful nudge. "You don't have to do that."

"I want to," she said softly.

Hunter turned to face her, his brows drawing together

as his eyes searched hers. "I really wanted to stay mad at you," he said quietly.

Daisy scrunched her nose. "That's really too bad for you."

And slowly, as they sat in that old house, the tension in his shoulders melted away.

And Daisy felt like something between them was changing.

The air between them felt magnetic, a force that drew them together. Hunter's gaze dropped to her lips for a heartbeat, and she let herself lean that one breath closer, knowing somewhere inside her head that it was a terrible idea.

Her eyes fell shut when his fingers curled through her hair, drawing her in. And . . .

Daisy pulled back, placing a steadying hand on his chest as reality broke through her momentary lapse in judgment.

There were a hundred reasons not to kiss Hunter Barrett. Only one of which was the fact that their fake engagement was just that. Fake.

"We should . . . we should probably call it an early night," she said, her shaky voice betraying her.

Hunter blinked, looking as dazed as she felt. "Right . . . yeah."

He climbed to his feet, reaching out to help her up. His hands were warm and strong and—Daisy needed to get out of there. Like. Immediately.

"Okay, good talk. See you tomorrow," she said, practically running for the door.

In what world had it seemed like a good idea to lean in for a kiss?

Hunter groaned, running a hand over the back of his neck as he tried to banish the mental image of Daisy's shocked expression from his mind. Closing his eyes, he breathed in the scent of coffee and donuts, anchoring himself in Good Day Coffee rather than the cold floor of the house, where Daisy had left him last night.

"Well, if it isn't Mr. Engaged," a voice called from behind him. Hunter turned to find Mia Jonathon Franklin. Her dark hair hung loose around the shoulders of a warm fall jacket. Hunter's mind flashed to Daisy again. She'd been lucky so far with a warm fall, but he was starting to suspect she didn't even own a jacket.

"Sorry, what?" he asked, trying again to get her out of his head.

"The engagement…?" Mia said, a slight frown creasing her forehead.

Hunter cocked his head in genuine bafflement and then—"Oh! The engagement—*my* engagement. Yes. So happy," he spouted, trying his best to sound convincing.

"Awww. Too twitterpated to even remember you're engaged?" Mia teased. "That's cute."

Hunter stood a little straighter. "Don't 'awww' me, Mia Franklin. I remember when you couldn't even ride a bike."

She grinned. "Sure, Hunter. I'll give you that one." She gestured to the line ahead of them, and they both stepped forward before she continued. "I'm just glad you found someone who makes you happy. Although I did think it was a little odd that she didn't mention you at all while she was looking for a house." She cast him a curious look, one brow ticking upward.

Hunter's neck heated. "I think she was as surprised by our engagement as everyone else. But . . . when you know, you know." He tried to string together enough truth for it to sound believable.

"Speaking of that fiancée of yours," Lyle Graves chimed in to their right, "where *is* the better half? Or am I just supposed to keep taking everyone's word for it that she exists?"

"Oh, stop it, Lyle," Vera chirped beside her husband.

"I'm just making conversation," Lyle protested. "So, Hunter, when's the wedding? Vera and I need to know if we should start planning our outfits."

Hunter nearly choked on air. "Um . . . I don't—we haven't really settled on a date yet . . ."

"Oohh, playing the long game," Lyle said, tapping his temple with a wink, as though Hunter should know what that meant.

Vera shot her husband a warning look before turning to Hunter with a sympathetic smile. "Don't mind him, honey. Lyle thinks he's a comedian. You two take your time. I mean, the engagement certainly came as a shock to everyone. It only makes sense that you'd have a little longer engagement. Really take the time to get to know one another."

You mean, before you do something stupid like, say, mis-

read a whole conversation and wind up trying to kiss her? Hunter suppressed another groan and stepped up for his turn at the counter. He ordered two coffees and two cherry tarts and was halfway out the door before he realized what he'd done.

Just in time for him to nearly crash into the very woman he'd been trying *not* to think about.

Hunter froze.

Daisy was dressed in her usual work attire. Those dang purple overalls again, this time over top a white turtleneck. Her hair hung down to her shoulders, kept away from her face by a black velvet headband. A few rogue strands hung around her face, and he wondered for a moment what it would be like to reach out and touch them.

Daisy smiled, a glossy sheen to her lips. "Is that extra cup for me?"

"What? No. Of course not," Hunter blurted out, sanity seeming to take a back seat while self-preservation grabbed hold of the wheel. He *had* bought the coffee for her. But apparently, that was something only a lovesick fool would do. What was wrong with him?

Daisy raised an eyebrow. "Okay . . . ?"

"You can have it," he backpedaled. "I—Jill gave me an extra by accident."

Amusement tugged at Daisy's lips. "Okay."

She accepted the coffee and took a sip. She let her eyes drift shut as she savored the caramel macchiato he had picked out just for her, and Hunter's heart lurched.

Oh wow, he was a mess.

Daisy turned her attention back to him. "Ready to head up to the house?"

Hunter's mind raced, trying to come up with any good excuse not to spend the day with her.

He came up completely blank.

"Ready."

Why did it suddenly feel like the house was ten times smaller today? Like every hall they stepped into was cramped and tight. Like no matter how much he tried to avoid her, Daisy was just . . . right there.

Hunter winced, pulling his attention back to his project as another gust of steam stung his arm. The wallpaper he'd been working on bubbled, and Hunter peeled it away with his scraper. Just behind him, Daisy worked on the opposite wall, so close he could almost feel her back against his.

"We've been getting great engagement on the videos," Daisy said, making conversation over the quiet tearing of paper.

"That's good," he said, trying and failing not to glance over his shoulder as she moved to a spot toward the front of the foyer.

"Yeah, I'm thinking, with our popularity, we might have a chance at winning the *HOME* New Year's Virtual Parade of Houses contest."

"Cool," Hunter replied absently, his gaze trailing again from the rising steam off the wallpaper steamer to Daisy. To Daisy stretching for a higher section of wall. To Daisy biting her lip as she focused on peeling away a large section of paper. To Daisy beaming in satisfaction at the finished section. To Daisy as she turned and smiled at him, making his heart race again. To—

"Hunter?" Daisy's voice snapped him out of his thoughts. "Are you okay? You've been scraping the same spot for five minutes."

"What? Oh, yeah. I'm fine. Just … being thorough," he mumbled, quickly moving to a new section. He wanted to thoroughly put his head through the wall. What was wrong with him?

"Are you sure you're okay?" Daisy asked again, closer now. "You seem a bit … distracted today."

"I'm fine." He scraped away another strip of paper, maybe a bit more aggressively than necessary.

From the corner of his vision, Hunter caught Daisy as she set down her steamer. A strand of hair slipped from her ponytail, brushing over her cheek, and there he was, thinking about the almost-kiss again, about his fingers threading through her hair.

Focus, Hunter.

He set his gaze firmly back to the wall.

Daisy's hand brushed his shoulder. Startled, he turned to face her. As he did, his boot caught in the steamer cord, throwing him off balance. His own steamer clattered to the floor as he stumbled forward, toward Daisy, and she instinctively stepped back, her back pressing against the wall. Hunter's hands came up to stop himself, and he managed to catch the wall with both hands, bracing himself, with Daisy effectively trapped between his arms.

For a moment, Hunter simply stared at her, as though

unable to understand what had just happened. He glanced down at his feet, still tangled in the cord, and then back at Daisy, who hadn't moved, her eyes wide with shock, her hands lightly pressed to his chest.

"Um . . . Hunter?" Daisy said, pulling him back to his senses.

"Sorry! I'm so sorry," he blurted out, his face burning with embarrassment. He quickly pushed himself off the wall, stumbling backward and nearly tripping over the cord again. "I didn't mean to . . . I mean, I tripped and . . ."

Daisy cleared her throat, a faint blush coloring her cheeks. "It's okay."

Hunter retreated to the door, suddenly desperate for the fresh air.

Outside, the trees were in full color, leaves piling across the recently mowed lawn. Hunter strode down the path, not stopping as his boots hit the street. He kept walking to the other side, where a stone wall marked the edge of Sunset Cove, overlooking the lake. He hopped up onto the wall and let his legs hang over the edge, savoring the cold stone beneath his palms.

Why was it that all of Hunter's most embarrassing moments had to do with Daisy Decker?

As though summoned, Daisy leaned up against the wall beside him.

"Well, that was . . . Wow," she said. "You've been off all day, but I think that was a whole new level."

To his own surprise, Hunter barked out a laugh, the cold air sweeping over the back of his neck as he hung his head. "Please tell me that didn't get on camera?"

Daisy winced, crinkling her nose the way she had the night before. "So sorry, Mr. Barrett, but that moment will live on. Probably forever."

His eyes flicked to hers. "You wouldn't post that . . ."

Daisy laughed, and Hunter relaxed into it. "No, I won't do that to you."

He let out a relieved breath. "Thank you."

Daisy nodded and hopped up onto the wall beside him, her shoulders brushing his ever so slightly. She let out a breath. "About last night . . ."

"I'm sorry about that too," Hunter said, running a hand over his neck. "I wasn't in the right head space. You were just being . . . well, you . . . and I read too much into it. But I'm good now. It won't happen again."

"Okay," she said, her voice lacking the usual lightness he'd begun to look forward to. Or . . . was that a hint of disappointment he detected?

They fell into silence again, the tension between them almost palpable, and Hunter suddenly wanted to take it all back. To ask her if he hadn't been reading into the connection she'd felt. If maybe . . . she'd felt it too.

"So, uh, about that *HOME* New Year's contest . . ." he began, relaunching their earlier topic.

Daisy seemed grateful for the change of subject. "Oh, yes! I think if we really push our social media presence and get some stunning before-and-after shots—those are due in December, by the way—we could have a real chance at winning."

As Daisy launched into her plans for the contest, Hunter found himself relaxing slightly. This was familiar territory—talking about the house, the renovation, their shared goal. He'd protect the family home. She'd go back to California. She'd forget he existed again. Easy. He could handle this.

All he had to do was remember that their fake engagement was just that.

Fake. As long as everything went according to plan . . .

Nine

THE CLATTER OF PLATES AND THE HUM of conversation filled the diner as Hunter and Daisy sat across from each other in a cozy booth inside Martha's on Main. The red cherrywood table between them held a massive plate of fries and several piles of paint samples, tiles, and fabric swatches, all grouped by color scheme.

"Okay, hear me out." Daisy leaned forward, popping a fry into her mouth as she rearranged one of the piles, her excitement obvious as she threw out her idea. "We do periwinkle for the door."

Hunter raised his brows. "*Periwinkle*?"

"Don't laugh," she said, laughing herself. "It's coastal. It's timeless. And it will be so pretty next to the lilacs."

"What lilacs?"

Daisy dipped another fry into the ketchup between them. "The lilacs we're going to plant next to the porch steps. Keep up, Barrett."

Hunter leaned his chin against his thumb, his knuckles brushing his lips as he gave her a thoughtful look. "Hard to keep up with the infamous 'girl with a plan.'"

Heat unfurled in his chest as her bright eyes dropped, her cheeks flushing.

"Aw, for the love of—" An exasperated shout carried across the room, followed by the sharp sound of cards being slapped onto the table. "That's it, I'm done. You fellas are cheating, I swear it!"

Hunter glanced across the diner, where the usual group of locals was engaged in a lively game of cards. Roger scowled animatedly across the table at Stuart "Mac" MacBride, sitting beside Randy Hart, the pair chuckling conspiratorially.

"Who needs to cheat . . ." Stuart started, his eyes on his hand.

"When you couldn't bluff your way out of a paper bag," Randy finished, followed by a roar of laughter.

Lyle Graves stood just behind Roger, leaning on his elbow against the booth. "I told you holding on to that seven of hearts was a bad idea."

Roger swatted at Lyle playfully. "Get outta here, you old busybody! If you hadn't been yapping about my cards the whole game, I might've had a chance!"

Hunter turned back to Daisy, chuckling.

Things had been easy between them the last twenty-four hours. They'd moved past the awkwardness and found their rhythm. Friends again.

He didn't hate it.

He plucked a fry and slumped back against the booth as

Roger stormed away with dramatic flair. Daisy glanced at Hunter and covered her lips, stifling a laugh with her hand.

It was becoming comfortable, sharing these moments with her. Easy.

He reached out and snatched a green paint sample, tossing it in her direction. "I'm still voting green for the door."

Daisy scoffed, pressing a wildly over-offended hand to her heart, and then shifted gears, pointing an accusatory finger back at him. "You listen here, Mr. Macho Contractor Man. I may not be an expert in contracting, but I do have a degree in design, and colors are where I really shine. You should take my advice. Periwinkle and all."

"All right, all right," he replied, lifting his hands in surrender. "Have it your way."

"Thank you." Daisy folded her arms over her chest in mock indignation.

Hunter took a sip of his drink and set the glass back down on the table. "It occurs to me, we never talked about Daisy the designer all those years ago. It was always renovation. Construction . . . *Decks*." He gave her a pointed look at that last one, and she rolled her eyes. "Tell me about this fancy design school you keep waving in my face. Where'd you go?"

Daisy tapped her straw in her drink, breaking up a chunk of ice. "I went to Cornell, actually."

"That's impressive." Hunter nodded approvingly. "Must have made your parents proud."

Daisy's smile faltered slightly. "Mom was thrilled. Dad"—she flicked the straw away—"not so much."

Hunter tilted his head, his brows furrowed. "He wasn't happy? That's one of the best schools in the country."

"He didn't exactly see design as a 'real career.' He thought I was wasting my potential."

"That's ridiculous," Hunter said, his voice gruff.

Daisy shrugged as she picked through the plate of fries. "I dunno . . . I guess I can see where he was coming from. Dad was always really focused on my achievements. You know? He'd make a point to show up when it mattered."

"Mattered to who, exactly?"

Daisy's gaze flickered upward, catching his own before dropping again.

She selected a fry, picking it up with her fingers. "He'd come to state debate championships. Honors Society banquet. My valedictorian speech," she said, listing off an impressive list of accomplishments. "So it was sort of a shock to him when I went into a field a little less . . ." She shrugged again, pulling the fry apart. ". . . impactful." Her eyes lifted for a moment, catching his before finding somewhere else to look. "Honestly, if I hadn't landed the show, I don't know if I could really call myself a success."

Again, Hunter frowned, his mind unable to match what she was saying against that lighthearted tone she couldn't seem to turn off.

"Anyway," she said, pulling that practiced "Daisy Decker" smile back onto her face. "Dad came around to it once the show took off. He calls every once in a while, asks how it's going."

Hunter couldn't stop himself. He reached across the table to take her hand, his thumb brushing her wrist.

"Seems like your dad really missed out," he said quietly. "Because it sounds like you were already something pretty special, even before all the success."

A mix of emotions played across Daisy's face. She opened her mouth to respond but was cut off.

"Hunter!" a gruff voice called from behind him. Hunter turned to find Asher Quinn strolling up to the booth, his hand clasped with his new fiancée's. They were a good-looking pair, with Sadie's blue eyes and dimpled cheeks, and Asher's square jaw and dark hair. Hunter had been harboring a secret jealousy of Asher's beard. He wasn't so sure he could pull that off.

Hunter quickly withdrew his hand from Daisy's. He nodded a greeting toward the approaching couple. "Good to see you, Asher."

Hunter had only met Sadie a few times, but she was friendly enough. "Nice to see you, Sadie."

"You too." Her eyes turned toward Daisy and then returned to Hunter expectantly.

"Right! Sorry. This is my beautiful fiancée, Daisy." Hunter gestured between the women. "Daisy, Sadie Hudson."

"How's the renovation going?" Sadie asked. "Asher mentioned he's seen the house a few times while passing by."

"It's going really well, actually," Daisy said, all traces of their somber conversation evaporating with her bright smile. "We were just discussing some design choices."

Sadie's gaze fell on the color palettes on the table, and her eyes lit up. "Oh, I love this one!" She tapped the periwinkle, and Hunter shook his head, a smile creeping across his face.

"I guess I shouldn't be surprised." He let out a sigh, smiling across at his partner. He glanced at the nearly empty plate of fries between them, then back to Daisy. "Looks like we need some reinforcements if we're going to tackle the rest of these design choices. I'll grab us another order."

He slid out of the booth, giving Asher and Sadie a nod. "Nice seeing you both. Enjoy your evening."

"Another one?" Vera asked as he rounded the corner, strolling up to the counter.

"It's thinking food, Vera," Hunter said, grinning. "Gotta keep the design juices flowing."

"I see," Vera said. "Well, maybe you ought to use some of those design juices to start planning your wedding."

Hunter coughed in surprise.

Vera chuckled and strolled back into the kitchen. She reemerged a moment later with a fresh plate of fries. "Here you go, honey," she said, setting it down in front of him.

"Thanks," he replied warmly and started back.

When he reached the corner, Hunter paused, a familiar voice carrying from the next room.

"I know it's none of my business," Martha Kelley said, her voice low, "but I would be remiss not to tell you to think twice about getting involved with the Barrett family."

"Excuse me?" Daisy's voice asked, and Hunter's heart picked up speed.

"They're good people. Bless their hearts. It's just that, well, everywhere they go, things just seem to go wrong.

You know, it was Barrett Construction that nearly drowned a woman with their failed boardwalk project. Then, of course, there were the lightning strikes and the house fire. And of course, that unfortunate situation with Belle. It seems to me that they may be more effort than they're worth."

A wave of cold washed over him, his chest tightening.

And then Daisy chimed in, and he froze, holding his breath.

"With all due respect," Daisy said firmly, "I think I know what I'm talking about when it comes to construction and contracting. So you can take it from me, Barrett Construction is one of the most reputable construction businesses in all of Michigan. They've won the GSA Construction Award three years in a row. They've won the Excellence in Business Award and the National AGC Safety Award. I was aware of their history when I decided to renovate with them. And I would have selected them to partner with even if I weren't engaged to Hunter Barrett."

Hunter stood there, unable to process her words for a moment. And then warmth rushed in, replacing all traces of cold.

He peered around the corner to see Martha's red face sputtering, "Well, I . . . I could be wrong."

"As for the superstition surrounding the Barretts," Daisy went on, "I didn't think I'd have to dignify that with a response, but apparently I do. So here it is. They are more than the sum of the things that have happened to them. And it breaks my heart to hear you call them more effort than they're worth."

Martha sucked in a sharp breath. Hunter almost felt bad for her.

Martha excused herself and walked away, and Hunter took a deep breath. He approached the booth, sliding in across from Daisy, setting the plate of fries down between them before meeting her eyes.

"Let's get out of here," she said, her eyes showing no trace of the conversation he'd just overheard.

"Gladly."

Daisy was thankful for the cold when she stepped out of the diner, her nerves still hot from Martha Kelley's unsolicited "advice." She sucked in a breath of frigid air, letting it wash over her as the roar of the diner faded away and Hunter stepped up behind her.

"You gotta excuse Lyle," Hunter said, laughing as he glanced back through the window, where the old man was now hiding his card from Roger, who still peeked over his shoulder. "Those guys always seem to get a rise out of him one way or another."

Hunter pressed a gentle hand to her back, leading her away from the busy establishment and toward the hazy glow of Main Street, Jonathon Island. The town still looked like a storybook to her, the vintage streetlamps tied with orange and blue ribbons for the fall, neat little piles of golden leaves piled up in the corners of the shops. It was a place you almost couldn't believe was real.

Daisy shivered as a gust of wind bit through her flannel.

"Here," Hunter said, already shrugging out of his jacket.

"What is this, a Hallmark movie? I'm fine." She laughed, even as another shiver ran through her.

"Sure you are," Hunter said, a hint of amusement in his voice. "But I don't want people thinking I let my fiancée walk around in the cold. Humor me."

He draped his jacket over her shoulders. The warmth of the fabric, still holding his body heat, immediately seeped into her as the smell of sawdust and pine filled her senses.

"Thank you," she said, lifting a hand to brush her wind-strewn hair away from her face, and she had to give the sleeve a little shake for her fingertips to find a way out.

Hunter nodded, his hands now shoved into his jeans pockets as they strolled toward the coffee shop.

It felt like so much had changed in the last few weeks, their relationship taking a turn the moment Hunter decided to stop keeping her at arm's length. And now they seemed to be in that warm, glowy place between friends and more than friends. The place where every interaction felt charged. Every glance seemed to hold some hidden meaning.

Daisy felt like she was standing just on the edge of falling. And she knew she shouldn't, but she craved the reckless thrill of inching closer.

They stopped in front of the coffee shop, the windows dark for the night, signaling the end of the day, but suddenly, she didn't want it to be over.

Daisy turned. "Do—"

"Do you want to keep walking?" Hunter asked.

Her answer was immediate. "Yes."

Hunter's eyes lit up, that smirk she'd just gotten used to spreading across his face. "Great. Let's go."

He took hold of the end of her sleeve—his sleeve—and tugged her along as he steered them away from town.

"Where exactly are we going?" Daisy asked, laughing as she stumbled over a branch. Hunter caught her easily, his warm hand enveloping hers, supporting her as he led them down a beaten path.

"What, I never told you about the old Barrett beach?" he said, his hand warming her back as he helped her over another fallen branch.

"You have your own beach?"

"Well, no," he admitted sheepishly. "But also . . . yeah, sort of."

The sound of waves grew louder with each step down the narrow trail. The trees thinned out, and Hunter reached out, pulling a branch aside to reveal the pebbly beach just on the other side.

Daisy let out a breath. "Wow."

The cold waters of Lake Huron were a cauldron of starlight, silver specks sinking into the deep. The waves hushed back and forth over the white pebbly beach, washing away all traces of the world around.

"The view never gets old," Hunter murmured, apparently just as awed by it as she was.

"Why do you call it Barrett beach?" Daisy asked, head tilting.

Hunter pointed inland, and she followed it up the hill, over rows of trees, to where the Barrett house overlooked the water. He took one more look and then clapped his hands together. "Come on, then." He gripped her sleeve again and tugged her farther onto the beach.

Her feet wobbled on the uneven ground, and it shifted with every step, causing her to thrust her arms out for balance.

"You good?" Hunter called over his shoulder from where he was now scouting the rocks—for what, she didn't know.

"All good!" she replied, lifting a shaky thumb.

"Good, now sit," he instructed, pointing to a dip in the rocks where he'd piled up a few twigs and branches.

Daisy did as she was told, feeling a bit silly as she tried to find a comfortable position against the icy rocks.

"Cold?" Hunter asked, concern lacing his voice.

"A little," Daisy admitted. "But it's beautiful here."

Hunter nodded, a small smile playing on his lips. "Just wait. It gets better."

He moved with practiced ease, gathering a few larger pieces of driftwood and arranging them into the loose shape of a teepee, and Daisy watched, fascinated, as he stuffed twigs and dried grass into the middle. He was a man in his element.

He stepped toward her, tugging her closer as he slipped a hand into the pocket of the jacket she was still wearing and pulled out a lighter. Within moments, a small flame flickered to life.

As Hunter added a log to the flames, feeding the fire as it rose higher, he turned to Daisy. A cocky grin spread across his face, his eyes reflecting the dancing firelight. He didn't have to say anything, his eyes said it all. *I am man, hear me roar!*

Daisy couldn't help but chuckle as she gave him a humoring clap.

"Thank you," he said, tilting his head in a bow. The rocks clicked together as he flopped down beside her, relaxing against his bare elbow like some sort of GQ model.

The fire crackled gently, sending sparks flying into the starry sky, the golden flakes mixing with the silver ones. Daisy nestled into the jacket, comfortable with the quiet, listening to the waves lapping against the shore.

Finally, Hunter broke the silence. "Thank you," he said softly.

Daisy pulled her gaze from the flames, turning to find him watching her intently.

"For what you said back there," he explained, dropping his gaze to the stone in his hand. He twirled it in his fingers, as though anchoring himself to it.

Realization hit Daisy, and she felt heat rise to her cheeks. The conversation back at the diner. "Oh," she said. "You heard that."

Hunter nodded. "Yeah, I did."

Daisy scooped up a rock of her own, trying not to pry. "You don't have to tell me about it . . . But, just so you know, she's wrong about you. And about your family."

Hunter dropped his stone, letting out a heavy breath as he rolled to his back, resting one hand on his chest, the other behind his head. The stars reflected in his eyes as the light of the fire was blocked out. When he spoke, his voice was low, tinged with an old pain. "She's not completely wrong."

Daisy stilled, waiting for him to go on.

His chest rose as he sucked in a deep breath. "I had this girlfriend. My high school sweetheart, I guess you'd call her. Belle." He spoke into the dark. "Belle came into my life just after everything fell apart at home. My dad had moved us to the mainland, but he was never really around. So, after school most days, my brothers and I would hop on the ferry. Hang around town with friends until the last ride out."

Daisy tried to envision young Hunter with his unruly brown curls and dark eyes. She had a feeling he wouldn't have noticed her in high school.

"Belle and I were friends. And at first, she was just a shoulder to lean on. But after a while, it turned into something more. Before I knew it, her mom was saving me a spot on their pew on Sundays, Pastor Arnie tossing an extra burger on the grill, making a place for me."

A complete family to replace his broken one.

Suddenly, Daisy didn't want to hear the end of this story.

"We dated for three years," he said, his eyes tracing constellations in the sky. "And when senior year rolled around, I was ready to follow her anywhere. She was an incredible athlete. And she'd gotten a full ride to play basketball for Michigan State. Her parents were so proud."

He paused, his voice heavy, and Daisy wondered how long it had been since he'd told anyone this story.

"Anyway, there was this party," he continued. "A bonfire

on the beach in St. Joseph." Hunter's jaw tightened. "I should have stopped her, but . . . I didn't. I'd spent years keeping Waylen out of trouble at these parties—"

"Waylen, the *cop*." Daisy frowned.

Hunter cast her a look. "He wasn't always a cop, you know. He used to get in trouble a lot before he turned things around. So I guess I had a lot of reason to think Belle wouldn't listen. So I went along with it . . . We showed up to the party, and she got it into her head to dive off the St. Joseph's lighthouse." He shook his head. "Belle had always been stubborn, and the alcohol only made it worse."

The fire crackled as a log fell into the flame, sending sparks across the sky.

"I'll never forget it. She hit the water, and I just knew something was wrong." He paused, collecting his memories. "We grew up around water. Jumped off the pier a hundred times. It seemed like no big deal. But it was dark, and we'd never jumped that lighthouse before. She misjudged the depth, hit a submerged rock, and shattered her leg."

Daisy's stomach twisted. He looked at Daisy, his eyes filled with regret. "If the Coast Guard hadn't been nearby, she might have died." Hunter drew in a ragged breath. "Just like that, it was all over. Her sports career, her college plans . . . everything she'd worked for, gone in one night."

"You can't blame yourself for that, Hunter," Daisy whispered, her whole chest aching for him and the weight he'd been carrying all these years.

"Sure I can," he said. "Her parents do."

Suddenly, the memory of the woman in the coffee shop,

her sad expression and Hunter's tense shoulders, came to mind.

"Tara is her mom," Daisy realized aloud.

"Yeah . . ."

"I don't think she blames you, Hunter." It seemed more like sadness—heartbreak—in the way Tara had looked at him in the coffee shop. Hunter sat up, his gaze searching hers. "Maybe."

A charged silence filled the space between them, and Daisy glanced away. "What happened with Belle?" she asked.

His chest sank as he let out a heavy breath. "She had months of physical therapy. I did my best to be there for her, but things just . . . fell apart."

A bitter laugh escaped his lips. "She called me up one day, said she couldn't do it anymore. That she didn't have room for a relationship in her recovery." He shook his head, his voice barely above a whisper. "Why is it, when things get tough, when everything falls apart . . . I'm always the first thing to get cut loose? What does that say about me?"

Daisy didn't know what to say to that. How do you respond to a person's most vulnerable moment? She reached out, curling her fingers over his.

"So there it is. Hunter Barrett's origin story." Hunter took a deep breath, as if trying to shake off the weight of his confession. He turned to Daisy, a small, forced smile on his face. "Okay, now you've heard my big bad secret. Tell me yours."

Daisy wrapped her arms around her knees, her hair

falling in a curtain around her. "I'm an open book. What do you want to know?"

Hunter bit his lip, thinking about the question before asking, "Why did you leave the show?"

Daisy blinked at him for a moment. She straightened, slipping back into the safety of that practiced smile. "I just thought it was time. Looking for a new horizon, so to speak." Her lips pressed together neatly at the end.

Hunter studied her for a moment, his brow furrowing. "Why do you do that?"

"Do what?" Daisy asked, her smile faltering slightly.

"That whole 'Daisy Decker' persona," Hunter said gently. "You know you're allowed to turn it off, right?"

Daisy's smile died, and she turned away from him, shrinking into herself. "Yeah ... I do ... I just ... it's easier to talk to people when I know what they're expecting from me." She picked up a nearby branch and poked it into the flames, watching it catch fire as she let out a heavy breath. "When the show first started, people would meet me in real life, and if I wasn't exactly as peppy or bright as they expected, they'd walk away disappointed ... So, I think I'm sort of stuck with it."

A long moment passed before she felt Hunter's arm wrap around her shoulder.

"We're really a pair, aren't we?" He laughed.

Daisy laughed too, feeling an instant lift in the air. "You're telling me!"

Hunter's thumb brushed over her shoulder, sending sparks through her skin. "For what it's worth, I'd really like to get to know Daisy without the Decker."

Daisy turned and found him looking at her, as though searching for something under all the layers of rules and plans, all the things she'd spent years building up so she'd never have to lose someone like him. And she wanted to believe that, for once, someone might want her just because of who she was rather than what she did.

And so she pushed aside the plan, the one that said this was all imaginary. The one that said the rush she felt every time he touched her was all a part of the show. And she leaned in. Her hand trembled as she reached for him, her fingertips brushing his neck.

Hunter closed his eyes, leaning into her touch, and when they opened, they met hers with an intensity that stole her breath away.

He reached for her without hesitation, one hand curling around the back of her neck, fingers threading through her hair, as the other wrapped around her waist, pulling her in. His gaze dropped to her lips for a split second. Long enough for them to wonder if this was a bad idea. And then.

Hunter Barrett kissed her.

Daisy melted into him, the warmth of the fire paling in comparison to the heat of his arms wrapped around her. This was not like the kiss she remembered from all those years ago. No. That kiss had been sweet. Timid. A bud in the spring.

This kiss was strong and sure. Wildflowers in bloom.

Hunter pulled back, his forehead resting against hers as they caught their breath.

His fingers traced over her face, drawing her back to him, his lips brushing hers again.

And suddenly, she was back in Chicago, waiting for a call that never came. And she remembered . . . A broken heart wasn't part of the plan.

She pulled away. "I'm sorry. I shouldn't have . . ."

Hunter's brows pinched together, and then the realization set in. "Yeah, sorry. You're right."

What were they thinking?

"I—we should go," she said, scurrying to her feet.

Hunter swallowed hard. "Right."

He doused the flames, leaving the stars to light their walk home. And when he dropped her off at the door, she almost wished a kiss had been part of the plan.

Ten

**EPISODE 5: ALL SAND AND NO PLAY,
UPLOADED (OCTOBER 24TH)**

The camera pans across the interior of the
Barrett house, focusing on the worn hardwood
floors before settling on Daisy. She stands in
the center of the foyer, wearing her signature
overalls with a cozy orange sweater underneath.
Hunter, wearing a plain white tee, leans up
against the wall behind her, his muscular arms
crossed over his chest, a smirk playing at his
lips.

Hi, friends! Daisy here," she beams, her
eyes sparkling with excitement. "Today, we're
tackling one of the most important parts of
our restoration project: the floors!" She steps
aside, gesturing to the floors with jazz hands,
and Hunter rolls his eyes, his smirk deepening.
"Lucky for us, this beautiful house still has its
original hardwood floors, but it's going to take a
lot of work to bring these gorgeous floors back

to life! So let's get started!"

Music plays as the camera cuts to a shot of Daisy and Hunter as they work together to gently pry the molding off the walls, a voiceover playing over the footage. "After carefully removing the antique molding around the floors, taping off doors, and nailing down any loose boards—" The footage cuts to a shot of Daisy sitting cross-legged on the floor while Hunter hammers a nail into the wood. He feels around, finding another loose plank, and glances at his tool belt for another nail and comes up empty. His eyes shoot to Daisy, who laughs, holding one out for him. He gives her a playful scowl and snatches it from her fingers. "—we're ready to start sanding. This process involves multiple passes with progressively finer grit sandpaper to smooth out years of wear and tear."

The camera cuts to Daisy pushing a large sander in a meticulous line along the wood grain. The shot speeds up as she makes short work of the rugged flooring, crossing the room end to end. When she's about halfway through, Hunter steps into the shot and begins work on the edges and corners with a smaller, handheld sander.

"While the drum sander takes care of the main floor area, it's crucial to pay special attention to the edges and corners. This ensures a uniform finish across the entire room."

The pair of them work steadily as shadows move across the space. Daisy backs into the final corner just as Hunter works his way there from the opposite direction. Startled, she spins around, nearly losing her balance as Hunter's hands shoot out to steady her.

"Oh! Sorry!" Daisy squeaks, her cheeks flushing.

Hunter chuckles, steadying her with a hand on her waist. "No worries," he says softly, their eyes meeting for a moment before they both look away.

"Sanding floors is no easy task. It requires patience, attention to detail, and plenty of breaks to stay hydrated and avoid fatigue."

. . . Hunter sits on the staircase, sweat staining his shirt as he takes a break, a bottle of water hanging from his fingertips. Down the hall, Daisy is crouched on her hands and knees, her sweater now gone, leaving her in a pink T-shirt under her overalls. She is working hard with a square of sandpaper on a remaining scratch, her brow furrowed in concentration.

Hunter glances over his shoulder, watching her for a moment, a soft smile playing on his lips. And then he stands up, walks over, and holds out the water bottle to her. Daisy pauses to look up, surprised, as Hunter nods for her to move aside. Understanding dawns on her face, and she gratefully accepts the water, stepping back as Hunter takes over the troublesome spot . . .

"What would I do without that guy?"

. . . Daisy and Hunter sit side by side on the steps, both covered in sawdust, their shoulders tight and their hair a mess. They look thoroughly disheveled.

Daisy's eyes travel over their finished work and land on Hunter. She laughs, taking in his haggard appearance, and a moment later, he joins in, his laughter bubbling over like water over stones.

"After hours of hard work, there's nothing quite like the satisfaction of seeing the transformation. These floors have stories to tell, and now they're ready for new chapters."

Daisy's eyes crinkle as she reaches out to brush some sawdust from Hunter's hair. He stills at her touch, his laughter fading into a soft smile. As Daisy turns her attention back to the camera, Hunter's eyes linger on her.

"That's it for today, friends! Thanks for joining us," she says, beaming at the audience.

Comments:

@User8978: Those floors are coming along beautifully! Can't wait to see the finished product!

@BookwormBarista: The way Hunter looks at Daisy when she's not watching . . . 😍 Anyone else seeing this?

@VintageGirlie: I'm learning so much from these videos. Thanks for breaking down the process, Daisy!

———

EPISODE 6: FALLING COLORS, UPLOADED (OCTOBER 31ST)

The camera opens on a sweeping shot of the Barrett house, standing stately against blue skies. The surrounding trees are adorned with the last of the fall colors, the rest of the leaves piled on the grass. Daisy and Hunter, wearing painting clothes, stand on the porch, surrounded by an array of paint supplies.

Daisy slips on her signature grin and speaks to the camera. "Hi, friends, and happy Halloween! Daisy here. We're taking advantage of this beautiful day to add some curb appeal to the house."

Hunter holds up a shutter, joining in the introduction. "I'll be giving these shutters a fresh coat of classic black . . ."

Daisy gestures to the front door. "And I'll be adding a pop of color to our entrance! But first . . ." She ducks out of the shot, Hunter's brow scrunching in confusion. A moment later, she pops back into the shot. In her open palm sits a single cupcake. "Rumor has it, it's a certain someone's birthday . . ." She laughs, her nose scrunching as Hunter shakes his head, a smile tugging at his lips.

"Yeah, all right," he says, eyes rolling.

Daisy turns to the camera. "Okay, everyone, all together now! Happy birthday to—"

"Oh no, no, no." He snatches the cupcake out of her hand and stuffs it into his mouth. "Tastes great. Thanks. Let's go."

And then he trudges out of the shot.

Daisy laughs, her cheeks growing a soft pink. "Okay then, let's get started!"

The camera pans to a new scene: Hunter and Daisy setting up their stations in the front yard, setting the door across two sawhorses. Daisy's voice enters. "When painting outdoors, it's important to check the weather forecast. You want a dry day with mild temperatures. Lucky for us, Jonathon Island has one more warm day for us this fall."

The shot cuts to Daisy carefully painting the door a periwinkle blue, then to Hunter and the black shutters.

"You'll want to make sure to use exterior paint for anything that will be exposed to the elements . . ."

As they work, Daisy steals glances at Hunter, his brows furrowed in concentration as he carefully brushes across the shutter slats. A mischievous smile slides across Daisy's lips as she dips her brush in her paint. She crouches behind her door as she waits for him to step away from his project.

Hunter sets down his brush and steps back, admiring his work, and then . . .

A grin splits across Daisy's face as she flicks her brush, sending a spray of blue across Hunter's white tee.

Hunter glances down at his shirt and then up in surprise. "Really, Decker?"

Daisy shrugs playfully. "Thought you could use some color."

A dangerous look crosses his face, and Hunter

darts for his brush, loaded with black paint.

Daisy's eyes widen. "Hunter . . ."

He crouches slightly, stepping closer. A lion stalking his prey.

"Hunter, no!" Daisy laughs, running as he lunges.

"We should note that this is definitely not an approved painting technique . . ."

The camera pulls back as Hunter chases Daisy across the grass, catching her around the waist with one arm while the other smears black paint playfully across her tattered T-shirt as she scream-laughs . . .

Comments:

@DIYDreamer: That periwinkle door is going to look amazing! Great color choice!

@Kimmiwiththekats: That paint fight was the cutest thing ever! They're totally falling for each other!

@Justthatgirl: The chemistry between these two is off the charts! Please tell me they're dating!

———

EPISODE 7: OUT WITH THE OLD . . . , UPLOADED (NOVEMBER 7TH)

The video begins with a shot of the interior of the house, focusing on the worn staircase. Hunter stands on the bottom step, looking handsome in a fitted tee and jeans. He flashes a charming smile as he steps down onto the landing.

"Hi, friends! Hunter here. Today we're tackling the—" he begins before being cut off as Daisy pops into the frame, a look of mock indignation splayed across her face.

"What are you doing?" she asks.

Hunter frowns. "What? I can't try my hand at being host?"

Daisy crosses her arms over her chest, standing her ground. "Stick to looking pretty, Mr. Contractor. I've got the intros covered," she says, playfully pushing him out of the shot before coming back to finish the intro with a sheepish smile. "Today we're focusing on the beautiful staircase, and we're finally going to be removing the old banister, making room for something new. Let's get started."

The video continues with a series of shots as Daisy and Hunter pull out the threadbare stair runner, sand the banister spindles, and finally set to removing the heavy wooden banister. As they finish, they step back to admire their work, shoulders brushing as they survey the scene.

"Now we just have to find the right replacement," Daisy says . . .

Comments:

@TheGreeneHouse: That staircase is going to be stunning when it's done. Can't wait to see what they choose for the new banister!

@CraftyKatie: The way Hunter tried to do

the intro and Daisy's reaction . . . they're so adorable together!

@User8978: I'm learning so much from this series. Thanks for making home improvement look fun and accessible!

@Kelsiewiththekids: I heard from a friend on Jonathon Island that Hunter and Daisy are engaged! Can anyone confirm?

———

WELL, WELL . . . LOOK WHO'S BECOMING a morning person," Miles teased through the screen of Hunter's phone. The inky morning loomed around him as Miles strolled the beach of Lake Michigan, the only light the sliver of sun peeking over the horizon.

"You're the only person crazy enough to like getting up this early. I've got a reason," Hunter argued, taking a sip of coffee from his travel mug. The heat warmed his hands in the otherwise frigid workshop. Outside, the cold morning watched from the windows, darkness kept at bay by the flickering fluorescents.

"Hey, I'm not complaining. Feels like it's the only time we get to catch up," Miles said, his eyes crinkling at the corners. "What exactly are you doing?"

Hunter set the mug down on the rugged wood counter and brushed his hands off, sending a puff of sawdust into the air. "I'm just putting the finishing touches on my project."

Miles raised an eyebrow. "And what might that be?"

Hunter lifted the phone until his project was visible in the background.

His brother gave an impressed whistle.

Hunter quirked a smile. "It's good, right?"

The camera shook as Miles crossed a rocky beach, the sound of stone clattering around his feet spilling into Hunter's workshop. Miles dropped to the ground and returned his attention to the camera. "Hunt, it's more than good. It's awesome. Dad would be proud."

The compliment felt odd in this space, as though they were remembering someone who'd died . . . But their dad wasn't dead. But he wasn't the man he'd been when he'd taught his sons how to work wood.

"Thanks, Miles," Hunter said. A beat passed, and he snatched up a worn square of sandpaper, running it again over the sleek wood.

"How are things going with the house?" Miles asked, his eyes on the brightening horizon.

Hunter paused his sanding, considering his brother's question. "The house is coming along. Better than I expected, actually."

"Yeah?" Miles prompted, his attention shifting back to the screen. "And Daisy?"

Hunter's hand stilled on his work. "Daisy is . . . complicated."

Miles chuckled. "You don't say."

"Don't you start with me." Hunter lifted an accusing finger, but there was no real heat behind it. He set down the sandpaper and leaned against the workbench. "I don't know, Miles. I think . . . maybe there's something between us." Hunter ran a hand through his hair, leaving a streak of sawdust. "But it's not like last time. That was . . ." Hunter didn't know how to describe the last time. He'd spent too long trying to forget it. "This just feels different."

Scarier.

Miles nodded, letting Hunter know he was listening.

"Daisy is this incredible force. She's creative and determined and . . ." His voice trailed off from the ramble, and he took a breath, recentering. "And I'm just trying to keep my feet on the ground." While he waited for the other shoe to fall.

For the Barrett name to catch up with them.

Miles frowned. "What exactly is going on between you two?"

Hunter tilted his head back, glancing at the ceiling with a humorless laugh. "I wish I knew."

He considered not telling him. But then, "We may have . . . accidentally kissed."

Miles's eyes widened in honest surprise. "Yowzah."

Hunter hung his head and spared a glance at his brother. "Like I said. It's complicated." He took a cleansing breath and turned back to his work. "And I don't know where the fake engagement ends and we begin. Are we pretending? Are we real?" He looked expectantly at his brother. "No really, tell me. I'm pretty lost here."

Miles chuckled and rose, turning the camera so the lake was behind him, the bright sunrise splitting sky from water. "I think maybe you should ask her," Miles suggested.

"Wow," Hunter said, blinking in sarcasm. "Thank you, Miles. You've solved everything." He swiped a bead of sweat from his forehead with the back of his hand. "It doesn't matter anyway. As soon as this project is done, she's headed right back to California. So . . ."

His brother gave him a pitying look, and Hunter suddenly wished he hadn't brought it up. He wasn't a lovesick fool.

"I gotta go," Miles said, the sound of tumbling rocks spilling through the phone. "Seriously though, Hunt. Ask her. What's the worst that could happen?"

Hunter switched positions again, crossing his arms, then dropping them, then striding across the room as he overthought his entire plan for the fourth time since he'd set up inside the house.

The morning sun spread across the gray skies, illuminating the newly refinished foyer with a warm glow. On the floor, beside the stairs, lay the secret project he'd been working on for weeks: a massive, intricately carved banister. Hours of work and a lifetime of Barrett tradition had gone into its creation. The presentation had to be perfect.

The sound of footsteps on the porch sent an excited jolt through Hunter's chest, and he threw himself against the wall, trying his best to look as though he'd been there the whole time, waiting patiently, coolly, for her arrival.

The door swung open, and Daisy stepped inside. Even in the dim light, Hunter could pinpoint the exact moment she noticed the banister.

Daisy froze, her hand covering her mouth in surprise. She approached it slowly, crouching down to trace her fingers over the intricate carvings, a look of wonder growing on her face.

Unable to contain himself any longer, Hunter shrugged away from the wall. "Morning, Decker," he said casually. No big deal.

Daisy sprang to her feet, spinning around, eyes wide. "Hunter! What . . . what is this?"

Hunter gave her a quizzical frown. "Looks like a new banister."

Daisy matched his frown, placing a fist on her hip. "Oh, thank you for that, Captain Obvious. Care to share where it came from?"

A sheepish smile tugged at Hunter's lips. "I made it," he said, running a hand over the back of his neck.

Daisy's jaw dropped. "You made this?"

Hunter nodded, feeling a warmth spread through his chest at her reaction. "Um, yeah."

"Stop. You didn't tell me you could do this."

"You didn't ask."

"Well, that's ridiculous. What other extremely helpful talents are you hiding from me, Hunter Barrett?"

Hunter chuckled. "Just that one."

Daisy stared at him, her eyes bright, her lips parted in a growing smile.

His chest tightened, and Hunter dropped his gaze, feeling the sudden need to fill the charged silence between them. "I . . . um . . . I was actually planning to be a carpenter. Before I joined the family business. It's kind of a family specialty." He ran a hand over the back of his neck. "Half the houses on the island have some sort of Barrett woodwork. It was just this thing we did when we completed a project. A little something to keep us on the island."

Daisy turned back to the banister, crouching again to trace the pattern along the edges. "It's incredible, Hunter." Then, she looked up at him, her eyes shining with something that tugged at Hunter's heart. "I want to see Barrett pieces all over this house when we're through."

All over this house. The implication in her words was not lost on him. It would take a lot longer than a few months to renovate this whole house . . .

Talk to her. What's the worst that could happen?

Hunter swallowed hard, the words on the tip of his tongue. *Would you stay? If I asked?*

Daisy glanced up again as if just remembering something. "Don't you have work today?"

He blinked, the fog in his mind clearing. "Yeah. Yes." He stepped back, shoving his hands into his pockets, sawdust and all. "I just wanted to be here when you saw it."

Her lips pressed together, hiding that beautiful smile, and his stomach flipped.

"Okay. See you tonight."

He wasn't ready for the worst that could happen.

No, he'd keep pretending.

As long as it kept her around.

Eleven

I T REALLY WAS PERFECT.

Daisy slouched back against the wall, staring again at the finished staircase. Her hands wrapped around a warm cup of caramel apple macchiato as she planned out her next steps.

The projects Hunter had agreed to were nearly done. The porch was finished, and the exterior had a fresh coat of paint, giving the house some much-needed curb appeal. The foyer had new wallpaper, refinished floors and stairs, and a piece of signature Barrett woodworking for the banister.

All they needed now was updated lighting, and then it would be ready for staging.

Daisy glanced around the house. There was still so much she wanted to do.

Her eye caught on the gaping hole above the sunroom door. The walls had been cleaned, the floor refinished, but

Daisy hadn't asked again to work on that room. Not after Hunter had told her what it meant to him.

But that transom . . .

She wondered.

Daisy set down her coffee cup and pushed to her feet before making her way toward the back of the house. She stepped into the old kitchen, pausing on her search to admire the potential of the space.

Daisy had done her share of snooping since they'd started the project. She'd seen every room, imagined the renovations she could do, all the ways she could turn this place from a house to a home for someone. She had a lot of ideas for the kitchen.

She'd move the island to make room for two between the oven and sink. Update the cabinets to be large enough to hide away appliances. Add space to sit around the counter. A place for kids to gather. A handcrafted pantry door made by this local woodworker she knew . . .

That's what she'd do.

If it were hers.

Daisy let out a quiet sigh and turned, her gaze catching on the windows that overlooked the backyard, her eyes following a recently worn path through the grass, leading to the weather shed tucked away at the edge of the property.

Bingo.

Hunter's workshop.

The door creaked as she pushed it open, the scent of sawdust and varnish enveloping her. Daisy's eyes widened as she took in the organized chaos of Hunter's workspace. Tools lined the walls, wood scraps were neatly stacked in corners, and various projects in different stages of completion leaned against corners and surfaces.

Daisy's fingers traced over piles of abandoned projects, delicately searching through them without luck. Dust floated in the air as she rustled through canvas and shifted stacks of wood. And then her eyes caught on a large cloth-covered object sitting on a stack of window casing, tucked behind a storage cabinet.

Daisy approached it and gently lifted the dusty cloth. Her breath caught as she revealed a corner of stained glass, its colors muted by years of concealment but still unmistakably beautiful.

With trembling hands, she pulled the cloth away completely, revealing the transom window in its entirety. The intricate pattern of browns and greens mimicked the roots of an ancient tree, telling a story of the Barrett family.

"Oh, Hunter," she whispered, imagining a younger version of him rescuing the window after the fire that had left his family in pieces. She could see him carefully wrapping it up, tucking it away. Just in case.

Daisy's throat ached as her fingers ghosted over the delicate glasswork. This window belonged back in the house. Back where it could bring light and beauty to the sunroom again.

Daisy glanced at her watch. She still had time before Hunter arrived back from work.

Quickly, she gathered the supplies she'd need—a hammer and nails. Wood glue. A level. The old window casing piled beneath the glass—and transferred them inside, next to a ladder. And then finally, she slipped the window from its hiding place and carried it inside.

In all her years of design, Daisy had likely installed dozens of transoms all by herself. So why was it that this one seemed absolutely determined to give her trouble?

Daisy set the level down on the sash again and watched the bubble slide past the little lines. She dropped her head onto her arms resting on the ladder. It was mocking her.

"Come on, Daisy. Pull it together," she muttered as she started in again, adjusting the sash one more time before setting it with nails and climbing down. Sweat beaded on her forehead as she carefully lifted the glass insert. It was heavier than she'd expected.

Balancing on the ladder, Daisy summoned all of her upper body strength and slowly lifted the glass into the window. Her arms trembled as she ran her fingers along the outer edge, pushing it into place.

Just as she thought she had the window aligned correctly, her phone began to vibrate in her back pocket. Daisy paused, pressing her fingertips to balance the glass as she slipped the phone out and placed it atop the ladder. Her finger hovered over the answer button and stopped.

Mom.

Daisy froze, her heart suddenly racing.

Her fingers trembled as she struggled to keep pressure against the glass.

What would she say? *Hey, Mom, sorry it's been months*

since I last called. My life imploded, and I'm just really swamped right now. But don't worry. I have a plan.

Yeah. No.

Not yet.

Daisy turned her attention back to the task at hand, letting the call go to voicemail.

The phone shifted, the vibrations buzzing it closer to the edge.

Daisy's eye caught on the phone as it tipped, and she instinctively reached for it.

In that split second of distraction, her hand caught on the sharp edge of the metal framing the glass. She jerked back reflexively, losing her grip on the window.

Time seemed to slow as Daisy watched the stained glass tip from its frame. The beautiful blues and greens that had been hidden away for so long now sparkled in the sunlight for one brief, terrible moment before gravity took hold.

The crash was deafening in the quiet house. Shards of colored glass scattered across the floor.

No. Oh no . . .

The air smelled like snow.

Hunter sucked in a deep breath, savoring the chill as he stepped off the ferry. He'd always loved the late fall, the anticipation that came with cold. The weather report had predicted the first snowfall of the season later that day—a little late in the year for them, but a welcome sight now that the exterior updates on the front of the house were done.

He glanced at his watch and winced at the pang of guilt for leaving early again, though it was short-lived. Renovations on the house would slow down soon, and he could catch up on work. Soon.

Ahead of him, the town was already buzzing with pre-Thanksgiving energy, despite it still being a few weeks away. The first snow had always had a way of sending everyone's holiday jitters into a flurry, and the modest decor that had peppered storefronts a week ago had now been ramped up into full turkey shrines and pumpkin memorials in every nook and cranny in sight.

As he made his way toward Sunset Cove, Hunter nodded greetings to the familiar faces throughout town. Linda Issacson arranged a cornucopia in the window of Doug's Market, displaying their Thanksgiving specials. Farther down, Fred Miller straightened a leafy wreath hanging on the front door of Miller Antiques.

Jill stood out in front of Good Day Coffee, stringing cranberries and popcorn around her sidewalk sign.

"Those are Christmas decorations, Jill," Hunter teased as he passed.

"They're multipurpose!" she called after him.

Hunter chuckled. The sight of the town flourishing for the first time in years filled him with a sense of pride and gratitude. They had so much to be thankful for this year. The newly opened realty office, with Mia's art covering the walls, stood as a testament to the island's growth.

Hunter's gaze fell on the empty storefront near the end of the street, and he thought back on Seb's request for his dad to bring his business back to the island . . .

They could even work out of the house once it was finished.

He pushed the thought away.

No sense in dwelling on things he couldn't make happen.

Daisy flashed in his mind. Her easy smile. Her bubbling laughter.

Really?

That was different, he lied to himself.

He turned onto the hill and began his ascent.

The trees, now bare, gave an extended preview of the lake view as he neared the end of the path. The gray skies made the lake look like used paint water, sinking from clear to dark against the shores. To his right, as he emerged from the trees, the house stood waiting for him. Daisy was waiting for him.

He crossed the porch and reached for the door just as a thunderous crash broke from inside the house.

"Daisy?" His heart leaped into his throat, pounding hard as he flung open the door. "Are you okay?"

Hunter stopped in his tracks, trying to make sense of the scene that greeted him in the parlor. Daisy knelt amid a sea of shattered glass, her hands trembling as she tried to gather the pieces, blood dripping from her palm.

"Daisy!" He was across the room in an instant, his boots cracking over broken glass as he reached for her. "What happened? You're hurt."

"I'm okay," she said, her voice watery, her gaze still fixed on the shards of blue and green across the floor.

"You're not okay," Hunter said. He reached for her hand, gently examining the cut. "Let's get you cleaned up."

He rose, ignoring the glass as he helped her to her feet. Briefly, his eyes swept over the scene, and recognition dawned as he saw the picture fully. The old transom window. He let out a breath.

Oh, Daisy.

"Come on," he said, leading her away.

Hunter cracked open a bottle of water and guided her hand over the sink as he poured it over the wound. Her hand trembled while he tended the cut, and he glanced at her, tried to duck into her line of vision.

"Daisy."

She sniffed, turning her face away.

"Daisy," he said softly, reaching for a clean towel to pat her hand dry. "Talk to me. What's going on?"

She sniffed again, lifting her other hand to brush a tear away, and Hunter broke. "Please, Daisy."

Finally, she peeked over her shoulder, her eyes brimming with tears as she let out a shaky breath. "I'm sorry," she whispered.

Hunter frowned. Did . . . did she really think he was angry at her? "Because of the window?"

A fat tear spilled to the dusty floor. "I just wanted to do something for you . . . I know how much that room means to you."

Oh.

"Hey, now," he said, stepping closer as his hands brushed her arms. He tried again to duck into her line of vision, but she'd gone back to avoiding his gaze. "It's just a window, Daisy. It's fine."

But she shook her head. "No, it's not. I feel like such a . . . such a failure."

The pain in her voice cut through Hunter like a knife. He opened his mouth to reassure her, but before he could speak, Daisy leaned forward, dropping her forehead against his chest with a heavy thud. Her shoulders shook with silent sobs.

Hunter's arms immediately encircled her. One hand cradled the back of her head, his fingers brushing gently over her hair, while the other pulled her in tighter. He could feel her tears soaking through his shirt, but he didn't care.

"Listen to me, Daisy," he said softly, his chin resting on top of her head. "You are not a failure. Not even close. That window? It's replaceable. You're not."

He held her close, letting her cry against him, offering silent support and comfort. After a few moments, he felt her breathing start to even out.

"I'm not going anywhere," he continued, his voice thick with emotion. "Do you hear me? I don't care about some old window. I care about you."

Slowly, Daisy lifted her head from his chest, her red-rimmed eyes looking for reassurance. Hunter cupped her face in his hands, his thumbs gently wiping away the remnants of her tears.

Oh boy, the lines were getting so blurry.

"Come on, I'll clean up the glass. You take a break," he said, stepping back.

Twelve

NOTHING WAS GOING THE WAY SHE had expected. But for once, Daisy felt a sense of comfort as she tried her best just to roll with it.

The crisp November air nipped at Daisy's cheeks as she sat on a bench overlooking the harbor. An open takeaway box from Martha's on Main rested beside her, a friendly note from Vera scrawled on a napkin peeking out from beneath. Daisy munched absently on her turkey club, her attention focused on the sketchpad in her lap.

Her pencil moved across the paper as she reworked the design she'd sketched out for the sunroom all those weeks ago.

So much had changed since then.

Her pencil traced the open space of the transom, a piece of the design she just couldn't make sense of.

There was a lot she couldn't seem to make sense of—like the way Hunter had reacted when she'd broken something so precious to him. The way that he hadn't been angry. Just kind. And gentle. And how there had been zero expectations attached to his forgiveness.

Or that kiss . . .

"Hey, you," a voice said from over her shoulder. Daisy turned to see Mia approaching, a warm smile on her face. "Mind if I join you?"

"Yes!—I mean no, I don't mind." Daisy stuffed the sandwich in her mouth, using her teeth to hold it as she moved her takeaway box, making room for Mia.

"A little cold to be sitting outside?" Mia said, glancing at the dusting of snow across the beach.

Daisy laughed. "Yeah. My mom would be very upset with me."

Mia chuckled, her eyes drifting to the sketchpad in Daisy's lap. "Is that the Barrett house?"

Daisy glanced down at the sketch, heat rising to her cheeks. "Oh, yeah. It's nothing . . ."

Mia frowned and reached for the pad. She picked it up gingerly, bringing it in for a closer look. "This is stunning, Daisy. Is this part of the plan? To redo the sunroom?"

"Oh, no," Daisy said quickly.

"It should be. It's really special. Touching." She handed the pad back, and Daisy took it, feeling self-conscious. "You've got to make the house your own. I mean, you'll be the one living there, after all."

Daisy's brows pulled together in confusion.

Mia pulled in a breath. "I just thought, with all the work you guys were putting in, that you and Hunter would be staying on the island after the wedding. But I guess that wouldn't make sense. Your job is in LA."

Daisy's heart squeezed at the thought. "We, uh . . . we haven't really talked about it yet," she admitted.

Mia winced. "Sorry. Didn't mean—"

"No, it's okay."

Mia nodded, understanding. "Well, I know you said you weren't planning on opening a business, but I know a lot of people who could use the Daisy Decker—or should I say, Daisy *Barrett* touch. Just something to think about."

Before Daisy could respond, Mia glanced toward the dock and the ferry, now loading a small group of passengers. "Oh, that's me." She hopped to her feet and took a few steps before pausing, turning back. "Let me know."

Daisy gave a polite nod. "Will do."

And Mia was gone.

Daisy brushed a hand over the design. Maybe it wouldn't be the worst thing in the world if the network never called. If her plans fell through.

She tried to imagine it. She could stay, open a design business. Renovate homes on the island and keep up her YouTube channel. Maybe she could even convince Hunter to partner with her—it would be good for his dad's company . . .

She'd buy a cute little house. Make it her own. Invite her mom to see it. Maybe even help with the renos, just like old times.

Warmth fluttered through her chest the more she thought about it.

And then, she remembered the biggest problem here.

She couldn't just *stay*. Eventually people would notice if she and Hunter didn't get married.

Unless . . .

Just then, her phone rang. Robin's name flashed across the screen.

Daisy answered. "Hey."

"Hey, babe!" Her friend answered. "Or should I call you love bird?"

A sad smile slipped across her face, though her friend couldn't see it. "Just Daisy will do."

"Suit yourself," Robin said. "But for real. Great job on the show so far. It's blowing up. Especially these last few episodes. I don't know what happened between you two, but the chemistry is insane."

Daisy let out a quiet sigh. "Thanks."

"Are we sure you can't keep him?" Robin asked playfully.

Daisy's heart skipped a beat, her cheeks warming. "Robin, come on," she managed, trying to keep her voice light.

"I'm just saying." Daisy pictured her friend shrugging, a coy smile on her face. "I wouldn't blame you if there was a little more going on there . . ."

The image of Hunter, his warm smile in the glow of the campfire, flashed through her mind. Then the memory of his arms around her as she cried against his chest. "There's not."

"Whatever you say . . ." Robin teased. "But seriously, the audiences are eating it up. Which brings me to the reason for my call—aside from my desperate need to talk to my bestie. The network has been buzzing recently with talk of picking up the show."

Daisy blinked in surprise. "Oh. That's . . . that's great."

Robin continued, "Word on the street is, there are a few showrunners eyeing your channel. They're salivating, waiting to see what you do next."

Daisy sucked in a tight breath. Good. This was good. "Awesome."

"Isn't it? You were right. This was the right plan." Her friend paused, waiting for Daisy to match her excitement, and then gave up, continuing without her. "Anyway, get ready for a call in the next few weeks. This is it. Your big comeback."

"Wow," Daisy said, her throat a little dry.

"I know. Very exciting. Okay, I gotta run, but I wanted to give you an update. Let you know that you're headed the right direction."

"Thanks," Daisy managed.

"Of course! Love ya." The call ended, and Daisy let out a heavy breath.

Her eyes skated over the icy water, over the rocky beach and the ferry pulling away. She glanced at the birds overhead, landing peacefully on the blue and yellow awnings, at the cozy storefronts and the people bustling around their little lives. And finally, her gaze dropped to the sketchbook.

She closed it.

This was good. The plan was working.

Now she just had to convince herself it was still what she wanted.

Hunter drummed his fingers on the steering wheel, humming along to the radio as he drove toward the office. A fresh dusting of snow lined the road, the sun sifting through the bare trees. A smile played on his lips as he thought about the past few days with Daisy. Everything felt . . . right. Perfect, actually.

So perfect, it had become difficult to get himself onto that ferry every day, knowing Daisy was just up the hill . . . waiting for him.

But the brightness of that thought dimmed as he remembered the growing pile of paperwork on his desk. Requests pouring in. Orders to fulfill. Estimates to finalize. Budgets to adjust. He'd been telling himself for days that he'd pull back and catch up on his real job. And yet, every day, when clock-out rolled around, Hunter found himself choosing Daisy.

She was like an addiction.

His phone rang, interrupting his thoughts as his truck rolled to a stop at a light. He answered through Bluetooth.

"This is Hunter."

"Hey, Hunt." Dawn's voice filled the car.

"Morning, Dawn. What's up?" he asked.

"Have you heard from your dad this morning?"

Hunter frowned as the light turned green. "He's not in the office yet?"

A slight pause and then, "Not yet."

It wasn't like him to be late. "I haven't heard from him.

Let me make a few calls and get back to you. I'm sure he's at one of the job sites."

Another pause. "Okay, thanks, Hunter," Dawn said, her voice tinged with worry.

The call ended, and Hunter dialed one of the site foremen. "Hey, Chuck. Have you seen my dad today?"

"No. He hasn't been around yet."

A knot began to form in Hunter's stomach. "All right, thanks. Let me know if he shows up."

Without hesitation, Hunter switched on his turn signal and veered off, pointing his truck in the direction of his father's house.

Fear coiled through his chest as Hunter hung up another dead-end call, his tires crunching as he turned onto the street leading to the small house on the edge of town.

"Come on, Dad. Where are you?" he whispered as he pulled into the drive.

Apprehension and relief fought for purchase in his head as he spotted his father's truck in the driveway. At least he was home. That was a start. But it wasn't like him not to show up for work.

His dad didn't take personal days. He didn't even take sick days.

Hunter slammed the door behind him as he climbed out of his truck.

"Dad?" he called out as he approached the front door. "It's Hunter. You in there?"

He gripped the handle and opened the door.

"Dad?"

A faint sound from down the hall caught his attention. Hunter rounded the corner, his heart pounding against his chest.

The door to the master bedroom hung open, and he pushed it aside to find his dad sitting on the edge of his bed, his hand on his chest, hunched over and visibly struggling to breathe. He looked pale, his eyes widening as he spotted Hunter in the doorway.

"Dad!" Hunter rushed into the room, gripping his father's shoulders. "Are you okay?"

He tried to wave Hunter off, but the gesture was weak. "I'm fine," he wheezed. "I was just . . . just about to head to work."

Hunter shook his head, placing a steadying hand on his father's shoulder. "For Pete's sake, Dad. You're not okay. Just look at you. You can barely breathe."

His father attempted to stand, but his legs wobbled beneath him. Hunter quickly supported him, easing him back onto the bed.

"It's nothing," his father insisted between labored breaths. "Just . . . a little chest cold. No sense crying about it."

Hunter felt a surge of frustration and fear. "This isn't 'nothing,' Dad. How long have you been like this?"

His father avoided his gaze, a telltale sign he was hiding something. "Just . . . just this morning. I'll be fine."

But Hunter could see the truth in his father's eyes— this wasn't a new problem. How long had his dad been struggling? How had he not noticed?

"We're going to the hospital," Hunter said firmly, gripping his dad under the arm as he helped him to his feet. "And don't even think about arguing. I'll drag you if I need to."

"I could take you," his dad gruffed.

"Not like this, you couldn't."

Hunter paced another lap around the sterile hospital room at Port Joseph Medical Center, the rhythmic nagging of the heart monitor filling his ears. His dad, clad in a patterned hospital gown, scowled from the bed, arms crossed over his chest as though Hunter was the one in the wrong here.

"Don't look at me like that," Hunter said.

His dad harrumphed. "This is ridiculous. I'm fine."

"Actually," a doctor said as she strolled through the open door, catching a dollop of hand sanitizer from the dispenser by the door before venturing in, "you did exactly the right thing by bringing him in."

Hunter straightened as the doctor stepped up to the bed, her eyes falling on his dad.

"I'm Dr. Patel. How are you feeling?" she asked, glancing at the monitors.

"Ready to get out of here," his dad replied firmly.

Dr. Patel smiled, a light of sympathy in her eyes. "I understand. Nothing worse than being poked and prodded in a hospital without answers. Trust me, I get it. But we need to discuss your condition before you can get out of here." She glanced at Hunter before continuing. "The echo we took showed that you've experienced what's called takotsubo cardiomyopathy, also known as stress-induced cardiomyopathy."

Hunter's father frowned. "In English, please."

"You have a condition that was brought on by intense stress, where the muscles of your heart become suddenly weakened, affecting its ability to pump blood effectively."

Hunter felt the air rush out of him. "Is it serious?"

"It can be," Dr. Patel replied. "But the good news is that it's usually treatable and reversible." She turned her attention back to his dad. "Have you been under unusual stress lately?"

He waved his hand dismissively. "No more than usual. Business is business."

Hunter felt a pang of guilt. "Dad, why didn't you say anything?"

His father shot him a look. "There was nothing to say. I've handled worse."

Dr. Patel interjected gently, "Your body is telling you otherwise. This condition is your heart's way of saying it needs a break."

"So, what now?" Hunter asked, looking between his father and the doctor.

"We'll keep you here for observation for a day or two," Dr. Patel said to Hunter's father. "Then, you'll need to make some lifestyle changes. Reduce stress, delegate more at work, maybe consider cutting back your hours."

Hunter braced himself as his dad scoffed.

"Dad," Hunter chided.

"What?" he replied, his shoulders rising. "I'm not going to sit around while my business dies."

Hunter ran a frustrated hand through his hair. How had it come to this? "I can handle the business, Dad. I promise."

His father's eyes softened slightly. "Hunter . . . you've got enough going on. Your own life . . ."

The tension in Hunter's shoulders eased in understanding. His dad hadn't said anything because he didn't want to bother him. "I've got it under control, Dad. Please."

A long moment stretched between them, and finally his dad gave a curt nod before turning back to the doctor.

She glanced between them, then nodded. "All right, so let's talk about your treatment plan . . ."

As the doctor continued explaining, Hunter's mind raced. He'd let his father down, let the business slide. All for what? A fake engagement? A home that had been abandoned for years? He pushed thoughts of Daisy aside. His family needed him now. Everything else would have to wait.

Thirteen

DAISY GLANCED AGAIN OVER HER shoulder, her eyes skating over the thin layer of snow on the street of Sunset Cove. She didn't know what she was looking for. She knew he wasn't coming. Even still, she glanced again.

Her breath swarmed the winter air as she turned back to her task, her cold fingers wrapping around the old, rusted light fixtures that framed the front door.

It had been a long week. Hunter had spent the majority of his time holed up in the office, trying to keep the business running on his own while his dad recovered from his medical emergency. Daisy had made the effort to go see Joe at the hospital. After all, he was her fake future father-in-law. But for the most part, she had been left to her own devices, given the space to let her imagination roam in these wild woods.

She'd spent the better half of the week throwing herself

at the renovation, making daily trips to the mainland for supplies. She'd ordered furniture for staging, picked out new light fixtures for the foyer and porch, installed the new stair runners, and anything else she could think of to keep herself from overthinking the fact that Hunter had simply disappeared.

She finished disconnecting the last of the old lights and frowned. Two . . . four . . . ten . . . Shoot. She'd miscalculated. She was short on wire connectors for the updated fixtures.

Sighing, Daisy climbed down the ladder and dusted off her hands. Another trip to Smith's Hardware was in order. She was starting to become a regular there.

Tromping down the steps in her new winter boots, she stuffed her frozen hands into her pockets and started down the hill.

Twenty minutes later, Daisy stepped out of Smith's with a fresh box of connectors. She was standing outside Martha's, contemplating an early dinner, when a familiar face stepped onto the street.

Daisy frowned, recognition snagging her attention. "Lino! Hey."

The man turned, his eyes trying to find the source. His eyes landed on Daisy, and his face lit with surprise. "Daisy!"

Beaming, he met her halfway down the sidewalk.

Lino O'Brien looked exactly how she remembered him. In his mid-fifties, he had the polished look of someone who spent most of his time in metropolitan boardrooms rather than on a remote Michigan island. His salt-and-pepper hair was expertly styled, and despite the cold, he wore a tailored wool coat that spoke more of urban fashion than Midwest practicality.

Daisy had always liked the producer.

"Crazy seeing you here. How are you?" she said, wrapping her free arm around him in a hug.

Lino smiled warmly, stepping back to look at her. "I'm good. You?"

"I'm good." Daisy slipped back into her safe, secure smile. "What are you doing here?"

Her mind swarmed with possibilities. Was he here to talk to her about picking up the show? Or maybe something else?

A flash of awkwardness filled Lino's face, and before he could respond, someone stepped out onto the sidewalk behind him.

Daisy felt dizzy. Like she'd been pushed through a frozen lake.

He was talking to someone, laughing, smiling. He was bundled up against the cold in a sleek, charcoal-gray wool coat that hugged his broad shoulders—a far cry from the casual attire he used to wear on set. His sandy-blond hair, once meticulously styled for the camera, was now slightly longer and tousled by the wind, giving him a more rugged look.

His face, still handsome in a way that used to make Daisy's heart race, turned to her. His strong jaw was covered in a light stubble, and his blue eyes lifted, met hers.

Logan Double.

For a moment, no one spoke. The tension was palpable, hanging in the frigid air between them.

Logan broke the silence first. "Daisy," he said, his voice a mix of hesitation and forced casualness. "I . . . didn't expect to see you here."

"It's no secret where I've been," she managed to say, her throat stinging. "What are *you* doing here?"

Logan glanced at Lino, who looked increasingly uncomfortable. "We're, uh . . . we're here on business," Logan said vaguely.

Daisy frowned, her eyes darting to the door they'd just stepped out of. *Miller Antiques.* "Sorry . . . I don't understand."

Logan's eyes darted to Lino. "Give us a minute?"

Lino nodded and turned to Daisy, giving her arm a polite squeeze. "It was good to see you, Daisy." He stepped away, leaving them alone on the snowy sidewalk.

Logan took a deep breath. "The network is really interested in Jonathon Island. They want me to do a holiday special, giving a facelift to one of the houses."

Daisy reeled back. "I'm sorry, what?"

"I'm doing a special short-run series renovating one of the homes, and then we're going to submit it for the *HOME* New Year's Virtual Parade—you know about that, right?"

"What? Yes. I know about that—but . . . the one-dollar homes are not up for grabs. There are none left. And even if there were, you have to open a business. You have to move here. Those are the rules. I checked," she said, her words stringing together in a jumble.

"I didn't apply for a one-dollar house." Logan's gaze dropped to her lips, the corner of his mouth tilting upward in a smirk. "I just had a great conversation with one of the owners up on Zinnia Boulevard, the Millers—nice family—and they've agreed to let us do a small reno, courtesy of HGTV, of course."

"Why?" Daisy blurted out.

Logan stuffed his hands in his pockets, brows raised at her outburst.

She blinked, cheeks flushing. "Sorry," she mumbled. "Why did they do that?"

"Why wouldn't they? I've got the show, after all," Logan explained, his tone careful. The unspoken words hung heavy between them. *I've got the show, and you don't.*

Heat rose to her cheeks, embarrassment welling behind her eyes. She was not going to let him see her cry. She nodded. "Got it."

She shouldered past him, heading toward her apartment. The light fixtures would have to wait.

"Daisy, wait."

She didn't wait. She didn't slow down.

She heard footsteps running after her, and then he was in front of her, blocking the sidewalk.

"What do you want, Logan?" she asked, her voice tight.

"You've got a lot of eyes on your channel right now. It's really a clever thing you two have got going. I'd forgotten about Hunter." He paused, a smirk touching his lips. "How'd you dig him up, anyway?"

"What do you want?" Daisy asked again, changing the subject.

"I thought maybe we could collaborate."

Daisy recoiled. "Collaborate? With you?"

Her eyes darted for an exit, and she turned, stepping onto the snowy street.

"I can get you your show back."

Daisy froze, just for a moment, and Logan seized the opportunity, stepping up beside her. "I talked to Lino. We think we could pull some strings, get you back on the show."

"I didn't ask you to do that," she whispered.

"I miss working with you. Please. Let me help you."

Her eyes stung.

She risked a glance up and found him staring down at her, those blue eyes imploring her to see reason.

"I have a show." She stepped past him, walked away, and didn't stop until her apartment door shut behind her.

He couldn't keep this up.

The door creaked open, well past dark, and Hunter stumbled in, exhaustion etched into every muscle of his body. He barely made it to the couch before collapsing, sinking face-first into the worn cushions with a heavy sigh.

Waylen emerged from his room, his police uniform slightly rumpled, the top button undone. "Oof, you've seen better days, my man."

Hunter let out a grunt in response, his eyes already sealed shut for the night. There was no way he was making it to his bed.

"How's Dad?" Waylen asked, crossing to the studio kitchen.

Hunter rolled over, his eyes still shut. "He's sick of turkey, and he misses salt."

"So, not liking the heart-healthy diet Doc put him on?" he said over the sound of the fridge opening, followed by the clinking of glass.

"Not liking it at all. Today, when I stopped by, I caught him red-handed, eating shredded cheese straight from the bag." Hunter dragged a hand over his face, wiping at the exhaustion. "Guy's lost it."

Waylen chuckled. "Sounds about right."

Hunter peeked an eye at his brother. "You know how it is, getting him to follow the doctor's orders. If I could just find a way to make him eat his veggies . . ."

He'd be okay. The doctor said his condition was reversible. Even so, Hunter couldn't help the sting of guilt.

Dad never would have run the business so hard if Hunter hadn't enabled it.

The worn leather armchair across from his crinkled as Waylen settled into it. "So . . . uh . . . I saw Daisy today. She was eating at Martha's . . . alone."

Hunter's eyes snapped open, a different kind of guilt washing over him. "Aw, man. I've just . . . I've had a lot going on."

"I know."

"The business is swamped."

"I know."

A heavy pause settled between them.

"Listen, Hunt. You know me, I don't like to poke my nose in where it doesn't belong—"

"That's not something I know about you."

"—but, it's been two weeks," Waylen continued.

Hunter ran a hand through his hair, sitting up. "I know, I know. I'll be there tomorrow, help her with the house."

Waylen frowned. "Help her with the house? How about just spending some time with her? She's your *fiancée*."

The words hit Hunter like a bucket of cold water. "Yeah. Yes, you're right. It's okay though. She gets it."

Waylen took a sip of his beer and leaned forward, his expression tight. "Maybe she does get it. But I wouldn't count on that lasting too long."

Hunter considered for a moment, a seed of worry sinking in. How long before Daisy realized she could do so much better?

They may be more effort than they're worth.

"Okay." Hunter nodded. "Okay, yeah. I'll get over there. First thing tomorrow."

Fourteen

THIS PLAN REALLY SHOULD HAVE BEEN thought through a little better.

Daisy groaned, her back aching as she set another box on the stairs, a gust of wind following her from the open door, which revealed a mountain of furniture and boxes piled on the covered deck.

Asher Quinn had been a godsend, using the horses to help haul everything up from the docks, but he'd had to leave for another delivery at the Grand. And now she was stuck, fifty boxes deep and alone again.

Where was Hunter?

Daisy glanced at her watch. Only a few days until Thanksgiving, and so much left to do. There were still episodes to put out, though she had a nagging voice in her head telling her that nobody would watch without Hunter in the background. Even so, she couldn't afford to wait for him.

Daisy breathed into her hands, rubbing them together for warmth, and strode back to the deck. Gritting her teeth, she hoisted up another box and began dragging it inside, careful not to scrape up the walls. It only took two more trips for sweat to begin beading across her temple despite the gusts of winter air, and Daisy felt her determination waver.

There was no way she could do this on her own.

"Need a hand?"

Daisy turned, her heart pitching in excitement to see Hunter. Instead, she found Logan.

He leaned against the porch post, arms folded across his chest. A scarf peeked out from the top of his warm wool jacket, his blue eyes standing out against the snow behind him. He looked more suited to modeling than furniture moving at the moment.

Daisy hesitated, her eyes skimming over the remaining items, and then, "Um, sure . . . Thanks."

Logan nodded and stepped forward, bending at the knees to take one end of the plastic-covered upholstered bench.

"It goes just in here," she said, directing him as they placed it in the hall and then put the rest of the boxes inside the empty parlor.

As last, she shut the door, blocking out the cold. Warmth seeped through her in its place. Despite the old single-pane windows and not having the heat turned on yet, the house really did hold heat pretty well. Daisy rubbed her hands together once more and then turned back to Logan.

"Well . . ." she said, crossing to the stairs, where she began opening boxes. "Thanks for your help, but I've got a lot of work to do, so . . ."

Logan let out an impressed whistle, and Daisy turned to see him wandering farther in, taking in the space. "So, this is the famous Bad Luck Barrett House."

His footsteps creaked over the floor as he examined Hunter's banister, reaching out a hand to trace the intricate carvings. Daisy had the urge to slap his hand away.

"We don't call it that," she said quietly.

"Oh?" Logan glanced at her. "Sorry. That's what I heard the locals calling it, so . . ."

Daisy turned away, focusing on the task at hand. She pulled a large framed mirror from one of the boxes and began to lift it, intending to hang it on the wall near the staircase.

"You know, there's another rumor going around town that you and Hunter are engaged." He chuckled.

Daisy pulled her pencil from the front pocket of her overalls, doing her best not to react. "We are."

She could almost feel his smug, amused smirk, but he said nothing.

Logan stepped closer. "Hang on, don't you think it would be better here?" He placed a hand on her lower back, gesturing to the wall opposite, with a hand held up to frame an imaginary space. "It would catch the light from the parlor better, make the hall feel bigger."

"I think I know what I'm doing," she said, pulling away from his touch. Though, looking between the two spots, she had to admit . . . "Yeah, okay. You're right. That is better."

Logan grinned, that dazzling smile playing with her as he took the mirror from her hands and lifted it against the wall. "How's this?"

"A little up," she said. "Yes, there." She stepped forward, ducking under his arms to reach the top, and left a mark on the wall.

He waited for her to retreat before lowering the mirror, turning. "See? We've still got it."

Daisy let out a heavy sigh and turned to face him, brushing the hair out of her face. "Look, Logan. I'm pretty busy. So whatever you're here for, can you spit it out, or leave so I can get back to—"

"I'm sorry."

Daisy blinked. "Excuse me?"

Logan leaned back against the wall, looking up at her under furrowed brows. "You wanted me to spit it out, so there it is. I'm sorry."

Daisy blinked again, shaking her head against the fog. Her chest squeezed as she dropped her gaze. She moved to the pile of boxes on the stairs, trying her best to keep working, but for the life of her, she couldn't remember where she'd left her box cutter.

"Daisy?" his voice said softly.

"I heard you."

"Could you say something?"

"What do you want me to say?" Daisy replied, the air struggling to escape her lungs.

"Anything. Whatever it takes to get us past this?"

Daisy whirled to face him. "To get us past this? There is no getting past this, Logan. You cheated on me."

"I'm done with that. I ended it with Cassie. I'm sorry!" Logan repeated, his hands reaching out.

"You said that."

"Well, it's true. I was an idiot and I took you for granted. And I'm sorry. I'm so, *so* sorry." He crossed the room, his hands coming up to hold her. His steely-blue eyes capturing her, holding her gaze. "Please, Daisy. Come back to California. Come back to our life."

Daisy froze, her heart hammering in her chest.

Their life.

She tried to wrap her head around what that life looked like. She and Logan. A power couple. Fame. Awards. *Success*. That had always been the plan, hadn't it?

Except... she wasn't so sure that was the life she wanted anymore.

Not with him.

Logan brushed a thumb over her cheek. "We can fix this."

Daisy placed her hands on his chest. "No, we really can't, Logan."

He frowned, his arms tightening as she tried to pull away. "So that's it, you're just going to throw away five years together because of one mistake?"

For a moment, Daisy actually felt bad for him. He really believed they could work this out. She reached up, brushing a hair away from his face, the way she used to do before the camera started rolling. "No," she said sadly. "I'm throwing away five years together because I can't remember the last time you looked at me the way he looks at me."

Logan's face contorted in confusion, then understanding dawned. "The contractor?" Logan's eyebrow raised. "The guy who's been too busy to help you with all this? Come on, Daisy. You deserve better."

His arms around her tightened, a hand sliding up her back to cup her head as his gaze dropped to her lips. "You deserve a man who won't hold you back."

Just then, a creak from the doorway caught their attention. She turned to see Hunter standing there, his face a mask of shock and hurt. The tension in the room shifted instantly, crackling with a new energy.

Daisy's eyes widened, her heart dropping to her stomach. "Hunter," she breathed, taking an instinctive step toward him.

But before she could say anything more, Hunter turned and walked away, his footsteps quick and heavy on the porch.

Daisy turned back to Logan, shoving hard as she pushed out of his grasp. "I can't believe you."

Logan scoffed, his eyes rolling. "Come on, Daze—"

"I'm going after him. Because I choose *him*." She turned toward the door. "Don't be here when I get back."

And here he'd been about to apologize.

Ten minutes earlier, he'd been waging words through his head—*I'm sorry I abandoned you.* The cold wind had whisked through his hair as Hunter trudged up the hill, two cups of coffee in hand.

He'd asked at the coffee shop for their best apology brew. "You know, something that says 'Sorry I've been too busy to spend time with my fiancée'?" he'd said as his eyes skimmed the menu.

Jill had done even better. Not two minutes later, a pair of Daisy's favorite drinks slid across the counter.

"So the lady can choose," she'd said with a wink.

Hunter savored the way the coffee aroma mixed with the smell of pine and the way the heat seeped into his palms. The gray sky overhead tried to be bleak, but it only served to make the red and orange leaves, peeking from under the snow, pop like flame.

Waylen had been right. Maybe spending a little time with his fiancée—fake fiancée—was exactly what he needed. And hopefully she wasn't too upset about the last two weeks.

His feet trudged up the path and paused outside the house. A set of horseshoe prints trailed down the street, and Hunter smiled. If he knew Daisy, she'd probably waited all of two minutes before dragging everything inside herself.

He stepped up to the door, a smile already tugging at his lips, and then he froze, his fingertips falling from the door handle as it swung silently out of his grip.

Logan Double was standing in his house.

With his arms around Hunter's fiancée.

"You deserve a man who won't hold you back."

The words had sliced deep, a quick sting that grew, burning through him.

He should have known.

As though sensing his presence, Daisy's head had snapped up, her eyes meeting his. If he didn't know any better, he might have mistaken that look of shock splayed across her face. But he'd been here before.

Without a word, he'd turned on his heel and walked away.

"Hunter, wait!"

Now the cold that hadn't touched him on the way up clawed over him as he reached the sidewalk. The coffees in his hands felt like lead weights, and he tossed them in the muddy ditch, not stopping as Daisy's voice called over the wind.

He couldn't believe he'd fallen for it. Again.

"Hunter, please!" Daisy called after him, her footsteps pounding against the sloshy pavement.

Hunter kept walking, each purposeful stride putting distance between him and the Bad Luck Barrett House. Long shadows grazed his face as he entered the wooded portion of the road, blocking the meager sun from what little warmth it could spread.

"Hunter, stop! It's not what you think!" Daisy's voice was closer now, breathless and pleading.

Hunter slowed, his jaw pulsing. He wanted to keep going, to disappear into the gray day, to leave her hurting the way he was hurting. But there was something in her voice that made him pause. Maybe it was desperation. Maybe it was that stubborn bit of him that refused to believe that everything between them had been part of the ruse. Slowly, he turned to face her.

Daisy stood a few feet away, snow crowning her honey-brown hair, her cheeks flushed from the cold, or maybe from running after him. Her blue eyes brimmed with emotion, wide and imploring. "Let me explain," she said, reaching for him.

Hunter's jaw clenched, emotions fighting for purchase in his head. All of him wanted to hear her out, to believe there was an explanation for what he'd just seen. And all of him wanted to throw the walls back up.

"Explain what, Daisy?" he finally said, his voice thick and low. "How you've been playing me this whole time? How all of this was a setup, a publicity stunt for your precious show? What was it, a ratings thing?"

Daisy flinched, her lips downturned, pressed into a tight line. "It's not what you think—"

"You want to know what I thought? I thought . . . maybe we were getting a second chance after all these years." He swallowed, his eyes searching hers as the words scraped from his throat. "But I guess it really was all part of the show. It's fine. I read into things. That's on me. But do me a favor. Stop acting like you care about me, because I can't keep falling for you."

Daisy's lips parted, her eyes bright with surprise. "Hunter . . ."

He stepped back. "We don't have to talk about it, Daisy. We're good. Let's just get through the next week, and then—"

He turned, meant to walk away, but Daisy's hand slid

into his, her soft fingers curling around his calloused palm. A moment later, she stepped into his path, the balls of her cheeks pink and wet. "Would you just let me talk for, like, two seconds?"

His lips pressed into a tight line. "Fine."

"Thank you," she said, an exasperated smile tugging at her lips.

She was really smiling.

He had bared his soul, and she was *smiling*.

He raised his brows. *Well . . . ?*

"First of all, *ouch*. To all of that," she said, though her voice held no bitterness. Her fingers curled into his, and for the life of him, he couldn't pull away. "Second of all, Logan showed up two weeks ago, right around the time your dad ended up in the hospital. He's doing a reno project in town. And I didn't tell you because I didn't want to add anything to your plate."

Hunter took a steadying breath, willing himself to listen. To hear her words for what they were.

"He stopped by today, asking me to come back to the show and to him." Her features softened with every word. "And I'll be honest, it made me think."

Hunter's chest expanded as his breath betrayed him. Of course . . .

"But I didn't have to think about it very long," she continued, "because the second he asked, I knew." She raised a hand to his cheek, shaking her head. "I don't want to be with him."

Hunter's heart thundered in his chest as he processed

her words. He stepped closer, his eyes searching hers, looking for any hint of a reason not to let himself believe her.

"He's not half the man you are, Hunter Barrett."

The last of his defenses crumbled.

Hunter's arms circled her waist, pulling her to him the way he'd wanted to do every day since she'd walked back into his life. He lifted a hand, his fingertips tracing the pink in her cheeks before threading through her hair, tilting her head back. She had snowflakes on her lashes. She was beautiful. He lifted her lips to his.

Daisy melted into him. Her fingertips brushed his chest, his neck, and curled around his shoulders as she returned his kiss.

Hunter pulled her closer, lifting her to her toes. His thumb grazed her cheek, memorizing the feel of her. The kiss deepened, and he poured into it all the words he hadn't said, everything he'd been holding back because he'd been afraid.

Daisy wanted him. She chose him.

Snow drifted through the trees, dusting them with white, but Hunter didn't feel the cold.

Fifteen

HUNTER COULD RENOVATE HOUSES, manage construction crews, and handle tough negotiations, but put him in a room with his grandfather, whose opinion could make or break his future, and he was a wreck.

"Stop, Hunter," Daisy said, her voice edging on laughter as she laid a hand on his, halting his nervous fidgeting with the doorknob. "I think you've checked it enough times."

Hunter blinked, emerging from his thoughts. The house was as ready as it could be—not that there was much to prepare, given the lack of furniture outside the items purchased specifically for the foyer and the porch. But Hunter ran through a mental checklist all the same. Kitchen, presentable. Living room, decent. Bathroom—actually, they shouldn't use the bathroom, the water wasn't turned on. He'd need to warn them—

"Hunter." Daisy stepped into his line of sight, lifting

his chin to look into her eyes. "It's going to be fine. Your family loves you, and they're going to see how much work you've put into this place."

Hunter took a deep breath, clearing his lungs. "I know. It's just . . . it feels different now." Now that he knew how much Daisy meant to him. Now that there was a bud of a future to protect. Now that he knew how much he wanted things to work out between them. And most importantly, how badly he wanted to make his family proud and keep the house.

Today was the day. His grandpa would be arriving any moment, and they really had to sell him on the renovations so that when Hunter came clean about the engagement and asked his grandpa to change the trust, he wouldn't be able to say no. Not with how much care Hunter had put into the house. He'd see.

Daisy brushed her thumb over his jaw, her gaze soft and reassuring as though she sensed his thoughts, and she lifted on her toes, drawing him down to her. But before their lips could touch, the front doors burst open.

"Turkey DAY!" Waylen shouted as he stomped through the door, followed by a cacophony of voices, each trying to outshout the others. He turned toward Daisy, his arms outstretched. But before he could reach her, Evan intercepted, scooping Daisy up in a bear hug.

"Too slow, Waylen!" He laughed, spinning her around.

"Interference!" Waylen shouted.

"Don't be a bad sport." This from Jude, who stepped in as Evan passed her off. He gave her a quick squeeze before pivoting to dodge Waylen's renewed attempt.

Miles stepped forward, waving his arms. "I'm open!" he joked.

"All right, all right," Hunter said sternly, pushing down his nerves to step in. His arms wrapped around Daisy's waist protectively. "She's not a football, guys. Cool it."

The family erupted in good-natured laughter and a chorus of playful boos.

"Lame!" Jude called out, but his grin was wide.

The crowd shuffled farther in and spread out, lingering around the door. Hunter's hand slid to Daisy's lower back as he led her through the group, grateful for her steady presence.

"Daisy, I'd like you to meet my brother Miles," he said, gesturing to his oldest brother. People said they looked alike, both sharing dark eyes and wide shoulders, but Hunter didn't see it.

Miles smiled warmly as he pulled Daisy in for a hug. Hunter watched, his heart swelling at how easily his family seemed to accept her.

"Hunter has told me a lot about you," Miles said, his eyes crinkling as he smiled.

Daisy echoed the sentiment. "Likewise."

Miles leaned in just a hair, as though about to say something more, and Hunter's breath hitched. Miles was the only one who knew about his and Daisy's arrangement . . . Hunter probably should have warned her. He went to cut in, but then another figure stepped through the door.

Hunter's breath caught in his throat.

"Ey!" Waylen shouted. "Gramps is here!"

"Sorry I'm late. Had to check in at the inn. I'll tell you,

it's a lot colder here than in Florida. I'm getting soft in my old age," he said between hugs for his grandsons. Tall and lean, their grandfather hardly looked like a man in his seventies except for his gray hair and wrinkled smile. He gave Miles a pat on the shoulder before turning, his gaze landing on Daisy.

"You must be Hunter's fiancée," he said, reaching out to shake her hand. "It's wonderful to meet you. I'm Richard, Hunter's grandpa."

"Daisy," she said, smiling brightly as she took his hand.

Hunter watched, his heart pounding, as his grandfather's hand came up to cup Daisy's elbow, pulling her in and dropping his voice. "I hope you know how truly blessed we are to have you join the family."

A soft pink rose to Daisy's cheeks, her fingers lacing through Hunter's. "Thank you. Hunter is a blessing to me as well."

Hunter's grandpa turned, glancing around the group. "Where's Joe?"

"He's going to meet us at dinner," Hunter said, trying his best to sound casual. His dad had refused to visit the house, even after Hunter had explained it was just a short tour.

Waylen let out a low whistle as he backpedaled through the foyer. "Look at this place . . ."

Hunter let out a sigh of relief as his brothers ventured into the house. He'd had himself halfway convinced they'd take one look at the changes and declare it ruined.

"This place looks amazing!" Jude called out from the parlor.

Daisy chuckled. "We didn't do anything in there, Jude. Just a little elbow grease on the soot and a little paint."

"You paint *good*," Evan chimed in next to his twin.

She stifled a laugh. "Thank you, gentlemen."

Miles took a step down the hall, toward the kitchen.

"Oh," she said, scurrying after him. "The kitchen's not done."

It didn't matter. The boys were already headed that direction. A moment later, they were all standing around the island, smiles plastered on their faces as they reminisced over the space.

Waylen hopped up onto the tiled counter, his feet dangling as he regaled them with a wild story about the time he and Jude had tricked Evan into playing hide-and-seek all alone for an hour.

"He really thought he was, like, the world champion!" Jude barked, wheezing with laughter.

"How about the time Evan convinced Miles his room was infested with beetles and then put raisins in his bed? I've never heard Miles scream like that." Hunter chuckled.

It was like old times, riffing with this lot. Easy and effortless. He slid an arm around Daisy's shoulder and pulled her in, pressing a kiss to the top of her head.

"You good?" she whispered.

"Perfect," he replied.

It was perfect.

Across the circle, his grandpa watched, his eyes crinkling with a smile. He would understand why Hunter had needed to lie for this place. He would.

Miles glanced at his watch and cut into the raucous

noise that hadn't stopped since the group had arrived. "I hate to break it to you, guys, but we're gonna be late."

Daisy frowned. "Late for what?"

His brothers exchanged looks of amusement, and then, as though it had been rehearsed, "The Jonathon Island football game."

"What?" Hunter asked, smirking. "You thought those halftime scrimmages in the backyard were just for fun? Oh no, that's all just practice. This is the real deal."

Daisy's brows rose as the Barrett boys and Richard strolled down the hill. They looked like the brute squad, all broad shoulders and scruffy jaws. She tried to imagine facing off against any one of them, let alone the group. "And everyone in town does this?"

Waylen stepped ahead, walking backward to face her. "Well, anyone brave enough."

He tripped and nearly went down, his brothers chuckling as they continued on.

"It's optional," Hunter explained. "But almost everyone in town shows up, either to play or to watch." He slipped his hand around hers, warding off the chill. It was a surprisingly warm day on the island. The sun had been out recently, and there were patches of dry grass throughout town. A good day for football.

Even so, she was glad to have finally purchased a jacket. She slipped her other hand into the pocket, savoring the warmth.

Main Street was alive with activity as they turned off

Partridge Lane. Daisy had gotten used to the quiet town these last two months, but it felt like more and more people were arriving every day. It seemed half the locals had family visiting, and they all bustled around the town with rosy cheeks and smiling faces.

Several storefronts held signs that read:

PLEASE JOIN US ON BLUEBERRY HILL.
CLOSED FOR THANKSGIVING.

It was a foreign concept to Daisy, the way this town seemed to invite everyone into the mix. Even going so far as to invite out-of-towners to their holiday traditions.

Richard's words returned to her. *I hope you know how truly blessed we are to have you join the family.* He hadn't realized the way his words had been a balm to her spirit. He didn't even know her, and yet he believed her to be a blessing.

Her own dad hadn't done that much. Not without something to earn it first.

The scent of cinnamon and apple pie wafted from Good Day Coffee as Jill stepped out from the shop and locked up.

"Heya, Jill!" Miles called out.

Jill glanced up, her eyes widening in delight as she caught sight of the entire Barrett family. "Well, isn't this just a sight!"

She stepped off the curb, wrapping Miles in a matronly hug, followed by Jude and then Evan. "I hope you two have been keeping out of trouble," she said, eyeing the twins.

"I wish I could say that was tru—" Waylen started, but Jude stopped him with a swift elbow.

"Of course, you know us." He gave her a cheeky wink.

Jill settled in among them as they continued their stroll through town.

"Is Brandon in town this year?" Miles asked, stuffing his hands into the pockets of his Patagonia jacket.

"Not this year," she said. "He's currently leading a three-day excursion through the Grand Canyon."

Daisy leaned toward Hunter. "Brandon . . . ?"

"Jill's son," he explained quietly. "He went to school with us. Was in the twins' class."

Daisy gave a nod. Ahh.

Miles gave an impressed whistle. "I did a weekend out there last year. It was incredible."

The coffee shop owner gave him a sad smile, and Daisy felt a pang of guilt. She wondered what her own mother was doing during the holidays this year.

They reached the end of the street, and Daisy was surprised to find people streaming in from every direction. Families and groups of friends padded down Blueberry Boulevard from the neighborhood up the road.

"Daisy!" a cheerful voice called as they stepped onto the grassy expanse, already dotted with picnic blankets and lawn chairs.

Children darted between adults, tossing a football and laughing cheerily. Daisy's eyes searched the surprising crowd for the voice. She spotted Holland and Jordi milling about. They both waved, and Daisy heard her name again. She turned and found Mia waving at her. She was settled on a checkered blanket, with another wrapped warmly around her shoulders. Beside her, a man in a Carhartt jacket reclined on his elbow, and next to him stood another couple—a good-looking man with his arms around a beautiful blonde woman. And beside them, a tall man rocking a pair of aviators had his arm slung over the shoulder of an adorable woman with lavender hair. They obviously all knew each other, but that was no surprise in a little town like this.

"Daisy, sit with us!" Mia called again.

Daisy veered that direction, tugging Hunter along with her. "Hey, you! Who's this?" she asked.

"This is my boyfriend, Cody," Mia said, beaming at the man reclined beside her. "And this is his sister, Lily." She waved toward the lavender-haired woman. "And her fiancé, Declan."

She took a pause, dramatically catching her breath, before continuing. "And this is my cousin, Dani, and *her* fiancé, Liam."

Dani gave a friendly wave, and Cody reached up a hand. "You must be Hunter's mysterious fiancée."

Daisy laughed, taking the hand and shaking it. "I don't know about mysterious, seeing as most of my life is broadcast to the world. But fiancée is spot on." And then it was her turn to beam up at her man.

"I've been watching your show," Lily said, her lavender hair falling over her shoulder. "I am absolutely in *love* with the new banister."

Pride swelled in her chest, and Daisy leaned toward the group. "Hunter made it."

"Come on now," Hunter said, hiding a sheepish grin.

"We've got to get you working on the Grand," Dani said. "We'd love to have some signature Barrett pieces to really anchor the renovations, right, Liam?"

"Absolutely."

Hunter's smile faltered. "Thanks, but Seb already tried convincing my dad to start taking projects on the island. Not gonna happen."

Liam nodded in understanding. "Let us know if you change your mind."

Before anyone could go on, a loud voice boomed over the crowd.

"Speaking of Uncle Seb . . ." Dani said, turning expectantly toward the older gentleman walking onto the field.

Daisy had heard about Mia's father, the mayor of Jonathon Island, but she hadn't had a chance to meet him yet. The man, tall with white hair, commanded the crowd with his presence, his easy smile connecting with friends and family.

"I want to welcome everyone to the Jonathon Island Thanksgiving football game. I see a lot of new faces in the crowd." He nodded toward the smiling faces of a few supposed newcomers. "And it's a great reminder of how much we have to be thankful for this year. I know we've had a rough stretch, but God always has a plan, and nothing could be more evidence of that than all of you here today . . ." His gaze moved over the crowd and landed on Daisy. "We're glad you're here."

Her too.

Seb turned, clapped his hands together, and tossed them into the air. "Now, who's ready for some football?"

The crowd cheered, and Hunter gave Daisy's temple a quick peck before jogging off with Liam, Declan, and Cody to join the game.

"Not playing?" Dani asked.

"I think I'll sit this one out, get to know a few of the locals," Daisy replied with a wink.

"Well, by all means," Mia said, patting the blanket in the spot that Cody had vacated.

Daisy settled in, grateful for the warmth of the sun on her face. "Where are the kids today?"

"Oh, they're around." Mia chuckled, pointing in the direction of her littlest one, who was showing an older woman a bright-red leaf she'd found. "That's my mom with Maggie."

A loud roar sounded nearby, and Daisy spotted Finn, making his best monster impression to Augo, who was pretending not to notice until the monster got close enough to tickle. Finn collapsed in giggles as Lucky bounded over, licking his ear.

Daisy had only met the kids in passing, but they seemed as sweet as could be.

She watched as Hunter joined his brothers, their playful banter and roughhousing eliciting a chuckle from her.

"So, Daisy," Dani said, leaning in conspiratorially, "have you two made any plans for the wedding yet?"

Daisy felt a nervous flutter, thinking of the lies accumulating between her and her new friends. Would they understand why when it was all over? "Oh, we haven't really had time to think about it yet. We've just been so busy with the house and the show . . ."

But even as she spoke, her eyes remained fixed on Hunter. He was laughing, his head thrown back as Evan attempted to tackle him. Jude joined in, and soon all three were a tangle of limbs and laughter on the grass. The sight made her heart swell, and suddenly, she could see it all so clearly.

She imagined Hunter standing at the end of a long aisle, his broad shoulders clad in a black tux, his brothers lined up in support for the man who never let them down. She imagined the look on his face as she stepped through the door, and the way her hands would tremble when she placed them in his. She could see it so clearly, she could practically smell the flowers, hear the bells.

"No . . ." she repeated distantly. "No plans yet."

But maybe someday . . . "Sorry," Daisy said, feeling a blush creep up her cheeks. "I guess I got a little distracted. But enough about me—what about you and Liam?"

"We're working on it," she replied warmly. "Planning a spring wedding."

"And you?" Daisy asked Lily.

Lily sighed. "We just resurrected my family's fudge shop, and Declan and I are just so busy running it that we haven't had a chance to set a date. All I know is that I can't wait to marry that man." With a smile, her eyes landed in the vicinity of her fiancé, who was currently running back to the starting line, a grin plastered on his face.

The sun continued to warm the field as the game went on. Dani and Mia told her all about the island, pointing out members of the community across the crowded park. They filled her in on the Grand Sullivan Hotel renovation, and Mia even touched on her children adapting to the new man in her life after the death of her husband over two years ago.

This town had been through so much. And yet they loved so easily.

Daisy wanted that.

But there was always that voice reminding her of the brutal truth. People don't just love you. Not without you earning it.

It was a lovely idea though.

A cheer erupted, and Daisy's gaze snapped to the game. Hunter was backpedaling, his eyes on the sky as the football soared toward him. He jumped. Caught the ball. And landed in the makeshift end zone, securing the win for his team.

The field exploded with cheers, and Hunter, flushed with victory and exertion, scanned the crowd until his eyes locked with Daisy's. A broad grin split his face, and he took off toward her.

Daisy stood, waiting for him. And when Hunter reached her, he swept her into his arms, lifting her off the ground. She laughed, head falling back as they spun.

"Kiss her!" someone shouted—it sounded suspiciously like Waylen.

Hunter's eyes held hers, the world fading around them, and he lowered her feet to the ground but kept going, dipping her back as he stole a celebratory kiss.

And the crowd went wild.

Sixteen

THE GAME WAS OVER, BUT THERE WAS still one more win Hunter had to secure. He just had to find the right moment to talk to his grandpa.

Hunter held the door open for Daisy as they entered Martha's on Main, the warmth and aroma of roasted turkey immediately enveloping them. The diner, though small, was already bustling with activity, filled with locals and visitors alike, who had lingered after the football game for Martha's annual Thanksgiving dinner.

The tables that were usually peppered throughout the floor, between the booths and the bar, were now pulled into two banquet-style lines, jammed end to end with chairs.

"Ey-yo, over here!" Evan's voice boomed from the far end of one of the long tables.

Hunter slipped his hand into Daisy's, leading her through the crowded diner.

"Saved you a spot," Jude said, scooting over to make room, and Hunter stepped back, letting Daisy shimmy in first. Miles and Waylen wedged themselves next to the wall on the opposite side, and Grandpa took the spot on the end.

A minute later, Dad stepped into the diner, his eyes searching the crowd.

"Joe!" Daisy shouted, her volume matching anything his brothers could muster up, and Hunter chuckled. He might make a Barrett out of her after all.

Dad took the remaining chair next to Grandpa.

And then their family was whole.

Almost whole.

"Glad you could make it, Dad," Hunter said, giving his dad a one-armed hug.

"And miss Martha's? You gotta be kidding." Joe chuckled.

Vera stepped up to the table. "Well, if it isn't the Barrett boys."

"And Daisy!" Waylen called from his distant spot at the end of the table.

Daisy buried her blushing face in her hands, and Hunter chuckled, wrapping an arm around her.

"And Daisy," Vera agreed. "We've got a whole turkey set aside for you all." She leaned in and placed down a platter overflowing with turkey, stuffing, and all the fixings. "Eat up, boys—and Daisy—there's plenty more where that came from."

"Oh, Dad here's on a heart-healthy diet," Hunter said, catching Vera before she could walk away. "You got any arugula? You can just bring him a heap of arugula. Or like . . . just raw carrots."

There was a chorus of ridiculous "healthy food" suggestions. Daisy tossed in a suggestion about quinoa.

"I'll be partaking in the *standard* Thanksgiving dinner, thanks, Vera," Dad said, giving the entire table a scathing look.

Chuckles all around.

Vera left, and the table erupted into a flurry of passing plates as food was piled high.

Platters were passed from the Barretts to the Jonathons, the Quinns, the Kelleys, and the Harts. And Hunter watched as Daisy dove right in, melding with the group as though it were where she belonged.

And he tried not to wonder what tomorrow would look like.

The evening died down, friends and families made their way home until only a small gathering remained at the diner. Hunter leaned back against his seat, his belly one turkey leg too full.

A game of rummy had broken out in one of the booths, the usuals having opened up a few chairs for newcomers. Mickey Harper sat across from Stu with furrowed brows, and Lyle let out a hoot as Mickey laid down a winning card. A chorus of shouts and objections erupted from the booth.

Hunter chuckled and turned his gaze toward the bar, where Jill was chatting with Terry and Bonnie Quinn, who were no doubt regaling her with tales of their recent cross-country RV trip.

At a nearby table, Jude and Evan were engaged in animated conversation with a pretty brunette—likely some cousin visiting family for the holiday. Their laughter carried across the room, adding to the low hum of conversation.

Miles, ever the responsible older brother, called out to them. "Hey, you two! How about rejoining the family?"

Jude glanced over his shoulder, a mischievous grin on his face. "Can't a guy multitask? We're securing plus ones for Hunter's wedding."

"Yeah," Evan chimed in. "It's important family business."

They sauntered back to the table, settling across from Hunter and Daisy.

Waylen plucked a piece of turkey from the nearly empty platter still sitting in the middle of the table and popped it in his mouth. "Speaking of weddings," he said as he leaned forward, addressing Daisy with a mouthful of food. "You're coming with us, right? We're renting an SUV and road-tripping out on Thursday morning. Nothing says future in-law bonding time like a seven-hour drive. Am I right?"

Hunter stiffened, unsure what her response would be. The conversation with Daisy from weeks ago replayed in his mind. Sure, she'd offered to attend the wedding with him. But it had been a pity offer. And once this whole arrangement was over, he didn't know what to expect. Certainly not to take his maybe-new girlfriend on their first date to his mom's wedding, never mind that he still wasn't sure if he wanted to go himself.

To his surprise, Daisy looked to him. *You still up for this?*

Hunter considered for a moment. He'd spent so long trying to hold on to the past, imagining that he could put everything back together so long as he let nothing change. And then Daisy had burst into his life, drawing him out of his shell, showing him how change could be good. The house was only one example of that.

His mother deserved a fresh start, and she wanted him to be a part of it.

He gave Daisy a quick nod.

She snuggled in beside him, her head resting on his shoulder. "I wouldn't miss it," she replied.

Hunter's arm instinctively tightened around her, a rush of warmth flooding through him.

"Glad to hear it," Miles said, raising his coffee mug in a mock toast. "Because guests get control of the radio, and I can't handle another six-hour trip while being forced to listen to one of Evan's board game podcasters."

"Hey now," Evan rebutted. "*The Dice Tower* is quality content. It's not my fault you're uncultured."

The table erupted in good-natured laughter, and Hunter found himself joining in.

"It'll be nice to slow down a little," Daisy explained. "I have a friend coming to take photos on the ninth so we can submit the renovations to the Home and Garden contest. Winner gets this huge cash prize, which could be really nice to have toward another project."

Hunter tried not to flinch as she said it. "Another project" could mean anything. Anywhere. It could mean back in California . . . But there were plenty of projects on the island too. They hadn't talked about what was next for them. Whatever they had growing between them, there was hope for it.

He threaded his fingers through hers.

Maybe they were playing a losing game, letting themselves fall for each other.

But maybe . . .

She glanced up at him, oblivious to his thoughts. "Hunter's beautiful banister was the perfect addition . . ." She returned her gaze to the group. "But I'm not sure it's going to be enough. I walked by Logan's Zinnia project earlier this week, and it's really incredible, even after just two weeks. He's already restored all the original lap siding, installed period-correct mullioned windows, and that wraparound porch with its tapered columns and river rock base is half finished. I guess we'll just have to wait and see . . ."

As if on cue, Hunter's grandpa rapped his knuckles on the table and rose, pressing a hand to his back, the other to his stomach. "Ohh, I think I'm going to be stuffed for a week," he joked.

To which Jude responded, "Preach it, Gramps. I'm about to enter my annual food coma."

Grandpa chuckled. "I think I'm going to head up to the inn. I'll see you all at your dad's tomorrow, right?"

A round of agreement filled the table.

"All right then, g'night, boys."

"And Daisy," Evan corrected.

A round of chuckles. "And Daisy."

He started toward the door, and Hunter pulled away from Daisy. "I'm gonna walk him home," he said, giving her a look as if to say, *you know, for the thing . . .*

"Oh—oh, right," she said, quickly glancing after his grandpa. "Okay. I'm probably going to turn in too. Still have episodes to edit. I'll see you tomorrow?"

"Count on it," he said, halfway out the door.

Warm light poured from the diner as Hunter fell into step alongside his grandpa. The night was colder than he'd expected, the earlier unprecedented warmth now faded below the horizon. Their breaths fogged in the lamplight as Hunter rehearsed what he was about to say. *Grandpa, there's something I need to tell you. About Daisy and me . . . It's a funny story, actually . . .*

"I was wondering when we'd get a chance to talk," his grandpa said, turning his shoulders to glance at Hunter.

"Me too, actually," Hunter said, stuffing his hands into his pockets. He took a deep breath, trying to summon the courage to speak.

The truth is . . . Daisy and I aren't engaged. We're not even dating. Well, maybe we are. It's complicated . . .

Wow. He was rambling even inside his head.

"I wanted to tell you how proud I am, Hunt," his grandpa said. "Of what you and Daisy have done with the house so far. And of everything you've done to hold your family together all these years. You've shown real strength."

Hunter's confession died on his lips, his heart hammering in his chest at his grandfather's words. "Thank you," he said, the words scraping from his lungs.

They continued on in silence for a moment, the sound of their footsteps echoing on the empty street.

"I was starting to think it might be time to let go of that old house," his grandpa started again. "To trust God to give it to the next right person . . . Call me sentimental, but I'm glad to see we've still got some time left with it."

Hunter swallowed hard, the lump in his throat growing. "Grandpa, about the house—"

"You know," his grandfather continued, "your father asked me, years ago, to change the trust."

Hunter stopped in his tracks, shocked. "What?"

His father paused beneath the streetlamp. "After your mother left. He knew he couldn't bear to live there anymore, so he asked me to give it to Miles. To ensure the family legacy."

Hunter frowned. "But you said no."

His grandfather nodded solemnly. "Do you know why we built the trust that way?"

Hunter let out a shallow breath. He had a feeling he wasn't going to like the answer.

"To create a legacy built on faith," Grandpa said, wrapping an arm around Hunter's shoulder. "It was never about the house."

"It was about faith," Hunter finished, feeling a knot form in his stomach.

Trust. Hunter wasn't sure that was something he really knew how to do. Even now, he was bracing himself for the end of him and Daisy. When it came to God . . . if Hunter's own mother could walk out of his life, it wasn't likely the Big Guy was going to stick around.

He thought back to his conversation with Miles the morning this all started. *But I think if you give Him a chance to come through for you, you might be surprised.* Maybe it was time he gave that a try . . .

His grandpa gave his shoulder a squeeze. "I'm just proud of you, is all . . ."

They stopped at the end of Main Street, the inn only a few buildings down, and his grandfather reached into his pocket. "There's something else." He pulled an old leather ring box from his pocket. The edges were worn, the clasp tarnished from years of use. He opened the box, revealing his grandmother's old wedding ring. The diamond was modest, set in a gold band with a simple filigree pattern around it. "I noticed Daisy wasn't wearing a ring yet."

Hunter's heart lodged in his throat. "Grandpa, no—" The truth clung to him, refusing to come out, so instead he just said, "I can't take this."

"I want to see Daisy wearing this tomorrow," his grandfather said, pressing the box into Hunter's hand. He gave Hunter a warm smile and a pat on the shoulder. "Now, if you'll excuse me, it's late. And this old man needs some rest."

His grandfather turned and walked away, leaving Hunter standing alone on the sidewalk, the ring box heavy in his hand.

This day had been a dream. A loud, raucous, inviting dream. And Daisy wanted more than anything to stay a part of it.

She hugged her jacket around her as she stepped onto the street, her cheeks still flushed from the warmth of the diner. The stars hung over Main Street, twinkling brightly down on the little town. It was a far cry from the bright lights of California, but Daisy felt more at home here than she ever had there.

Her footsteps echoed as she rounded the end of the coffee shop, her little slice of the town emerging in the alleyway. There, the old wooden staircase led to her second-story apartment. Since they'd slowed on renovations, Daisy had taken to decorating, despite her looming departure from the island. The wooden rail had been wrapped in leafy garland, and fake potted plants sat on the treads leading up to the door.

Her mom would have been proud.

Daisy paused on the steps, the guilt aching through her chest. She pulled out her phone and found her mom's name. Her thumb hovered over the contact for a moment, and then she sighed and scrolled to Robin's name instead.

She'd call. Soon.

"Babe! Hi!" Robin's voice answered after a few rings.

"Happy Thanksgiving, beautiful!" Daisy said, sinking onto the stairs. "How are things going?"

She heard Robin shuffling around, the noise around her growing louder and then fading again. "Sorry, had to step outside. My parents decided to host the cousins this year. It's a madhouse in there." She let out a breath. "I'm good. Very excited about my top client's impending comeback."

Daisy imagined a cheeky wink, and she smiled. Robin

had always been good at making her feel special. Maybe that's why they were best friends.

"How are things with lover boy?" Robin asked, her voice dropping low as though hoping to exchange secrets.

Daisy blushed, a smile tugging at her lips as she thought about their victory kiss on the football field. Hunter was different now. Relaxed. Trusting. "It's good."

"Yeah."

"Yeah," she said. "It's just . . . Robin, I'm not sure what we're doing anymore."

"What do you mean?"

"I mean, at first, it was all just an act. I mean, I know this whole thing started out as a fake engagement. He needed a fiancée. I needed content. It made sense . . . at the time. But then . . . Logan showed up offering me a chance to go back to the way things were."

"Oh . . ."

"And I realized I didn't want that." Daisy shifted, slumping against the cold wall, savoring the chill against her warm back. "Logan and I, we worked because we wanted the same thing. We were both out to win. To be the best. But Logan didn't build me up. He was actually pretty terrible to me. He was manipulative and controlling. He belittled me while, in the same breath, he took credit for my ideas."

"You never told me any of this . . ."

"I never told anyone." She ran her nails down the seam of her jeans. "I was afraid of what fans would think. He's HGTV's golden boy. I was afraid of needing to rebuild everything I'd worked so hard for if I raised a fuss. It wasn't worth it."

She paused, brushing her hair behind her ear as her next thought brought a wave of heat to her face. "Hunter has never made me feel like that. He sees me, you know?" She brushed a thumb over her knee, remembering that night on the beach. *I'd really like to get to know Daisy without the Decker.*

"The Barrett family is incredible. All of them. They're loud and messy and hilarious. They're close. And I think a lot of that is because of Hunter. There was a time in their lives when everything fell apart. Hunter was the one who held them together . . . He still does. It breaks my heart sometimes how hard he holds on to them. Like one little crack and he could lose them all . . ." She hadn't realized how much she'd really learned about Hunter since this all started. How much she respected him. "It's crazy, because I know it's a *fake* engagement, but I could see myself being a part of all that. I could see myself staying."

Robin was quiet. "That's big, Daisy."

"I know." Daisy let out a heavy breath. "And I don't know what to do, because he's talking to his grandpa right now, trying to get him to change the trust so he doesn't need to be engaged in order to inherit the house. And then that's it. It will be over."

The words sank into her with a heaviness that made her heart ache.

She was about to get everything she'd planned for.

And nothing she wanted.

Robin cut through her thoughts. "Does it have to be?"

"What do you mean?"

"You said it yourself. You can see yourself staying. So what's stopping you?" A loud wave of voices sounded from Robin's end of the phone, and she hurriedly said, "Oh, love, I wish I could stay and talk. That's all so much. But my mom's calling me in. I think she needs reinforcements."

"It's okay," Daisy said. "You go. We'll chat later. I'll be back in LA in a few weeks."

"Love you, babe. Hang in there."

"You too."

The call ended and the silence closed in around her, the cold November night seeping through her jacket. Her breath clouded in the air as she let the question sink in. *What's stopping you?*

Things had changed so quickly between her and Hunter, they hadn't had a chance to make a plan. Could she really stake her future on someone who hadn't promised her a life?

She stood and started up the stairs when a sound from the street caught her attention.

A figure strolled across the entrance to the alley and paused, glancing toward her.

Logan.

"Daisy," he said as he stepped into the circle of light from the exterior lamp beside her door. "Is this . . . is this where you live?"

Daisy glanced uncomfortably up at her door. Had he been listening in on her conversation? "Um, yeah."

"Looks . . ." His eyes scanned the faux potted plants and the garland. "Very you."

"What do you want?"

"Relax," Logan said, stuffing his hands into his pockets. "I wanted to apologize for the way I acted the other day. It's obvious that you're happy here with . . . with Hunter." He said the name as though the taste of it made him sick. "But I also know how things are on the set. And that's what the house is, right? It's the set for your show. I know how emotions can get a little . . . tangled."

"Spit it out, Logan."

"Fine," he said, his tone carefully neutral. "I just . . . I don't want to see you corner yourself here, Daisy. So, just in case things don't work out, let me know. I'm having a meeting in a week with the HGTV execs to talk about the future of *Double Decker*. I'd love to have you there."

Daisy shifted uncomfortably, wrapping her arms around herself against the cold. "Thanks, but I'm busy that day."

Logan gave her a long look, and then, nodding, he stepped back. "All right. I can take a hint," he said, a bitter edge to his voice. He turned to leave, then paused. "The offer stands though."

He walked away, and Daisy hurried into the apartment, locking the door.

Seventeen

WOULD YOU TWO CLOWNS STOP waving that mistletoe around?" Hunter growled, dodging the leafy branch for the fifth time in as many minutes.

Evan and Jude, clad in matching green-and-red-striped sweaters, looked each other over, head to foot. "We're not clowns," Evan said earnestly.

"We're *elves*," Jude corrected. "Why? Do we look like clowns?"

Hunter's dad chuckled from across the room, where he was "directing" the decorating process from his La-Z-Boy. "Leave him alone, boys. He's just anxious for Daisy to get here."

Miles popped his head in from the kitchen, the scent of spiced cider wafting from behind him. "I was gonna ask. Where is she, Hunt?"

Hunter, who was trapped in the conversation by the

armful of garland he was helping Waylen drape over the archway to the small dining area, glanced at the clock on the wall. "She should be here soon. She had a few edits to make to the most recent episode of the show. She said she'd catch an Uber from the ferry."

"She'd better hurry," Waylen said, pinning up another swathe of garland. "Otherwise, she'll miss all the decorating fun."

"Is that sarcasm?" their dad asked. "Because I won't accept bah humbugs in this house."

"Not sarcasm," Waylen replied, grunting slightly as he stretched toward the corner. "Though I don't know why this couldn't wait another week."

"Oh," Miles said, crossing the room to set down a plate of cookies on the coffee table. "I think that's my bad."

Dad stood just long enough to grab a cookie and settled back into his chair. "It's not every year I get all my sons home at the same time." He cast a warm smile toward Miles. "Who knows what you'll all be up to next year. We have to take advantage."

"Oh, someone's taking advantage all right," Waylen complained, sending his dad the stink-eye as he snatched up another cookie. He finished pinning the last of the garland and stepped down from the ladder.

"You gotta be kidding me," Jude's voice exclaimed from the kitchen.

Miles's gaze shot up.

"Miles put Red Hots on the gingersnaps again!" Evan cried.

The twins hurried into the living room with fistfuls of

red-dotted cookies. Jude lifted the cookies in his brother's direction, shaking them for good measure. "Why? Why, Miles?"

Wide-eyed, Miles glanced at his other brothers.

"Don't look at me," Hunter said, lifting his hands in surrender. "I don't know where he got that."

Waylen frowned. "What? That's how Grandma used to do them."

The twins mirrored each other's looks of disbelief, scoffed, and started back toward the kitchen. "Don't worry, guys. We'll fix them," Jude called out as they vanished around the corner.

Miles surged to his feet. "Don't you dare!" And then he vanished as well, with Waylen following close behind, never one to miss the action.

The merriment continued in the kitchen, but Hunter savored the quiet, settling on the sofa across from his dad.

His dad smiled, his eyes trailing over the decorations. "I'm sorry I couldn't make it out to see the house yesterday," he said, his gaze fixed on the garland. "The boys told me the place looks great."

Hunter meant to go for a smile, but it came out as more of a grimace. "It's okay, Dad."

His dad shook his head. "It's not, but I appreciate you saying that."

Hunter eyed the plate of cookies on the coffee table as the comfortable silence shifted.

"You know, I've been watching the YouTube channel."

Hunter blinked. "Really?"

His dad nodded. "You've done some quality work up there."

"Thanks, Dad." It meant more to Hunter than he knew. "You know, I've been getting requests, inquiries for custom projects, ever since that episode aired—the one with the banister."

His dad remained quiet, so Hunter went on. "I know you don't want to talk about it, Dad. But don't you think it's time to stop letting the past hold you back?"

He let out a heavy breath. "I know you want to move the business back to the island, Hunt . . . but it's a big risk. I've spent so long trying to make up for my mistake. Trying to make sure everything is perfect so that nothing like the boardwalk ever happens again. The town's just getting back on its feet . . . and what's to say I won't let them down? Or worse, what if something happens? I couldn't—I can't, Hunt."

The air felt heavy, the years of fear and stress suddenly making his dad look decades older.

"I get it, Dad," Hunter said, ducking his head to meet his father's downturned gaze. "Really, I do. But I'm starting to think that maybe you and I, we spend too much time afraid. Afraid of what might happen if we loosen the reins. And maybe, just maybe, if we let God take the reins, He'll surprise us with what's in store."

The sound of Christmas music drifted down the hall, the great Christmas cookie battle apparently over, and Hunter heard footsteps coming to end the conversation. He reached out and clasped a hand on his father's shoulder. "Think on it, okay?"

His dad lifted his gaze again, his eyes red. "I'll think on it."

Just then, Waylen strode into the room, popping a Red Hot into his mouth.

"All right, Dad. What's next?" Hunter asked, hopping to his feet, shaking away the heaviness.

Crumbs spilled across his dad's sweater as he looked around and said, "Why don't you head down to the basement and grab the tree?"

Hunter nodded and started for the stairs.

A buzz filled the space as Hunter flicked on the fluorescent lights, which dangled over a maze of boxes and old furniture. On one side of the room, his dad's small workstation sat forgotten, unused for years. Hunter let his eyes graze over it, searching for the holiday decor.

His dad was a funny guy. He didn't maintain his yard. He didn't give a thought to curb appeal. But give him a blow-up Santa for the roof, and he was all over it. Hunter spotted the large container marked *Christmas Tree* in his dad's messy scrawl, and he made his way toward it.

As he bent to pick it up, the small box in his front pocket slipped out, tumbling across the floor.

The ring.

Hunter paused what he was doing and reached for it, his chest squeezing as he lifted the box and opened it.

His stomach sank.

What was he going to do? He'd just given his dad a whole speech about trusting God, and here he was, scheming to get his way. He couldn't continue lying to everyone. Eventually, the truth would come out.

Unless . . .

The diamond caught the light, glittered.

His conversation with Miles all those weeks ago rang in his head.

Ask her. What's the worst that could happen?

He didn't think this was exactly what Miles had meant, but the sentiment was the same. Maybe they had a shot at making this work. If anyone was willing to put in the effort, it was Daisy Decker.

What if he asked her to . . . to what, marry him?

He shifted the ring, and the light in the diamond dimmed. *Come on, Hunt. Be real. It's just a matter of time until things start to go wrong. And then what? You're back where you started, picking up the pieces.*

He snapped the box shut and shoved it back into his pocket.

Hunter hefted the Christmas tree box onto the landing and shut the basement door. "Oh, don't worry about me, guys. I'll get it," he said sarcastically as he carried the box into the living room.

He froze.

The festive atmosphere from earlier had evaporated, replaced by a tense silence that made Hunter's skin prickle with unease. His brothers were huddled together, their faces etched with concern.

"What's going on?" Hunter asked, setting the box down. His eyes darted from one face to another, searching for answers in their grim expressions. Miles met his gaze, a look of pity in his pressed lips.

Waylen's face was tight, his jaw pulsing angrily. He wouldn't even look at Hunter.

Evan and Jude exchanged glances, a silent conversation passing between them. Finally, Dad stepped forward, the disappointment clear in the lines of his face. "There's something you should see."

He handed Hunter his phone, the screen frozen on a familiar sight. He felt lightheaded as the video began to play, the words hitting like static in his ears.

Hunter's stomach dropped. "What is it?"

"We were hoping you'd tell us."

Okay, new plan. Daisy's fingers traced the edges of the manila envelope in her lap as she rode in the back seat of the Uber.

Daisy had had a full morning, the early hours of the day spent video editing, prepping social media for the week ahead, and making room in her schedule for the upcoming road trip with Hunter and his family. But even as she'd busied herself checking items off her mental to-do list, her head was still spinning around the conversation she'd had with Robin last night.

And she knew what she wanted to do.

Robin's words had been churning inside her head all morning. *What's stopping you?*

She wanted to stay. To see where things between her and Hunter went, even if it meant slowing down on her career.

So the new plan all started with the envelope.

Her phone buzzed, and Daisy fished it out of her pocket, sliding her thumb over the screen.

Robin ♥
What's going on?

Daisy
???

Robin ♥
Why are you trending on socials?

Daisy
Am I?
I didn't post anything.
Lemme check.

She swiped the bottom of the screen, her apps menu opening. She tapped into Insta and frowned.

She was blowing up, her notifications going wild with scathing comments.

@ParkzFam: Poor Hunter, he deserves better than this.

@MidwesOpe: I knew it was all for show. Daisy's just another clout-chasing influencer.

@BookwormBarista: Can't believe she'd use someone like that. Disgusting.

Daisy's eyes widened in horror as she clicked on the video she'd been tagged in, her heart pounding in her chest.

DAISY DECKER CAUGHT IN A LIE.

The blood drained from her face as her own face filled

the screen. She sat on the porch of the Barrett house, wearing her lilac overalls and mittens. It was an outfit she'd worn in a video weeks ago, footage from the YouTube channel . . . but the words. She'd never said any of that.

"It was all just an act," her voice said, shrugging casually. "This whole thing started out as a fake engagement."

"Hunter had to be engaged in order to inherit the house, so it just made sense." Daisy felt sick as she watched herself continue, her eerie smile in conflict with the words she was saying. "He needed a fiancée. I needed content."

Daisy was dizzy, the air trapped in her lungs. "But then . . . Logan showed up. And I realized I didn't want Hunter." The Daisy on the screen brushed a hair behind her ear, blushing. "Logan and I, we worked because we wanted the same thing. We were both out to win. To be the best . . ."

Daisy really was going to be sick. She leaned back, closing her eyes as she pulled in a stale breath, the final words of the video ringing in her ears, laughing. "I didn't want to have to rebuild everything I worked so hard for when everything fell apart because of Hunter Barrett. He isn't worth it."

Robin 🖤
This is bad, Daisy . . .

Daisy

I never said those things. I don't know where that video came from. But it's a total fake.

Daisy called Hunter. She had to warn him. Explain to him . . . what? She hadn't said those things . . . but she didn't have an explanation. Who would have even done this? Maybe Logan, but he wasn't tech-savvy enough to create a fake video like this. Was he?

The call went to voicemail.

She dialed again and again. The call was ignored.

Daisy's heart raced, the blood rushing through her ears. Her fingertips felt numb, prickly. The air inside the car felt stifling. Hot.

She looked up, realizing the Uber had stopped. They were outside Hunter's dad's house. The windows were lit with Christmas lights. Daisy stepped out of the car, her knees wobbling as she clutched the envelope with white knuckles.

He would understand. Hunter knew her. He trusted her. He'd listen. He had to.

Daisy's boots made no sound as she made her way toward the house, up the steps. Before she could reach the door, it swung open, and the walkway filled with warmth and light. Hunter stepped outside, closing the door behind him.

Daisy stilled.

Hunter's face was a solemn mask. Emotionless. Distant.

He crossed his arms over his chest, leaning a shoulder against the doorjamb. "I don't think you should be here."

"Hunter, please, let me explain." Except there wasn't anything to explain. She had no idea where the video had come from, let alone the things she'd said.

"I don't want another explanation, Daisy."

"Hunter—"

"Every time I hear you out, you somehow convince

me it was all just a misunderstanding. I'm done." Hunter wouldn't look at her. His dark eyes scanned the surrounding neighborhood, the sidewalk, the melting snow. But not her.

"Please, Hunter." Her voice broke as tears built up behind her eyes.

His jaw pulsed as he shook his head. "I can't believe you did this to me again."

"I didn't—Hunter, the video's not real."

"I'm not blind, Daisy. I watched the video. I know your voice. I know your face," he snapped, his gaze finally meeting hers. "Maybe I am blind for trusting you again." Daisy's breath caught in her chest at the wounded look in his eyes. "You know the worst part? You couldn't even wait for things to fall apart before cutting me loose."

He pushed away from the door, turning his back to her.

Daisy scrambled for something to say, anything to make him stay. "What about us?"

Hunter stiffened, the lines of his broad shoulders tightening. He spared a glance over his shoulder, his eyes flashing with anger. "What part don't you understand, Daisy? There is no us. We are over. And I hope it was worth it. Because it looks like you've been canceled. Your followers are dropping like flies."

She opened her mouth to speak, but Hunter continued, his words laced with bitterness.

"And boy, you really had me fooled." He laughed humorlessly, shaking his head. "But I see the real you now, and you were right. I am disappointed."

Tears spilled down her cheeks, and Daisy stepped

down, the envelope slipping from her fingers and fluttering to the ground.

Hunter's gaze swept over her one last time. "Go home, Daisy," he said, his voice firm. Resolved. "It's over."

He turned and stepped inside, shutting the door behind him.

Eighteen

THE EARLY-MORNING SUN SIMMERED in the steam off the lake, lying like fog upon the water. Hunter sat on the dock, the sounds of ice chunks crushing against one another over the quiet harbor, his elbows resting on his knees, head hanging low. In his hand, his grandma's ring weighed him down, the stone cutting into his palm. He couldn't look at it anymore. He closed the ring box and tucked it back into his pocket.

The last week had been a nightmare. First there had been the video itself. The words cut deep, etched into his memory. And then there had been the reactions. His dad's. His brothers'. But worst of all, his grandpa's. Hunter's face burned just thinking about the look of betrayal and disappointment that had been heavy in the old man's eyes.

Things were fraying already. It was just a matter of time . . .

And what was he doing? Sitting on a cold dock, waiting

for a ferry to meet up with his brothers so he could watch his mom marry someone he'd never met.

A pair of footsteps thumped quietly against the dock, and Hunter lifted his head.

Tara Chamberlain stood beside the bench, her winter coat cinched tight at the waist. She held two cups of coffee in her gloved hands, a soft smile on her lips. "Good morning, Hunter. Do you mind if I join you?"

He let out a breath. This was not what he needed right now. He scooted over. "Have at it."

Tara quietly perched on the bench. Extended one of the steaming cups toward him. "I spotted you on my way to Good Day. I wasn't sure if you'd still be here, but I grabbed you a coffee."

Hunter frowned in surprise. "Thank you."

An uncomfortable silence stretched between them as the ferry appeared in the distance.

"Where's Daisy today?" Tara asked, taking a sip from her cup. "I'd gotten used to seeing you two together."

Hunter turned the cup in his hands, letting the heat warm his palms. "She's gone. It's over. I guess she finally saw what everyone does about me."

It was a heavy statement. Not something he wanted to share with someone so familiar with his failures. But he couldn't seem to hold the words back. Tara had been like a mother to him once, and maybe there was a part of him that really needed that right now.

Tara tilted her head. "What is it you think everyone sees in you, Hunter?"

Hunter licked his lips, discomfort creeping up his

throat. He glanced away, focusing on the sheets of ice in the bay reflecting the sun. "I think they see every bad thing that's happened to me as one more piece of baggage . . . I think they see a million broken pieces. The ruins of an old house. They see me as too much work."

"Is that what you think I see in you?" she asked quietly.

"I think it's why you look at me the way you do." The words scraped his throat. "I think I let you down when I didn't protect Belle the way I should have. I think you realized that the people in my life end up getting hurt or getting out. You got out. And who would blame you?"

Again, the heavy silence.

"Hunter Barrett. It was not your responsibility to protect Belle," Tara said, her breath hanging in the air. "She made the choice to jump into that water. It was a choice I wish she hadn't made, but never for a moment did I blame you for it . . . But I couldn't look at you without seeing that terrified look on your face when we showed up at the hospital. When I look at you, I relive the most terrifying night of my life. And that's not fair to you . . . I'm sorry."

Hunter lifted his head. All these years . . . "Thank you."

The ferry pulled up to the dock, and Hunter swallowed a heavy breath.

"Where are you headed?" Tara asked.

"I'm supposed to be heading to my mom's wedding . . ."

"You know," Tara leaned toward him, her shoulder bumping his. "Sometimes people leave when things get hard . . . but sometimes they stay, Hunter. And sometimes they come back . . . if you let them."

Hunter thumbed the seam of his coffee cup. "That sounds like a pretty good way to get hurt all over again."

Tara let out a peaceful breath. "Yes, it does. But God calls us to trust Him that when we get hurt, He'll stick around to pick up the pieces."

Do you know why we built the trust that way? . . . To create a legacy built on faith.

Hunter's brow furrowed as he absorbed her words. He swallowed. "I'm not sure I know how to trust God."

"That's a hard one to learn, so I'll just tell you what helped for me." Tara wrapped an arm around his shoulder, giving it a motherly squeeze. "It takes practice, and prayer, and most importantly, listening. God's not going to hide from those who seek Him. He doesn't walk away, Hunt."

The ferry began to load with passengers.

"You getting on?" she asked.

Hunter took in a deep breath. "Yeah, I think so."

Daisy's dreams were dead. And so were her plants. Maybe that was being a little dramatic, but as she stood at the window of her Los Angeles studio apartment with her cute little watering can and tried to revive a crispy brown pothos plant, she wasn't so sure.

Giving up, Daisy set the watering can aside and turned back to the pitiful little apartment. She'd arrived home a few days ago, and still the studio smelled like dust and stale air. Daisy shuffled the three feet to the couch and slumped face down into the cushions.

"Yoo-hoo!" Robin called from the front door.

Daisy groaned in response.

Her friend lived conveniently across the hall and had been "popping by" to check on her every few hours since Daisy's return. Apparently, there was just something about her that screamed *I'm not okay!* She couldn't imagine what it was.

"Oh," Robin said, edging gently into the living room area. "All right, we made it out of bed. That's a start."

"Yaaaay," Daisy said flatly.

"Okay, sweetie, why don't we sit up. I'm a little worried about airflow," Robin said, pulling Daisy up. "Great job, babe." She stood and glanced around the room, apparently taking note of the lack of change since she'd last been there. "So, how did your little assignment go?"

"What assignment?" Daisy mumbled.

"Your assignment to do just . . . one thing."

Daisy pointed at the laptop, sitting open on the coffee table, her bathrobe slumping down over her finger. "I edited the last episode."

Robin's brows rose in surprise. "Okay! Well, that's something."

"Don't think I'll upload it though . . . not sure what the point would be. We've got, like, three followers left. And I'm pretty sure two of them are in this room."

Robin let out an exasperated breath. "Come on, Daisy. This isn't you."

Daisy looked at her hands and dropped them back to the couch dramatically.

Okay, sure, she was being a little melodramatic. But her career had been catastrophically destroyed, her love life torpedoed, and all her plants were dead. What did this woman expect from her?

"Okay, well. I'm going to need you to do whatever you gotta do to pull yourself together because . . . I got you into that meeting with the HGTV execs! We're flying out Monday morning, and we'll be in the office by that afternoon," she announced, as though that were the greatest thing to ever happen to both of them. "It took some convincing, but they are willing to hear us out and talk options for the future."

Daisy tried to muster a weak yay, but it came out more like a gurgle.

"Daisy," Robin said flatly, her brow furrowed with concern. "This is your career we're talking about. You've got to pick up the pieces or you'll be left behind."

Then came a suggestion that made Daisy's stomach churn. "I think the first thing we should do is clear the air. Release a statement about the video," Robin said, her voice cautious. "People need to know you didn't say those things and the video is fake."

Daisy wanted to cry. They'd never believe it. She had no proof it was a deepfake. And despite her suspicions over Logan's involvement, she couldn't publicly accuse him of something like that. Especially not when he held her career in his hands.

She pulled her knees up to her chest, burying her face in her arms, and let out a long groan of frustration. How had it come to this?

She felt Robin sink down on the sofa beside her, a comforting hand start circling her back. "You know I'm just trying to help, right, babe?"

"I know," Daisy replied, her voice watery.

"Okay."

Another minute ticked by before Robin whispered, "I gotta get to work, but I'll be by tonight. We can workshop something. You don't have to play nice with Logan if you don't want to."

Daisy felt a kiss on the top of her head, and then she was alone again, tears stinging her throat. She lifted her head to wipe her eyes and spotted her phone, abandoned on the coffee table. She reached for it and opened her contacts, found who she was looking for, and hit the Call button.

The phone rang twice before a familiar voice answered. "Daisy. Hey, sweetie."

"Mom," Daisy choked out, her voice cracking with emotion.

"Oh, honey. It's okay," her mom said, her voice soft. She didn't ask what was wrong. She'd probably seen it all over Daisy's social media pages. And she didn't ask if she was all right. She knew. "It's okay. You're okay."

"I'm sorry I didn't call," Daisy whispered, a fat tear trailing down her cheek. "I just . . . I didn't want you to see me fail. I didn't want to call until I was back on track."

"Daisy."

"I just . . . I told myself I'd call as soon as I had my life under control . . . and I don't know what I'm going to do now. Everything's a mess." And she wished she was back home, in that little house they'd made their own all those years ago.

"It's okay, sweetie. I knew you were waiting."

"You did?"

Her mom let out a quiet laugh. "Yes."

"How?"

She half expected her mom to say her standard answer of "mom magic," but she didn't. Instead, she said, "Because you always wanted everything to be just right. You never let me step in and rescue you. Never asked for help. But I always hoped you knew it was there."

"I knew," Daisy whispered. A comforting quiet filled their call, and then Daisy said, "Mom, can I ask you something?"

"Anything."

"You remember the day you came home with all the painting supplies? The day we started renovating together?"

"I do."

"What happened?" Daisy asked. "What happened to make you do that?"

There was a moment of silence on the other end of the line. "It was something your dad did. Or rather, what he didn't do."

"What do you mean?"

"Do you remember your Knowledge Bowl competition back in middle school?"

Daisy nodded, then remembered her mother couldn't see her. "Yeah."

"Your father … he decided not to come home to see you compete. Said he'd show up if you made it to the championships. When you did something . . . worth seeing.

And something in me just snapped." Her mother's voice grew stronger. "You deserved a better dad, Daisy. One who didn't see you as just the sum of your accomplishments. Because no matter how hard you tried, you could never live up to his impossible standards."

Daisy felt tears rolling down her cheeks, but she remained silent, listening.

"I couldn't give you a better dad, but I could give you a place that felt safe and special. So I went out and bought whatever I thought we needed to create a home where you could just be you, without the pressure to achieve something great. No blueprints. No plans. Just you."

"Mom," Daisy whispered, her voice cracking again.

"I've been so proud to see you successful in your career, honey. But do you know what my favorite thing was? When you were just starting out. When you were doing that YouTube channel, helping people turn their average homes into places that felt special and safe. You were doing for others what I tried to do for you."

Daisy was reminded of the church service Hunter had taken her to that first day they were "engaged." *Fortunately for us, God's grace is sufficient. He doesn't tally up our good works. He doesn't compare them against the saints, or the celebrities, or even our neighbors. He gives life we don't deserve, out of a love we could never earn.*

Daisy wiped a tear from her cheek, her face hot and her throat thick. "I love you, Mom."

"I love you, Daisy. All of you."

Nineteen

GET IN. EAT CAKE. GET OUT. THAT WAS the plan.

Hunter adjusted his suit as he stepped through the heavy wooden doorway of the church. Piano music sifted through the quiet crowd, drawing guests in to sit down. Hunter searched for a quick, inconspicuous path to the pews, hoping to avoid any cousins, aunts, or well-meaning friends of his mother. He just wanted to slip in unnoticed, do his duty as a son, and leave.

Evan gave him a nudge and pointed toward the front of the church. To Hunter's horror, there was a small sign that read: *Reserved for sons of the bride.*

Reluctantly, Hunter followed his brothers up the long aisle.

"Don't—" he started to say as they all filled in the pew, leaving him to sit at the end, exposed.

All right. Now all he had to do was sit here. He could do that.

A quiet female voice cut through the murmurs of the crowd. "Excuse me, I'm looking for Hunter. Does anybody know Hunter?"

He hesitated. He could just sit there. Do nothing. For all he knew, she was asking so she could kick him out. No need to draw attention.

"I'm looking for Hunter," she said again.

He let out a heavy sigh and rose from his seat. "I'm Hunter."

The woman, a brunette with a clipboard, let out a sigh of relief. "Oh, thank goodness. Your mom is asking for you. She's in the bridal suite."

Hunter exchanged glances with his brothers, a mix of surprise and apprehension on their faces. Miles gave him a slight nod, reminding him that he didn't have to be in control. Maybe this was just one of those things he needed to trust God about.

So he followed the woman as she led him through the church, their shoes padding across the red carpeting throughout, and down into the basement, to another set of heavy wooden doors.

She knocked gently before opening them. "Ms. Sherman? I found Hunter."

Hunter stepped into the room, his heart pounding.

The room was quiet; the music from the sanctuary faded into the distance. On one side of the room, a makeup station had been set up along a wide folding table. On the other side, a large screen closed off a portion of the space for changing. Hunter swallowed as she stepped out from behind the screen.

It had been more than ten years since he'd seen his mom. The last time had been his high school graduation. She'd come with a date, and he'd punched the guy . . . if he was remembering correctly. It hadn't been his best moment. He'd been a different man then.

And she'd been a different woman.

The woman who turned to face him now wasn't the broken, haunted figure from his memories. She looked . . . happy. Healthy. Her eyes held smile lines he'd never seen before. Her hair was a beautiful gray, bringing out the blue in her eyes.

Her gaze met his, and for a moment, neither of them spoke.

"You look nice, Mom," Hunter finally managed, his voice thick with emotion.

She smiled, but tears were already welling up in her eyes. And that smile trembled.

And Hunter crumpled.

"Don't," he said. "Don't cry."

He crossed the room in two strides, sweeping her into his arms, willing those tears not to fall. "I'm sorry."

His mom let out a loud sniffle and stepped back, the tears pouring down her face, leaving tracks in her foundation.

"You're sorry? I'm the one . . ." Her voice broke, and she sniffled again. She snatched a tissue from the nearby table, dabbing it to her eyes. "I'm the one who should be sorry. I never should have left you. I never should have said it wasn't worth it to be a . . . a Barrett . . . anymore." Her words came out in a string of tears and sniffles. "Because I'm so proud that you are one."

Hunter swallowed hard. "It's okay, Mom."

"No, it's not." She shook her head, her mascara blotting. "And I couldn't get remarried without you knowing that. I am so . . . so proud of my Barrett boys."

Hunter pulled her in again, wrapping his arms around his mom as she wept.

After a few moments, she pulled back, wiping her eyes and trying to compose herself. "You know, I ask Miles about you all the time. I just . . . I didn't want to bother you. I wasn't sure if you wanted a relationship with me after . . ."

"I know, he's told me." A knot formed in his chest. "And I'm sorry I shut you out. I'm . . . I'm learning a lot about rebuilding relationships." He grabbed another tissue, stepping up to dry her tears. "Do you think . . . maybe we could have a fresh start?"

"I'd like that."

There was a knock at the door, and the wedding planner poked her head in again. "Two minutes, Lisaaah—oh, your makeup!" She blinked. "I'll get someone in to touch that up."

The wedding planner vanished, and Hunter's mom gave a little chuckle. She glanced back at him, a hopeful look on her face. "I was going to ask one of my boys to walk me down the aisle. Would you . . . ?"

"Of course." Hunter felt a smile tugging at the corners of his mouth. "Yes," he said again, surprising himself with how easily the word came. "Yes, I'd be honored."

"Ey! Look who it is!" Evan shouted from their table in the crowded reception hall.

"If it isn't the big man!" Jude joined in the heckling, a wide grin splayed on his face. "How'd it feel, walking Mom down the aisle?"

"Did you feel strong?" Evan asked.

"Manly and heroic?" This from Jude.

Hunter chuckled as he slid across from his brothers. He leaned back, slinging his arm over the chair as he took in the space.

The venue, a fancy place in downtown Chicago, had been set up with a timeless look. Soft, white fabric was draped from the ceiling, creating a billowing canopy. Twinkling fairy lights were woven through the fabric, mimicking a starry sky and casting a warm, golden glow over the entire room. The table itself was decorated with white floral centerpieces set in gold vases atop crisp white linens.

Miles gave him a hefty pat on the back, bringing his attention back to the table. "You did great, Hunt. I don't think I've ever seen Mom so happy."

Before he could say more, the DJ made an announcement, his voice booming through the space like a sports announcer. "Ladies and gentlemen, please rise and join me in welcoming the newlyweds for the very first time . . . Mr. and Mrs. Carlisle Hansen!"

The guests stood, a wave of anticipation rippling

through the room as the music swelled. Hunter and his brothers rose from their seats, turning toward the entrance.

The double doors swung open, revealing the bride and groom. Hunter's mom beamed, her smile widening as she glanced up at her new husband. The music reached a climax, and they turned back to the crowd as they swept into the room.

In the center of the dance floor, Carlisle lifted his wife's arm, spinning her out, her dress twirling around her. He pulled her back in, his eyes bright as he kissed her earnestly. The crowd cheered and Hunter smiled.

She was happy and taken care of, and maybe that's all that mattered, really.

The music faded, and the happy couple settled at the sweetheart table.

The caterers made their way around the space, releasing tables for dinner, and it wasn't long before Hunter's mom and Carlisle made their way through the room, greeting their guests.

Waylen slid back into his seat, frosting coating his lips, a chocolate cupcake half devoured in his hand.

"Aw, come on, Waylen," Miles groaned. "Don't you know you're supposed to wait until the cake is cut to go in for dessert?"

Waylen blinked. "Really?"

Miles dropped his head into his palm.

Evan and Jude surged to their feet as their mom stepped up to the table.

"You look stunning, Mom." Evan wrapped her in a hug, while Jude shook their new stepdad's hand.

And then they traded. "Really beautiful, Mom," Jude said.

The twins had made the trip out to Chicago a few times, along with Waylen. And of course, Miles lived out here. It seemed Hunter was the only one who saw the man as a stranger when his mother's new husband stepped up beside her.

Mom turned to the table, her smile bright. "Carlisle, I want to introduce you to my youngest, Hunter."

Carlisle extended a hand, and Hunter took it, gave it a firm shake. The man looked to be in his late fifties, with graying hair and a thick mustache, a strong jawline, and brown eyes. He fit in next to his bride.

"It's nice to meet you," Hunter said, stuffing his hand back into his pocket.

"Likewise."

"What do you do?" Hunter asked, making the effort to get to know the man.

The man lifted a shoulder. "I work in the FBI. I investigate fraud. Digital forensics, actually." The way he said it made it sound as though that should mean something to Hunter. "It's a shame, that video of your fiancée. Linda told me about it," he went on. "Hope you know it's a fake."

Hunter frowned. "What?"

Carlisle cocked his head, as though this was information everyone should have already known. "It's a deepfake."

All eyes at the table turned up to Hunter, who studied Carlisle, trying to wrap his head around what he was being told. "How can you tell?"

Carlisle's brows lifted, and he pulled his phone from his

pocket. "I'll show you." He opened his browser and pulled up the video, Daisy's face filling the screen. "First of all, let's zoom in on her mouth as she speaks." He enlarged the video. "It's hard to tell, but in just a few places, the words she's saying aren't completely in sync. Just a word here and there."

He zoomed back out and scrolled to a later part of the video. "And here." He paused the video, moving it forward frame by frame. He pointed to Daisy's smile. "See how there's no outline on her teeth here?"

Hunter frowned, staring at the image.

"And most importantly . . ." Carlisle scrolled forward again. "Listen." He lifted the phone so that Hunter could hear over the dinner music. The sound of distant traffic layered over birds and waves.

"Cars," Hunter breathed. Whoever made this video obviously had never been to Jonathon Island.

"Bingo," Carlisle said, one eyebrow cocked in self-satisfaction.

Hunter couldn't believe it. His chest loosened, letting him take his first real breath in days. The video was a fake.

Hunter slumped back to his seat. What had he done?

Waylen cleared his throat, and Hunter glanced up at him. "I don't know if this is a good time, but . . . I picked this up outside the house. I was waiting for the right time to give it to you. It's from Daisy."

He slid a dirty envelope across the table, and Hunter picked it up, his fingers numb, and opened it.

He studied the contents for a moment, his heart racing.

And then turned back to his brother. "Go grab Evan and Jude. We gotta go."

"Yessir!" Waylen said, grinning as he scrambled out of his seat.

Hunter turned back to his mother. "I love ya, Mom. Congrats to both of you . . . I hope it's okay, but—"

"Go," his mom said, beaming up at him.

"Thank you." He strode across the dance floor, headed for the door, his phone already pressed to his ear. "Hey, Dad, we're coming home. I really need your help. I know it's asking a lot. But do you think you could meet me at the house tomorrow morning?"

"If you need me, I'll be there."

"Thank you, Dad. I'll send you a list of supplies once I get on the road."

This time, he wasn't letting Daisy Decker out of his life without a fight.

"Thank you all so much for meeting with us," Robin said as she and Daisy entered the executive boardroom at HGTV's Knoxville headquarters.

They had spent the better portion of their six-hour flight preparing for this meeting, rehearsing and drilling any possible questions or concerns. Daisy had done this a hundred times. Just get in, tell them what they want to hear, and get out.

She pressed a poised smile onto her lips and slipped into one of the chairs opposite the *Double Decker* showrunner, who sat alongside the show's creative and management team, and then finally a few HGTV execs. Logan sat on Daisy's side of the table, a few seats down, clad in a pressed suit and designer shoes—a stark contrast to what viewers saw on the show.

Outside the impressive boardroom, green hills surrounded the building, creating a sense of intimate seclusion, like they were about to have a meeting in the middle of a sunlit field. It made looking at the gray walls and white boardroom table hard on the eyes.

A woman from the creative team, early fifties with sleek black hair, leaned forward, placing her hand on Daisy's wrist. "It's nice to have you back, Daisy," she whispered.

Daisy smiled. "Thank you."

They settled back as the showrunner for *Double Decker*, a man in his early forties with graying temples and a pressed suit, stood, taking position at the end of the table. "Why don't we get started?"

"First off," he continued, "we want you to know how much we loved your Jonathon Island show, Daisy. The small-town feel really resonated with our viewers."

"Likewise," the woman across from Daisy said, turning slightly toward Logan and his agent beside him. "We've seen great success on the Thanksgiving pilot episode of your short-run holiday special. But everyone said it was missing one thing. The one thing that Daisy's show had and yours didn't."

Daisy held her breath. Don't say it—

"Chemistry."

Shoot.

"Which is why we're proposing a new show: *Double Decker: Small-Town Edition.*"

The screen at the end of the table lit up as shades lowered across all the windows. An image appeared, displaying Daisy and Logan, a shot pulled from one of their earlier seasons. But instead of one of their California beach houses, they stood in front of a beautiful old Victorian home.

Daisy's brows rose slightly.

"The concept," the first executive explained, "is that you'll travel to small towns across the US, doing quick renovation projects. It'll be similar to what Logan did on Jonathon Island, but with both of you working together, like what you and your contractor—"

"Hunter," she provided.

"Right." The showrunner glanced at her. "Like what you and Hunter did. We'll showcase not only the progress but also the relationship you two build as the show unfolds."

Logan shifted in his seat, glancing at Daisy.

"We want to capture that same charm and authenticity," another exec added. "We're thinking of downplaying the production aspect, making it feel more like your YouTube channel, Daisy. Really showcasing the natural chemistry between you and Logan.

"As for the video circulating social media right now"— the lead executive's tone grew more serious—"we want to put all the . . . unpleasantness behind us. This show could be a fresh start for everyone. But for that to happen, we'll need to make viewers believe in you two as a couple. They need to see Logan as the right choice for Daisy, instead of seeing Daisy as the woman who broke some guy's heart. We need to know that you two can make this work. That you can be successful together on-screen and off . . ."

Broke *some guy's* heart.

That's all he was to them. Just some guy.

And they wanted her to just replace him, as simple as that.

". . . we've been looking at potential locations," one of the execs was saying, but Daisy's mind was far away. "There's this adorable little town called Deep Haven that we think would be perfect for—"

"I'm sorry," she interrupted, her voice cutting through the executive's spiel. The room fell silent, all eyes turning to her in surprise.

She took a deep breath, glancing at Robin, who gave her a reassuring nod. "You know what the problem was with *Double Decker*?" she asked, turning her attention back to the table. "It was all curb appeal. It was surface-level. Fake."

She looked up at the photoshopped image of her and Logan. "We'd roll up to the house, fresh from our trailers, pretend to do some modicum of work, dust off our gloves, then roll to the next house, reapply the dust, and do it all again. We never looked at those houses as homes, never asked what we could do to leave an impact."

Daisy looked down, clicking her nails against the table. "I don't want to do curb appeal anymore. I don't want to be fake anymore. I'm tired of putting on a persona so that people won't be disappointed by the real me. And I'm tired, so tired, of working so hard for even an ounce of success."

God's grace is sufficient.

Daisy stood. "I appreciate you for meeting with us today. I'm sorry to have wasted your time."

She didn't wait for a counterargument. She just walked out.

A moment later, Robin burst through the glass doors, hurrying after her. "That was . . ." Daisy braced herself for a lecture. "Incredible! Daisy, you're my hero. I can't believe you did that . . . We're going to have to talk about maybe discussing these kinds of decisions with . . . oh, I don't know . . . your *agent* next time. But wow!"

Daisy heard footsteps behind them, then Logan's voice. "Daisy, wait up!"

She kept walking, but he caught up to her just as she and Robin reached the elevator. He stepped in front of her, blocking their path.

"Come on, Daisy," he said, his voice fraught with frustration, his brows scrunched tight. "This isn't you. You're a winner. A go-getter. You said it yourself, we want the same thing. We both want to win."

Daisy froze. What did he just say?

"When?" she asked, turning slowly toward him.

"What?" Logan frowned.

"When did I say that?" Daisy snapped, daring him to answer.

Logan's face fell, confirming her suspicion. She knew it.

Logan and I, we worked because we wanted the same thing. We were both out to win. To be the best . . . That's what she'd said that night he'd come to her outside her apartment.

"You recorded me." Her voice came out barely above a whisper, but it echoed through the sterile hall.

Logan's eyes darted away, and he shifted, licking his lips. "What?"

The boardroom door opened quietly behind them as a few of the network execs stepped out into the hall.

"That night, outside my apartment, you recorded my conversation."

"I don't—"

"You recorded me. And then you hired someone—because let's face it, we both know you can't do anything yourself—to manipulate footage from my show to make me look bad. To get me canceled. To drive a wedge between me and the man I love . . . and for what?" Daisy took a bold step forward, chin raised.

"For you," he snapped. "Everything I did, I did for you."

"Yeah?" Heat built in her chest, her voice rising. "How about when you *stole* the design that got us our show in the first place? Did you do that for me, Logan?"

He ground his teeth together. "I did that for us."

"There is no *us*, Logan. How could there be? You're already in a committed relationship with yourself." She glanced over his shoulder toward the crowd of people now gathered behind them. "Logan Double is a thief and a liar, and he'll do whatever he can to get ahead. If you're smart, you'll think twice about doing business with him."

She stepped into the elevator, Robin at her side. She wasn't going to lose what she and Hunter had together. Not again. "Change of plans—"

"Way ahead of you. First flight from Knoxville to Port Joseph, Michigan, leaves tomorrow morning."

Twenty

EPISODE 8: HOME FOR THE HOLIDAYS, UPLOADED (DECEMBER 10 TH)

The shot opens on the closed door to the Barrett house's sunroom. The edges of the door are stained with soot. Above the door, an empty gap hangs where a transom once was. Dust floats in the air, carried on the warm sunlight pouring through the parlor windows.

Hunter Barrett steps into the frame, his dark hair pulled away from his face, the hint of a five-o'clock shadow on his chin. He smiles into the camera, his gaze warm and inviting.

"Hi, friends. Hunter here," he says, his voice a warm rumble. "Welcome back to *House to Home*. As you can see, my beautiful cohost, Daisy Decker, isn't with me today . . . so I brought in some reinforcements to help me with a special project I'm working on."

Three handsome men step into the shot.

Hunter sets a hand down on the first man's shoulder. "Now, you've all met Waylen before."

"Ladies," Waylen says, winking at the camera.

"But I'd like to introduce Evan and Jude, two more in the Barrett family."

The twins share matching grins, framing up behind Hunter and Waylen to fit in the shot.

"Today we're going to be tackling a massive project."

They part, revealing the now-open door to the sunroom. The camera pans through the doors and across the room, showing peeling wallpaper, soot-stained walls, worn wooden floors, and a massive hardwood mantel hanging precariously from a stonework fireplace. Many of the stones above the mantel are missing, leaving gaping holes in the plaster. Hunter and his brothers lift a sheet over the fireplace, covering that part of the project.

Hunter steps into the shot again, standing next to the old fireplace. "We've got a lot to do if we're going to transform this place in the next forty-eight hours. Let's get started."

The shot splices into four feeds, each corner showing a Barrett brother working a different job. Waylen starts on the floors, carefully working them over, hammering down loose boards. Evan works to remove the old wallpaper, tearing out the fire-damaged portions underneath, tossing aside drywall. Hunter and Jude set to work on the fireplace, removing the massive mantel and carrying it from the room.

Hunter's voice comes over the footage. "Now that we've got the mantel down, I can step into the workshop for another special project."

The camera cuts to a new scene, Hunter standing inside the shed, the lights giving his skin a warm, tanned glow. A new figure steps into the shot, another man, older, with the same sheepish smirk.

"Friends. I want to introduce my dad, Joe Barrett. He's a master of woodworking, and while the other guys are hard at work inside, he's going to help me out in the shop today."

Joe nods, clapping his hands together as he steps up to the workstation. The shot speeds up, watching as Hunter and his dad collaborate on the project, kept carefully out of sight, moving in sync as they drill and measure and carve and sand.

At last, Hunter steps back into the sunroom, a large canvas now hanging over the fireplace. The walls are rebuilt and repainted, the floor refinished. The windows are no longer framed by soot, and the ceiling's no longer gaping with charred holes.

Hunter faces the camera. "I don't know what Daisy usually says here. So I'll just say this. I can't wait to show you the finished product, but if you want to see it, you'll have to check it out on *HOME*'s New Year's Virtual Parade of Houses. The contest starts tomorrow, so be sure to check it out and give the sunroom some love. And Daisy, if you're watching," his eyes soften as he looks into the camera, "please come home."

———

DAISY BLINKED DOWN AT THE SCREEN, her heart racing as she replayed the ending again. This hadn't been there when she'd boarded her flight this morning. Daisy swiped her screen, opening up her messages, her hands shaking as a gust of wind buffeted the ferry.

Daisy
Where did this come from??

Robin 🖤
EEEP! Hunter reached out while you were on the plane. He asked me to upload it to the channel.
Are you freaking out? I'm freaking out.

Daisy sucked in a deep breath as the ferry pulled into port, the automated message echoing through the speakers. "On behalf of everyone at Jonathon Island, we'd like to welcome you to the island . . ."

Daisy
I just got here. I'll call you later.

She stuffed her phone back in her pocket and climbed from the boat.

The little town was just as she'd left it, except now, the streets were tucked under a layer of snow. Christmas lights twinkled from every window, red and green ribbons adorned the lampposts. Potted Christmas trees sat in every corner, with strings of garland and glittering ornaments. The air smelled like cinnamon as she strolled down Main Street.

The wind swirled around her, carrying flurries of snowflakes as she climbed the hill toward Sunset Cove, and when she crossed into the tree-covered portion of the trail, it was like stepping into a dream. White everywhere. Her footsteps crunched through the fresh powder and she emerged out the other side. The sun poured across the lake, reflecting off the bobbing sheets of ice.

And the Barrett house stood, waiting. The front porch was wrapped with Christmas lights, a white wreath hanging on the door. The porch lights were lit, calling her in.

Daisy hesitated.

Daisy, if you're watching . . . please come home.

She pulled in a nervous breath and climbed the steps to the door.

The house was quiet, the light low except for the glow coming from the far end of the parlor, from beneath the closed sunroom doors.

She reached out and pulled the handle, light pouring out of the room.

Her breath caught.

It was her design. The one she'd meant to give him. The beautiful stonework fireplace stood with the same wooden mantel, reclaimed and refinished, but above the mantel, set into the stones, was a gorgeous hand-carved tree, its roots sinking into the stone.

It was exactly as she'd imagined it.

"I didn't think you'd come back," a voice said behind her.

She turned.

Hunter leaned against the open doorway, his hair peppered with soft snow.

"Well, your show left me on a cliffhanger," she said, taking a step toward him. "I had to see the finished result."

"And?" he asked, pushing away from the door. Taking a step closer.

"It's beautiful," she said. Closer.

"Yeah," Hunter agreed, his eyes dipping to her lips. His smile faded, his eyes softening as he pulled in a breath. And then he closed the distance between them, his hand lifting to brush the hair out of her face. He tilted her head back to look at him, and they both started speaking in a jumble.

"I'm so sorry, Daisy—"

"—the video was a fake—"

"I know. But I wish I'd trusted you. I'm sorry I said any of those things. I never cared about the followers or the show or any of that." His jaw pulsed as he let out a heavy breath. "I'm sorry."

"No matter how many times life falls apart, Hunter Barrett," she lifted to her toes, kissing away that heaviness between them, "I promise I will always stay to rebuild." She pulled back, looking into his eyes. There was a light there, hope and trust flourishing where once there had only been doubt. "I love you."

Hunter pulled back, his eyes wide, his lips parted and grinning. "You love me?"

"I lov—"

He crashed into her, his lips capturing hers. His arms wrapped around her waist, pulling her closer as they continued up, one hand pressed against her upper back. Her heart hammered in her chest, squeezing for breath, but she didn't need air. Not right then.

"I love you, Daisy." He kissed her again, this one soft and slow. And while they were falling in love, the snow was still falling outside.

Daisy pulled back, nestling against Hunter's chest, and he turned back to look at the completed sunroom. He slid an arm around her shoulder, keeping her close. "It's really too bad."

Daisy quirked a brow, head tilting back to look up at him. "What's too bad?"

"Oh, we'll have to sell it," he said matter-of-factly, looking up at the mantel. He glanced down at her again, his gaze tracing her lips, her cheeks, her eyes. "Unless . . ."

Daisy's lips curved into a smile, turning to stand fully in his arms. "Yes?"

"Eh, forget it," he said, his thumb grazing her neck, his fingertips curling into her hair. "It's a crazy plan."

"Haven't you heard? I'm all about crazy plans."

He pulled her in for another kiss, his lips brushing hers softly, like words unspoken. Promises made.

Epilogue

OVER THE SNOW DRIFTS AND UP THE hill, under white-coated pines, and atop Sunset Cove, the snow drifted past the frosted windows of the Barrett house. It had been nearly a week since Daisy had come back to him, and now the house burst with warmth and laughter, filling it to the brim.

Hunter leaned against the doorjamb, looking in at the ongoing engagement party.

Asher stood near the Christmas tree, regaling Vera with a recent tale from the stables while Sadie sat on the nearby couch, Augo's dog, Lucy, in her arms. Augo, Roger, and the rest of the gin rummy crew were huddled nearby, arguing animatedly over a recent game. Or maybe it was a future game. They didn't seem to need much of a reason.

Beyond them, the Barrett brothers—minus Miles— had taken over the sunroom, their booming laughter mixing with the Christmas music playing softly through the house.

In the corner, Dani and Liam were deep in conversation with Seb Jonathon, while Mia was perched on the arm of Cody's chair, both of them stealing bites from identical plates of Lily and Declan's famous fudge. And across from them stood his fiancée—his real fiancée.

She was beautiful. Her honey-brown hair was pulled up into some sort of bun, wrapped up impossibly into itself. Her lips tugged upward at the corner, hinting at some inside joke as she conversed with Cody and Mia. Her gaze drifted and found his.

Aw, she caught him.

Pushing away, he sifted through the crowd.

"Two plates?" Hunter asked low in her ear as his arms slid around her waist. "Who brought the fudge?"

"Lily and Declan. Separately." Daisy laughed, leaning back against his chest.

Hunter let out a satisfied breath, his hand curling around her delicate fingers. His thumb brushed over his grandmother's ring, perfectly set on her finger. He'd never get used to that.

Suddenly, a muffled knock sounded from the front door, barely audible over the din of conversation and music.

Daisy frowned, glancing around. "Who would that be?"

"Let's find out." He tugged her toward the door, fighting to keep the smile from his face. He'd been checking his phone all evening, waiting for this moment.

"Hunter?" She glanced up at him, suspicious now.

He gave her hand one more squeeze and reached for the door.

Outside, the snow had created a winter wonderland, and standing on the porch, with snow in her hair, was a woman with Daisy's smile.

The woman did a little jazz hands. "Surprise!"

"Mom?" Daisy's hand flew to her mouth as she launched herself into her mother's arms. "I can't believe you're here!"

Daisy's mother held her for a long moment before pulling back. "Of course I'm here. I wouldn't miss my own daughter's engagement party!"

Hunter grinned, watching the moment play out.

Daisy pulled back just enough to look at him, her eyes shining with tears. "Did you do this?"

He shrugged, trying his best to play it cool.

Clasping her mother's hand, Daisy dragged her into the house. "Come in! You need to meet everyone . . ."

They vanished into the crowded parlor, Hunter trailing behind. He posted himself on the edge of the fray, leaning against a wall as he listened to Daisy gushing out introductions, beaming.

Mia worked her way through the crowd, Cody in tow.

"Well, well," Mia said with a knowing smile. "Look who's a big ol' softy now."

Hunter shot her a sideways look. "No idea what you're talking about."

She suppressed her smile. "Sure you don't."

Hunter's phone vibrated, pulling his attention away, and he took it from his pocket. His screen lit up with a text from Jonah White, Holland's brother and his oldest friend from Jonathon Island.

<u>Jonah</u>

Hey, man. Sorry this is last minute, but I'm standing on the docks and it looks like I missed the last ferry. Would you be able to come grab me?

Cody, who leaned against the wall next to him, gave his shoulder a nudge. "What's wrong?"

Hunter grimaced. "It's Jonah. Apparently, he's come by for a surprise visit. And missed the ferry."

"Oof."

"Yeah." Hunter angled the phone toward Cody. "And now he wants a ride. Except he doesn't know I sold my MasterCraft."

Cody glanced at the ongoing party. "Let me take care of it."

"Thanks, man," Hunter said.

"Don't mention it." Cody turned and gave his girlfriend a quick peck on the cheek before pushing away from the wall. "I'll make sure he gets home."

Hunter waited for Cody to step out the front door, and then shot a quick text back.

<u>Hunter</u>

Ha! Just missed it. Hang tight, we'll get you here.

Hunter watched as Daisy introduced her mom to his brothers, who had the pair completely surrounded, before making his way toward the sunroom, where he'd last seen his dad.

He found him standing beside the fireplace, his eyes

running over the room he'd built for the love of his life, the one he'd repaired for the love of his son's life.

"Hey, Dad," Hunter said, stopping in front of him.

"Hey, Hunt." His dad glanced at him, the lines of his face not so deep tonight. "You should be real proud of the renovations. The house looks great."

Hunter followed his gaze, tracing the memory of the damage that had been fixed. "Thank you."

His dad released a relaxed breath, a smile tipping on his lips. "Just had an interesting chat with Seb and Liam," he said nonchalantly.

"Yeah?"

"They were admiring the mantel." He glanced back at the beautifully carved family tree. It really was his best work. "Got to talking about custom work." He took a sip of his drink, a mischievous glint in his eye. "Looks like I might be taking on some local projects. Maybe slow down a little bit."

Hunter's brows drew together. "What happened to 'it's too risky'?"

His dad smiled, a peace settling over his features. "You know, son, I think I'm gonna try letting God take the reins for a change."

The words hit Hunter square in the chest.

"Just like that?" Hunter asked.

"Just like that." His dad's gaze drifted to where Daisy and her mother were laughing with the rest of Hunter's family. "Sometimes the best things in life come when you stop trying to work it out yourself. I think you know a little about that."

He glanced over at Daisy. Smiled. "I think I do."

This night had been . . . everything.

Daisy's feet were tucked up into a cozy blanket as she curled up on the couch in the sunroom. A fire crackled under the new mantel. Her mother, sitting at the other end, brushed her fingers over Daisy's hand, examining the ring in the soft lamplight. The house had finally quieted, the last of the guests trickling out into the winter night.

"It really is beautiful, sweetie." Her mother smiled, letting the ring catch the light.

"It was Hunter's grandmother's." Daisy touched the delicate setting. "Can you believe it?"

"I can, actually." Her mother squeezed her hand.

Daisy beamed again. Her cheeks were going to be sore tomorrow from all this smiling.

Her mother's gaze trailed through the house with a familiar look, as though she'd been here before. "You've done such a wonderful job with this house, Daisy. You really do have such a gift."

Daisy glanced over her shoulder to where Hunter was dutifully cleaning in the parlor. "I didn't do it alone."

They fell quiet for a moment, the Christmas lights twinkling across the windows.

"When do you find out about that renovation contest?" her mom asked.

"Couple of weeks." Daisy's heart fluttered at the thought. "The prize money would help a lot with finishing the renovations. Or . . ." She bit her lip, letting the idea she'd been tinkering with slip out. "Maybe even starting a design business. Hunter and I have been talking about it. We could put a couple of desks in the parlor, some comfortable chairs for meeting with clients . . ."

Her mother's eyes lit up. "I can see it." She glanced around the sunroom, taking in the carefully restored details. "I think God's going to have a lot of fun watching you and Hunter turn houses into homes."

Daisy leaned back. "I think maybe you're right."

Her mother's gaze flickered toward the door, a smile tugging at her lips. Hunter leaned against the door, hands in his pockets. "I'll give you two a moment."

She exited, giving Hunter's shoulder a soft pat on her way out.

The room fell into a warm quiet, the Christmas tree lights and the crackle of the fire enveloping them as Hunter sank onto the floor next to her, laying his head in Daisy's lap. She brushed the hair away from his forehead, placing a soft kiss above his brow. Hunter's eyes drifted shut, a smile sliding across his lips.

She leaned back again, stroking her fingers through his hair. Her gaze wandered again, over the room where it all began. "You know, I knew this house was special the moment I saw it. But . . . I had no idea just how special it would be. This house . . . it's like family to me."

Hunter glanced up at her with those dark eyes.

She brushed her fingers over his brows and cheekbones, tracing the glow of the fire against his skin. "It's funny, isn't it? How God knows what we need, even when we don't?"

"It's a little exciting," Hunter said, turning to look at her fully now. "To know we can trust God with the planning from now on. And to know He'll be present in the good times and the bad."

She grinned. "Exactly."

Daisy Decker said goodbye to the girl with a plan.

Bonus Epilogue

Thank you for reading *Meet Me at Sunset Cove*. We hope you loved this story. Find out what happens next for Daisy and Hunter with a Bonus Epilogue, a special gift, available only to our newsletter subscribers.

This Bonus Epilogue will not be released on any retailer platform, so scan the QR code to get your free gift. You acknowledge you are becoming a Sunrise Publishing, Sarah May Warren subscriber. Unsubscribe from any newsletter at any time.

Thank You

Thank you so much for reading *Meet Me at Sunset Cove*. We hope you enjoyed the story. If you did, would you be willing to do us a favor and leave a review? It doesn't have to be long—just a few words to help other readers know what they're getting. (But no spoilers! We don't want to wreck the fun!) Thank you again for reading!

We'd love to hear from you—not only about this story, but about any characters or stories you'd like to read in the future.

Contact us at www.sunrisepublishing.com/contact.

READ ON FOR MORE FROM

Jonathon Island

Return to Jonathon Island in book 6
**Meet Me at the
Christmas Cottage**
by Christen Krumm.

When a cynical novelist and charming military doctor become accidental roommates over Christmas, 'tis the season for unexpected romance!

Bronte Parker is a successful very-much-non-romance writer who gave up on her own happily-ever-after long ago. With a looming deadline and a bad case of writer's block, Bronte decides to rent a quaint cottage on Jonathon Island for some holiday peace and quiet. But her plans for solitude are completely sleighed when the cottage owner's brother, Jonah, shows up unexpectedly. Now Bronte is stuck sharing eggnog, Christmas movies, and way too much time with her new accidental roommate—and the last thing she needs is a distraction.

After two years away, Army surgeon Jonah White is finally going to be home for the holidays. And he's got a big decision to make about his future—something he needs to talk through with his parents. Except, much to his surprise, he arrives to find his family gone on a tropical Christmas cruise and a seriously uptight author in their place. And thanks to a blizzard, he can't even escape.

Determined to make the best of it, Jonah pushes Bronte out of her comfort zone and tries to help her overcome her writer's block by showing her a real Christmas—something foster kid Bronte has never had. And as the unexpected pair are swept up in the magical Jonathon Island Christmas festivities, they start to envision a different kind of life for themselves...one where maybe a happily-ever-after could actually exist.

But with a looming book deadline and their temporary living situation nearing an end, can they be brave enough to rewrite their expectations about love and family?

One

STANDING ON THE OPEN DECK OF A ferry in near freezing temps probably wasn't the best idea, but Bronte preferred if no one overheard this conversation with her agent. Not to mention needing to escape a baby screaming its lungs out since they had boarded.

Bronte lifted her face to the sun, letting it warm her. The Jonathan Island Ferry Company boat cut through the lake on its way to the island, and she found the slight bob relaxing. Zipping the front of her coat a little higher, she shifted her phone to her opposite ear and resisted the urge to "accidentally" drop it into the water.

"Okay, run me through this again. You have how much written?"

Bronte winced, not wanting to admit just how little she had done. Maybe she could just fall over the side of the boat, but all that would probably get her was wet and freezing. "Lexi, don't make me say it."

"Are you in a wind tunnel or something? I can barely hear you. How much did you say?" Bronte's best friend and agent practically yelled in her ear.

Bronte sighed and moved out of the sun and wind to tuck herself into the alcove by the door. At least here, she'd still be able to watch their arrival to the island in relative silence. She could still hear the baby's cries, muted though they were through the door. A pang shot through her heart, but she shook thoughts of babies and families from her mind as she turned from watching the Michigan shoreline grow smaller.

"Twenty-seven. That's how much I've written." Waves lapped against the side of the boat as it cut through the glassy water. "And I'm on a ferry heading to Jonathon Island. Remember? I told you I booked a place here for Christmas."

"Twenty-seven thousand's not bad, Bront. You're at least, what? Twenty percent done?"

Oh, the faith her friend had in her.

"No, just twenty-seven. Two, seven." On the book that needed to be at least ninety thousand words.

"Does my mother know you only have 'two seven' written on this project?" Lexi choked out.

"She would if I would actually answer any of her calls. I'm not sure why I need to answer her calls anyway. You're my agent now." Bronte sank onto the bench that ran the length of the boat. She could imagine this would be a coveted seat in the summer, the perfect location to watch the island growing closer. In the winter, the wind cut through her layers like knives. Bronte didn't mind. The cold felt good, refreshing, after being in airports all day. Besides, it rivaled the winter wind whipping down the plains in good old Oklahoma, which had been her home for just a little over two years now.

Bronte's fingers gripped the bench seat as they passed under a bridge. Should she hold her breath or did the "holding your breath" rule only apply when driving through tunnels? "And you'd better not tell your mother just how far behind I am."

"First of all, I would never. Second, I'm only your agent-in-training. My mother is still technically your agent. I'm not sure ghosting her is the best choice."

Bronte snorted. "First, just because you're an agent-in-training, doesn't mean you aren't my agent. You are. Also, Margot will be fine because she'll never know how far behind I am. The newest installment of the Pike Family Saga will be on both of your desks by January fifth."

"January fifth?" Lexi squeaked. "Bronte, that's three weeks."

"Saying it's due next month sounds so much better, don't you think?"

"Bronte!"

"I know, I know." Bronte dropped her forehead into her hand. "But it's fine. Totally fine. I'm going to get it done."

"That's, like, thirty thousand words a week. Over four thousand a day."

"That's so helpful. Thank you."

"Sorry. It's just . . . a lot."

Bronte wanted to squeeze her eyes tight and pray the deadline just went away. "I know. And I've never been this behind before. But there was the press tour and movie stuff this year."

"Which you have never let get in your way before."

"It did this time." And then there had been the surgery . . .

"This is all Brad's fault."

A heavy silence followed. Bronte's chest tightened, and she blinked against the cold wind that was causing her eyes to well up. No, she wasn't going down could-have-beens. She squared her shoulders. All of that had happened ten months ago—practically a year. Brad was behind her now. She didn't care about him. She had a manuscript to write and a plan to execute.

"Okay, okay. No numbers, but I need you to hurry up and finish that book so the publishers can do their thing and we can go on tour again. You know you need your number one agent to shield you from all your raving fans."

Bronte's chest tightened. "Oh yay. Tour," she deadpanned. Why had she chosen a career that required her to fly to different cities to meet hundreds of strangers? *Calm down. A tour won't happen for at least another year.* "If they mauled me, they would never find out what happens to Theodosia, Marisol, and Vivian at the end."

"Are you going to finally give them their happy ending?"

Bronte stood and stepped back over to the railing, not caring if Lexi couldn't hear her over the wind. She was tired of this discussion. Digging her fingers into the metal railing she replied, "You know I don't write happy books."

"I think you should. Wrap the entire series up in one big happy bow."

"And how is that going to be realistic?" Bronte pressed.

"Sometimes it's okay to give someone a happy ending," Lexi said gently.

"Happy endings don't exist." At least, not in Bronte's experience.

"Bronte—"

"Stop, it's fine. I know there are authors out there that write happy books. That's just not me. Write what you know, and what I know is not happy endings."

"All right, I get it." Lexi paused. "So, speaking of Brad—"

"We weren't speaking of Brad," Bronte interjected.

Lexi ignored her and continued. "You've been staying off social media, right?"

"Yes . . ."

Lexi huffed out a breath. "Good. Good. That's good."

"What does my staying off socials have to do with Brad?" Bronte pulled in a deep breath. In the warmer months, she'd be able to smell the verdant greenery lining the lake and enjoy the fresh breeze, but not now while her nose was frozen.

"Well . . ."

"Lex, just spit it out already," Bronte snapped, a little more sharply than she wanted. She chewed her bottom lip to keep from snapping again.

"Brad is engaged."

All the air whooshed from Bronte's lungs. "Good for him." She somehow managed to get the sentiment out. Sucking in the cold air and willing it to freeze her heart, she reminded herself she'd traveled all the way to Jonathon Island to get away from any thoughts of Brad. Dreams of holing herself up in the cutest little cottage that she had ever seen, head down, words flowing, started melting from her mind.

She would *not* give Brad anymore brain space. She imagined herself taking a broom and sweeping Brad out of every crevice in her mind. He wasn't welcome there any longer. He'd made it very clear in February that he'd decided he wanted a family. He wanted the noisy babies, and as Bronte couldn't change her mind on the matter, he didn't want to be in her life. And now he was engaged. It didn't get any clearer than that.

"Bronte? Did I lose you? Oh gosh, I shouldn't have mentioned Brad. What was I thinking?"

"I'm here, but hey, the ferry is almost to the island." They were only halfway there. "I'm going to have to let you go."

"Sure. You have a wonderful time, Bronte. Seriously call me once you get settled—"

Bronte shook her head even though Lexi couldn't see her. "I've got to write."

"Fine, send me a text. Send a carrier pigeon."

Shifting the phone to her other ear, Bronte asked, "Do those even exist anymore?"

"Just let me know you got in and settled okay."

"Yes, mother," Bronte replied sarcastically.

With well-wishes of Christmas, Bronte ended the call and dropped her phone into the pocket of her oversized black peacoat. Wind whipping at her hair, she curled her fingers tighter around the railing to keep them from doing something silly—like looking at her ex's social media accounts. She didn't need to see Brad and his fiancée. She had already swept Brad out of her mind.

But would one little peek really hurt? Once she arrived at the island, she'd put thoughts of her ex and his happiness out of her mind for good.

Ignoring the scenery she had been so looking forward to taking in, Bronte pulled her phone from her pocket and with laser focus, scrolled through the apps on her phone until she found the icon she was looking for. Fingers seemed to fly over the face of her phone as she typed Brad's username from memory. The first image contained him and Marie, with Marie flashing one of the largest rings Bronte had ever seen.

"Look at that rock."

Bronte startled, almost dropping her phone into the lake, as a girl in a camel-colored trench coat came to stand next to her. She was a bit shorter than Bronte, but then again, Bronte had always been called a giant. Five nine wasn't that tall, but that hadn't stopped boys in middle school from giving her the nickname. It wasn't her fault she'd been head and shoulders taller than them at that age.

Of course, it was better than them teasing her for being a foster kid.

The girl's blonde hair shone in the sun and was tucked perfectly into her scarf and layers. Blue eyes sparkled, and all of her features were a perfect kind of petite that Bronte had wished for her whole life. After traveling all day, Bronte had swiped the last of the mascara off her face in the airport bathroom and had to wrestle her untamed curls into a knot on top of her head—which she was pretty sure resembled a bird's nest at this point.

"Oh, sorry. I didn't mean to scare you." The girl took a step back, eyes wide. "Aubrey Jennings." She thrust her hand in Bronte's direction.

Bronte clicked her phone off and dropped it back in her pocket, taking Aubrey's offered hand. "Bronte. Parker. It's fine. I didn't need to scroll anyway."

"Right." The girl smiled and leaned against the railing next to Bronte. "Would you look at that?"

A large white building flanked in scaffolding loomed in the distance. Dirty snow glittered on the ground and covered a crane sitting quietly to the side. The Grand Hotel. Bronte remembered, after deciding to come to Jonathon Island, reading reports about the rebuilding of the hotel after it'd burned in a tragic accident years before. She wished she had been able to get a room at the hotel, but since they hadn't opened it to the public yet, she'd been compelled to find other lodgings.

"I'm so glad to see they're rebuilding the hotel. It's going to be gorgeous when they get it done." Taking a big breath, as if coming to the island was clearing her head, she turned to Bronte. "Is this your first time to the island?"

Putting her hands in her pockets, Bronte nodded. "You?"

"Oh, no. I grew up here. My grandmother still lives here."

"Back for Christmas?"

Aubrey clicked her knee-high boots as if she were Dorothy in *The Wizard of Oz*. Bronte half expected her to sigh *There's no place like home.* "Yep. Staying until New Year's."

Her heart clenched. What would it be like to have family to visit for the holidays? A grandma waiting for her on the other side of this ride. Maybe with a steaming cup of tea and the world's best snickerdoodle cookies. When she had deadlines looming, she could visit her grandma, who would insist on making sure she stayed fed while Bronte's fingers flew over her keyboard, creating characters and entire worlds. A family didn't have to be noisy and in the way. Did it?

"What brings you to Jonathon Island?"

Aubrey's question snapped Bronte from her daydream. Probably for the best. She didn't need to spiral down the what-if tunnel. She'd accepted that wasn't a life she'd ever have a long time ago. "Just visiting. I rented a cottage out for the next few weeks." *I'm on deadline. I have a book to write*, she finished silently. Five bestsellers in, and she still found it hard to tell people what she did for a living.

"You're going to love it on Jonathon Island. The Christmas season is my favorite. There are so many fun activities planned. Oh, and this year, I've heard they're bringing back the ball."

"The ball?" She vaguely remembered reading something about a ball when booking her rental, but she hadn't looked too much into it since she was here to write her book.

"Yeah, the Christmas ball. I remember going to the Christmas balls when I was a teenager, but then the hotel burned down, and there hasn't been anything like that on the island in ages. I'm so excited they're bringing it back."

On any other trip, attending a ball might have been fun. "I've never been to anything even remotely resembling a ball. Unless line dancing counts? I've done that a few times." Bronte made a face.

"Maybe not quite the same." Aubrey laughed. "Oh, and I hope they have the lights up in the town. It's so magical."

That word—*magical*. It sobered Bronte right up. There was nothing magical about Christmas. Not for her.

Not for anyone who was alone.

Bronte just nodded and tucked her chin further under her black silk scarf. She hoped the lights weren't up. Didn't matter though. She'd be hunkered down in her cottage the whole time, writing.

They fell into silence, watching the waves go by in a quick clip.

"So, what is it you do?" Aubrey asked.

Bronte hated this question. It always made her feel self-conscious. She accepted having to talk about being a writer when she went on tour, almost to a point where she enjoyed it, but in her everyday life? Nope. Why hadn't she become something simple? Like an accountant. "I'm a writer."

Hopefully there wouldn't be any more questions after that, but Bronte knew better.

Aubrey's eyes lit up. "That's great. I always wanted to write a book. What do you write?"

Bronte's second most-hated question. "Oh, just some family sagas."

"I love to read. My ex and I used to have contests to see who could read the most books every year." Her smile wavered just for the briefest moment before returning. "Are you published? Anything I might have read?"

She almost brushed off the question, but she'd just look more ridiculous when the truth came out. "The Pike Family Saga." Almost six years since her first novel had launched her career, and she still felt awkward talking about it.

"Like the movie?"

Despite herself, Bronte relaxed. Fans of the movies were easier to handle than fans of the books. "Yes. *Color of the Stars.*"

Aubrey snapped her gloved fingers. "Yes, that's it. Wow, so you're like a celebrity."

Bronte winced. "Not really."

"So, are you working on the next in the series? Are there going to be more movies?"

"I'm working on the last book in the series." Why she had been so adamant about that, she'd never know. Now that the end was here, she didn't want to say goodbye. "But there should be more movies coming out. The rights were bought for the entire series."

"That is so exciting." Aubrey continued rambling about celebrities and movies and asked something about Liam Hemsworth, but Bronte's mind wandered. All the movie, book, and Pike family questions were always the same.

She should talk to Lexi about asking the publisher if they could extend the series. Bronte knew they would be on board with that idea. But if she wanted to ask for more books, another contract, she needed to make sure this last book was the best one so they couldn't tell her no. Maybe Vivian Pike would run from the love of her life and move to an island. Or maybe her love would be the one to leave her, and she would still go to the island, vowing to live out her days alone. She could take over the apothecary shop, just like her mother had always wanted her to. Where would the series go from there? Maybe she should throw in a secret love child.

Bronte wrinkled her nose. No. There would be no secret love children.

"Don't you think?"

Bronte snapped back to the conversation at hand. Drat. Aubrey had asked a question, and Bronte had completely missed it.

The intercom crackled. "On behalf of everyone at Jonathon Island, we'd like to welcome you to the island. We'll be docking in just a few minutes, so please remain seated until the vessel has been secured to the dock and luggage carts have been unloaded. Please take this opportunity to collect your things. And lastly, please be courteous to your fellow passengers as you exit the ferry. Thank you, and have a nice visit."

Saved by the boat.

"Well." Aubrey pushed off the railing and turned to go back inside. "I guess that's our cue."

Turning, Bronte couldn't help but sneak one more glance at the approaching island—her home for the next two weeks. Tall, bare trees peeked over the tops of the colorful buildings that dotted the shoreline.

She had studied the map of Jonathon Island for the last month, ever since she'd decided this would be where she hid away to finish her novel. She could picture the shops along Main Street and the friendly smiles of the people who lived here year-round. Jonathon Island was the perfect place to write the last Pike novel. Bronte could already feel the inspiration calling to her from the island.

Okay, right. She could do this.

Nothing would get in the way of her finishing this novel.

Bronte was ready to hunker down and start working on this book. Now she just needed to find Mia Franklin and get the keys to the cottage she'd rented.

Having secured their luggage, Bronte and Aubrey disembarked and walked down Ferry Street. The cutest row of white and gray shops—adorned with multicolored awnings, twinkle lights swaying in the slight breeze—lined both sides of Main Street, and fine, it was a little bit magical, decorated for Christmas with its lights and wreaths and ribbons.

Even with a few of the shops vacant, Bronte could tell this was the hub of the island. She had loved what she'd seen of Jonathon Island on the House to Home YouTube channel—yes, she was that person that would rather follow a YouTube series than watch anything on primetime television.

She couldn't believe she actually stood here.

"Where are you headed?"

Bronte pulled her phone out of her pocket and scrolled to her messages. "I need to find a Martha's on Main and a Mia Franklin to get the keys to the place I'm renting."

"Martha's on Main is that way." Bronte's companion lifted her hand and pointed up the street. "I'm headed this way to catch a ride to my grandma's."

Bronte looked around, expecting to spot a car or Uber. She didn't see any.

"Thanks."

"Hope you have a great time while you're here. Maybe we'll bump into each other again."

They said their goodbyes and went their separate ways.

The wheels on her suitcase complained as they rattled over the cobblestones, catching on the uneven walkway and threatening to spill. That's all Bronte needed—for her suitcase to spill open on Main Street.

Bronte's suitcase jerked her back as it got stuck on a divot in the street. She shivered as a gust of cold air blew. The sun was deceiving. It looked like it should be a nice day with no frigid air cutting through her coat to slice her bones. Deceiving or not, Bronte couldn't see how there were snowstorms predicted for later. Not even cotton-ball clouds dotted the sky.

With one more jerk, the street gave the suitcase back, sans a wheel.

Bronte groaned. "Are you kidding me?" At least it wasn't a busted zipper. Pocketing the rogue wheel, Bronte half dragged, half carried her suitcase the remaining three shops to Martha's on Main.

Warmth of the restaurant enveloped her as she pushed

in from the cold, suitcase dragging behind her. The door clambered shut as all the eyes of the patrons swung in her direction, and there were many. For a random Monday a week and a half before Christmas, the place seemed packed. Two older gentlemen played what looked to be an intense game of checkers, and there was another group of five, who looked to be deep in some kind of meeting, and she recognized a few people from the ferry.

"Just find an open seat, and we'll be with you in a moment," someone from behind the bar directed.

"I just need to meet up with Mia Franklin? She has the keys and directions to my rental."

"Rental? There aren't any rentals on the island." A larger woman with gray streaking through her dark hair, piercing blue eyes, and a too-gruff voice handed a plate to a waitress, who turned on her heel to deliver it to a nearby table.

"I, uh, am renting from Holland White?" Bronte rifled through her messenger bag, looking for the rental agreement she knew she'd printed out.

"Yes, yes, Martha, you remember. Holland is renting out her place while they're in the Bahamas." A dark-haired woman, no more than twenty-five, dressed in jeans and a white sweater, came up beside Bronte. "Hi, I'm Mia Franklin. You must be Bronte."

Bronte took Mia's proffered hand.

Martha huffed. "I still don't know why the Whites had to go off to the Bahamas for Christmas. Who has heard of such a thing?"

"Sunshine, sand, and warmer than twenty degrees, Martha. Anyone could see the appeal," Mia shot back.

Martha harrumphed, turned, and pushed through swinging doors disappearing to, Bronte assumed, the kitchen.

"Don't mind her. I hope your trip here was good," Mia said, leading Bronte back over to the dark wood booth where she had papers spread over the entire surface of the table. Putting one knee on the booth seat, Mia leaned over to dig through her briefcase. "Give me one second, and I'll get you the keys. Sorry about the mess. I'm working from here today since my kids are sick and at home with my mom. Honestly, my office was just too quiet. I'd rather be where there's people. You know?"

Bronte didn't know.

Mia continued muttering to herself as she pulled her bag closer. It must be like a Mary Poppins bag with all the digging Mia was doing. Bronte shifted on her feet, not sure if she should offer to help or find a seat to sit down and wait, maybe get something to eat before heading out.

"Ah-ha!" Mia held up a set of keys on a dark-blue plastic keychain, like one you'd find at a vintage hotel. "Found them." She held them out toward Bronte. "I went over there earlier today to make sure the heat had been turned up. The Whites have been gone for a few days already and aren't scheduled to be back until after you leave. If you need groceries or anything while you're here, Doug's Market is right down that way." Mia thumbed the direction toward the grocery store. "Of course, you'll also find Good Day Coffee, Island Pizzeria, and Kelley's Bar & Grill, which, if you need something to do in the evenings, is the place to go. They generally have line dancing or trivia night or something. Always a good time. And of course, there's Martha's." Mia swept her arms out.

"Great." Bronte flashed what she hoped was a thankful smile. After talking with Lexi and confessing exactly how much she had to get done out loud, it'd started sinking in.

What had she been thinking, waiting until the very last minute? And maybe she did have twenty-seven words down, but what she hadn't told Lexi was that she'd written those months ago. She didn't even know if they were going to stay.

What was her first line again? It didn't matter. She was here now, and this book would get written.

"Is there an Uber I can call or . . ." Bronte trailed off at the amusement in Mia's eyes.

"There are no cars on Jonathon Island."

"Oh. Right." Bronte knew that from watching the show, but hadn't that been more of a reality TV stunt? "How do you get around, then?"

"Depends on the season. From Memorial Day to Labor Day, we walk or bike. The Quinns are working on getting horses back on island next season, and Asher Quinn—yes, *that* Asher Quinn—has started up a carriage tour business with the few horses still here."

She actually didn't know *that* Asher Quinn but promised herself she'd google him later. "That's so . . . interesting."

"It really is. If you just give me one minute, I can drive you over on a golf cart." Mia started gathering her papers, tapping the stacks on the tabletop before slipping them in her briefcase and donning a coat, scarf, and hat.

"Oh, I couldn't—" Bronte started.

Mia shot a pointed look at the missing wheel on Bronte's suitcase. "Of course you can. You do not need to be dragging that thing through the streets of Jonathon Island. Besides, I'm done here anyway, and the Whites' place is basically on my way home."

Bronte took a step back to let Mia finish gathering her stuff, letting her gaze shift up to the white-tiled ceiling and pendant lighting. Martha's was a cute little restaurant, and from how many tables were full, the food must be good too. Most everyone had gone back to whatever they were doing before Bronte stepped in. *Thank goodness.*

Mia straightened, pulling the strap of her bag onto her shoulder. "Ready?"

"Don't forget this." Martha thrust a plastic bag filled with takeout containers in Bronte's direction.

Bronte stared at the bag dangling from two of Martha's fingers. "I didn't order anything."

Martha jiggled the bag. "I'm sure you're tired from traveling all day. I know Mia went up earlier and made sure there were some groceries and the like, but figured a little more couldn't hurt. And I live in the big white house only a few houses down from Holland's, so if you need anything, just come by and ask."

Bronte's face warmed, not sure why Martha would care about whether or not she had enough food. "Oh, thank you." She took the bag, scents of something savory curling up with the steam. A pang shot through her stomach. Maybe she was a little hungrier than she realized.

Grabbing her suitcase by the top strap, Bronte stuck

out her hip to help heave it up so she could hobble-follow Mia back out into the cold December air.

"Sorry it's so cold." Mia led them over to a blue golf cart. "And the ride over is going to be a little chilly, but luckily the Whites' house isn't too far away."

They stored the suitcase in the back, securing it with a bungee cord. Bronte sat in the front next to Mia. Holding on to the handle, Bronte shifted as far over as she could on the golf cart's seat. There wasn't much room on the bench seat, but she didn't need to be sitting in Mia's lap.

Sighing, Bronte let her head fall back on the seat rest, head lolling to the side so she could at least see where they were going. Or maybe she didn't want to know. If she didn't know, she would be less likely to want to get out and explore instead of staying put and getting the writing done. Not that that wasn't the plan to begin with.

They passed the cutest houses painted in white and dark blues. Bronte spotted a few houses' landscaping showing off, even in the winter months. After only two minutes of driving, Mia whipped the golf cart into a driveway.

The Whites' cottage looked exactly as it did in the photos Holland shared online—white rock skirting the bottom third, giving way to dark, moody siding and black windows. Bronte couldn't wait to get inside. This place, this house, something about it put Bronte at ease, and she knew for the first time that she would get a huge chunk, if not all, of the next Pike Family Saga written here.

"Thanks for the ride." Bronte slipped out of the golf cart and unhooked her suitcase from the back.

"Anytime." Mia followed Bronte out of the golf cart

and up the sidewalk to the front of the house. "There are goodies in the cabinets, but if there's anything that you need, please don't hesitate to reach out. I know you have Holland's number, but I don't think she'll be available since they're on a cruise ship."

"That's really nice of you. Thanks." Bronte clutched the bag of takeout containers while also keeping a grip on the top strap of the suitcase. The zipper could still decide to fail her.

Mia fell into silence next to Bronte, and they stood on the sidewalk. Bronte wanted nothing more than to escape inside, get settled, and start writing. *Ninety thousand words. Ninety thousand words.* The reminder beat a rhythm in her head.

"Well." Mia clapped her hands together with a slap. "I'm going to get home and make sure my mom's not going crazy. Call me if you need anything. Anything at all!" Waving, Mia got back inside the golf cart and, after backing out of the driveway, continued down the street.

Sitting back under trees and foliage, the house seemed to say *Welcome. You are going to get so much work done.*

"I hope so," Bronte mumbled to herself as she jammed the key into the lock.

The inside was just as inviting, if not more, than the outside. Even though there weren't any Christmas decorations (thank goodness), it still smelled of cinnamon and citrus.

Leaving her suitcase next to the front door, Bronte went farther into the house. The small entryway led down a short hallway to the open kitchen and living room.

The kitchen was the perfect kind of homey, with its

speckled granite countertops and mossy green cabinets with gold hardware. A wall of windows in the breakfast nook showed a big backyard. A large island separated the kitchen area from the living room, and on that island, a pile of chocolate chip cookies sat on a Santa plate with a folded card sitting next to it that said, "Welcome to the White house, Bronte."

Smiling, Bronte exchanged the bag of food from Martha for a cookie and continued her exploring.

The living room was the stuff of dreams, so different from her two-bedroom apartment that she'd never quite found the time—or energy—to decorate. The mustard velvet sectional made Bronte's heart pitter-patter. She couldn't wait to sink into it with her laptop and get to work. A large, white fireplace took up most of the wall, flanked only by a dark wood piano. She plunked at two keys while leaning over and studying the various pictures of whom she could only assume was the White family that covered the top of the piano.

She could almost watch the family grow up through the frozen images. A man with sandy brown hair, the only indication he was older being the deep grooves in his face, sat next to a beautiful older woman with salt-and-pepper hair. They were surrounded by—one, two, three . . . Mercy, five kids, four of which were girls. That poor brother. A handful of the siblings had dark hair, with one lone blonde sister. The solitary son stood behind his parents, his smile making Bronte feel as warm as the picture looked. Another photo showed the son in military garb. The intensity of his face in the photo made Bronte do a double-take to make sure it was the same person. Serious or not, it did nothing to detract from his handsomeness. A face like that—strong jaw, defined chin, thick eyebrows sitting on top of blue eyes that sparkled with kindness—would give any Hollywood heartthrob a run for their money.

Taking her cookie, Bronte wandered up the stairs to the second floor. There were four rooms, way more than Bronte could ever need, but this house would be perfect for pulling inspiration for the last Pike family book. The room at the end of the hallway had an evergreen wreath bearing a placard with her name expertly calligraphed in gold. After retrieving her suitcase from downstairs, Bronte unpacked, setting her folded clothes into the antique dresser. She warred between tucking herself into the window seat alcove that overlooked Jonathon Island or heading back downstairs. But with the quickly setting sun, the picturesque image would soon be painted in black.

Bag unpacked and decision about where to work made, Bronte grabbed her notebook and laptop and headed back downstairs to find a cozy spot to start working.

Settling on the velvet couch, she opened her laptop, trying to ignore the large picture windows that led to the backyard. Holland had said in the listing that this was her childhood home. What would it have been like growing up in a house like this? Having four siblings to play with. Constant activity, running in and out, sports, homework, extracurricular activities. It must have been like a dream.

She'd hoped maybe one day she'd have that. Now . . .

A prick stung the back of Bronte's eyes. She blinked furiously. She needed to stop being ridiculous and get to work. Having overactive retrospection wasn't going to help her get anything done. She let out a quick breath. Yes, work. Writing. Getting the last Pike family story down. The last one. This was it. After this she would move on to . . . to what? Did she have anything after this?

"Focus, Bronte," she told herself, ignoring how hollow and alone her voice sounded.

She stared at the blinking cursor. Fingers poised over the keyboard, Bronte closed her eyes to imagine the words she needed to write.

Her eyes flew open. She hadn't texted Lexi to let her know she'd arrived.

Toggling over to the message app on her laptop, she fired a quick text to her friend, letting her know that she'd made it and all was good.

That finished, she moved back to her open document, closed her eyes again, and tried to conjure up the first line.

Her finger *tap, tap, tapped* against the side of the keyboard.

Ugh, this wasn't working. Her brain must be too tired from all the travel.

Bronte slammed her laptop closed. No matter. She'd rest tonight and get started first thing in the morning.

She had waited this long to get started—one more night wouldn't hurt.

Acknowledgments

Way back at the start, before Daisy stepped foot on dear, sweet Jonathon Island, when I was still thinking up the story of the Bad Luck Barrett House, I was blessed to have my own home completely upended. I'll never forget leaving my house in the pouring rain because of the toxic sewage quickly filling my basement (which, by the way, our bedrooms were in). I remember chuckling, as one does when their life is spiraling out of control, and thinking about how this was going to give me great insight into my characters. At that time, I had only three months until my manuscript was due, and I'd planned to spend the summer working on it...And now my family was living on a mattress in the living room, with every spare inch of our house (including my office) filled with bags and tubs from the salvages of our basement. Suffice it to say, I was pretty nervous about being able to finish this book.

All that to say, I would be remiss not to thank everyone who helped us pick up the pieces of our life last summer. From the outpouring of people who donated clothing to my daughter, who lost her entire wardrobe, to the people who ventured into the toxic depths of our basement to rescue what they could. To my in-laws, who let my family of four (plus two dogs) camp out in their living room for almost a month, to my parents, who went full mamma-and-pappa-bear mode.

Truly, I would not have been able to write this book without all of you.

When I say the flood was a blessing, I really mean it. God blessed us. I have never felt so surrounded by my community. Thank you.

On that note—I have to thank my hubster-dubster, Neil. You, above all the rest, were my champion last year.

I also want to thank the Sunrise team. Another great blessing in my life is being able to work with such amazing people. And of course that includes a big thanks to Lindsay Harrel, who knew the story from the beginning, saw what it was becoming, and helped me take it there. Thank you!

And of course, give a little shout out to my beta readers, Whitney, Meredith, and my whole mom-crew. I'm honored that you chose to step into this story before it was all polished and pretty. I'm so thankful for all of you.

And finally, thanks to Susie, who, despite her children's groans and gnashing of teeth, took the time to pause every movie and teach the boys and me how to craft a story. You did it, Mom. I'm a writer now. Can we play the movie?...Love you.

Growing up in a writer's household, Sarah May Warren always knew she was doomed to catch the writing bug—and she did, right around the time she met and fell in love with her now husband, Neil. She finally started writing her first full length novel while pregnant with their first child, and she hasn't stopped since. When she's not writing a story, or adding another book to her endless TBR, Sarah can be found volunteering with her Church's worship team, coordinating weddings, or cuddling up for movie night with her two amazing daughters—oh yeah, and that scruffy hubby of hers.

Visit her as SEWarrenFiction.com.

Jonathon Island

Where faith, family, and romance meet small-town, beachside charm. Whether you spend a weekend at The Grand, take a stroll down Lilac Lane, or cozy up in the Christmas Cottage, you'll fall in love with this heart-warming contemporary romance series, full of second chances and unforgettable love stories!

Check out the full series at sunrisepublishing.com.

We solve the problem of what we read next.

Available on Amazon

Where southern charm and romance intertwine...

"Heartwarming, genuine, and utterly captivating."

–SUSAN MAY WARREN
USA Today bestselling author

We solve the problem of what we read next.   Available on Amazon

Home to Heritage

SUSAN MAY WARREN and **TARI FARIS**

with **Mandy Boerma** and **Andrea Michelle Wood**

We solve the problem of what we read next.

Available on Amazon

**WHERE EVERY STORY IS A FRIEND,
AND EVERY CHAPTER IS A NEW JOURNEY...**

Subscribe to our newsletter for the latest news, weekly giveaways, exclusive author interviews, and more!

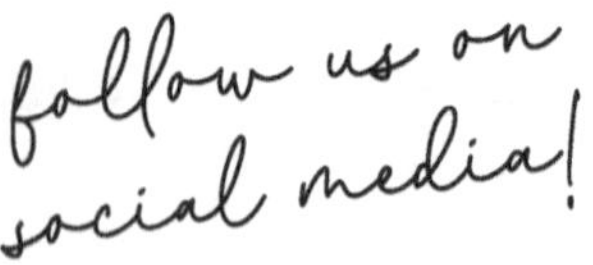

Shop paperbacks, ebooks, audiobooks, and more at
SUNRISEPUBLISHING.MYSHOPIFY.COM